SO MUCH THINGS TO SAY

My Life as Bob Marley's Manager

Don Taylor

with

Mike Henry

BLAKE

Published by Blake Publishing Ltd,
3 Bramber Court, 2 Bramber Road, London, England W14 9PB

In association with Kingston Publishers Ltd,
LOJ Industrial Complex,
7 Norman Road, Building 10, Kingston CSO, Jamaica

First published in Great Britain in 1995

ISBN 1 85782 119 X

British Library Cataloguing-in-Publication Data:
A catalogue record for this book is available from the British Library.

Typeset by Pearl Graphics, Hemel Hempstead

Printed in England by Clays Ltd, St Ives plc

1 3 5 7 9 10 8 6 4 2

In memory of
Kyle Donald Taylor
1988–1993

Song Lyrics

PAGE	
Jacket	'So Much Things To Say' (Bob Marley Music/Blue Mountain Music Ltd)
3	'Sun Is Shining' (Bob Marley Music/Blue Mountain Music Ltd)
22	'Talkin' Blues' (Bob Marley Music/Blue Mountain Music Ltd/Rondor Music)
26	'No Woman No Cry' (Bob Marley Music/Blue Mountain Music Ltd)
27/241	'Ride Natty Ride' (Bob Marley Music/Blue Mountain Music Ltd)
30	'Trench Town Rock' * (Words and Music by Bob Marley © 1983, Cayman Music Inc, USA)
95	'Babylon System' (Bob Marley Music/Blue Mountain Music Ltd)
104	'Johnny Was' (Bob Marley Music/Blue Mountain Music Ltd/Rondor Music)
105/147	'War' (Bob Marley Music/Blue Mountain Music Ltd)
134-135	'Smile Jamaica' (Bob Marley Music/Blue Mountain Music Ltd)
200	'Who the Cap Fit' (Bob Marley Music/Blue Mountain Music Ltd)
210	'Want More' (Bob Marley Music/Blue Mountain Music Ltd)
238	'Redemption Song' (Bob Marley Music/Blue Mountain Music Ltd)
239	'Slave Driver' * (Words and Music by Bob Marley © 1979, Cayman Music Inc, USA)
239	'Zimbabwe' (Bob Marley Music/Blue Mountain Music Ltd)
242	'Roots' (Bob Marley Music/Blue Mountain Music Ltd)
243	'Survival' (Bob Marley Music/Blue Mountain Music Ltd)
244	'Confrontation' (Bob Marley Music/Blue Mountain Music Ltd)
247/251	'We and Dem' (Bob Marley Music/Blue Mountain Music Ltd)
253	'Rasta Man Chant' (Bob Marley Music/Blue Mountain Music Ltd)

Contents

Contents

Acknowledgements

I could never have achieved the successes I have had were it not for the following persons, beginning with my early years as a promoter and on through to the present.

To the following I acknowledge my sincere appreciation: Stephen Hill, Snr, the R&B family of 1958–68, Ben E. King, Jerry Butler, Chuck Jackson, the late Jackie Wilson, the Shirelles, especially Shirley Owens, Walter Godfrey, the Drifters, the late Tammi Montgomery Terrell, Betty Everett, Little Anthony and the Imperials, especially Anthony Gourdine, that great contributor Henry Wynn who was a guiding light at 'sweet' Auburn Avenue, Bobby Schiffman, owner of the Apollo, and Murray the K, the 'fifth Beatle', who was responsible for so many shows at the Brooklyn Fox; to Patti LaBelle and the Blue Belles, Dick Griffey, Kendal Minter, Vivian Scott, Danny Sims, Janet Davidson and Jackie Davidson, and in later years the Top Line crew of Marcia Davis, Bagga Davis and my close confidant, Danny Marks. Thanks to all the 'Wise Guys' that I have met and worked with in the world, for being 'stand-up' people. I would also say thanks to Mrs Ermine March, Nari and Hotu Chatani, Nicky Nicholas, Tom Tavares-Finson and my other mother, Aunt Daisy Belizario.

Thanks to all the street people from Kingston to New York, via Brooklyn, Chester, Pennsylvania and Nassau, Bahamas.

In the life of my association with Bob special thanks must go to all those who played a part in his success and indeed by extension my own success. In this category I place Chris Blackwell, Rita Marley, Cedella Booker, Judy Mowatt, Marcia Griffiths, the Wailers Band, 'Family Man' Barrett, Carlton Barrett, Tyrone Downie, Alvin 'Seco' Patterson, Al Anderson, Junior Marvin, Alex Sadkin (deceased), King

Sporty, Captain Curry and of course Bob's children. I will be forever grateful to Bunny Livingston and Peter Tosh who together with Bob formed the original Wailers; without them I would have no story to tell today. Thanks also to Frankie Crocker of WBLS NY, and all DJs and programme directors, and all the Island Record licensees around the world, who played their part in building Bob's career. I am also immensely grateful to Apryl Taylor, my former wife, who did so much for Bob while he stayed with us in Miami.

With respect to the book itself I must pay special thanks to co-author Mike Henry, and to Camille Hines-Henry for bringing Mike and myself together to make this book a reality. Many thanks also to Dawn Chambers who transcribed the tapes as I recorded them, spending endless hours typing and retyping. To Abe Dabdoub for his legal advice and the typesetters Dwight and Christine Simons of WRR. Special thanks to Kim Robinson-Walcott for her incisive editorial advice, and editor Annie Paul who helped to bring coherence to the manuscript as well as being responsible for text design and layout; and to Susan Anderson who worked on various aspects of the book including the cover design and photographic layout.

I wish to acknowledge the role played in my research by such publications as *Catch a Fire*, by Timothy White, *Bob Marley: Reggae King of the World*, by Malika Whitney (a former secretary of mine) and Dermot Hussey, *Reggae International* by Stephen Davis and Peter Simons, *In His Own Words* (Omnibus Publishers), *Reggae Report* magazine (owned by Peggy Quattro, also a former secretary of mine), and the *Daily Gleaner*.

My eternal thanks to the medical fraternity who saved my life: I refer specifically to Dr William Bacon of Miami, Florida and Dr Phillip Thompson of Nassau, Bahamas. And finally, I must thank my wife Sonia, who has shared in the birth of this book.

DON TAYLOR

Prelude: Miami 1980

Bob Marley's eyes were yellow. Like the eyes of a wild mountain cat. And there was a rage in him I had never seen before.

Slowly he cocked the trigger of the huge, black, automatic 9mm pistol and held the muzzle inches from my right eye. Behind him his road manager Allan Cole held an identical gun.

'Sign the paper Don Taylor or I am going to blow you away,' Bob whispered. 'Just do it man.'

I read the document he waved in front of my face and saw that Bob was ordering me to sign away every verbal and written agreement the two of us had ever made.

For me this was the ultimate betrayal. I had dedicated years of my life to Bob's career. In my small way I had helped him to grow from a ghetto 'Tuff Gong' to a poised, respected, multi-millionaire global superstar. Now he was determined to wrench away everything I had worked for.

The afternoon had started routinely enough. Bob was staying at his mother's mansion in Miami, resting between concert tours of Europe and the Far East. He had telephoned me at my home nearby to ask me to come over to chat about something that was worrying him. At first we talked by his huge, shimmering swimming pool. But, as the conversation grew more raucous, he commanded Allan and me to move to his room.

Within minutes a tussle developed between the three of us, and it was then that Allan pulled the two evil-looking pistols from a wooden bedroom wardrobe.

Even with the weapons pointed at me I tried to stay looking cool. It wasn't that I wasn't frightened – it went through my mind that it might happen, he might just shoot me. But you have to remember I understood the old Jamaican thing about attitude and intimidation. Like Bob I'd grown up on the streets. I knew all about intimidation, how people used it to get what they wanted. It rarely led to anything. I'd be more frightened to be in that situation today. Today in Jamaica intimidation leads to instant action.

Bob was trying to intimidate me, but because of our relationship, and all the things we'd been through together, I didn't think he'd actually shoot me, and I knew Allan well enough to know he wouldn't. He went on shouting and pointing the gun at me: 'You're going to sign – what you trying to do to me?'

I just looked coldly into his eyes and told him: 'I'm not going to sign.'

At that moment one of the little children came through the door. I think it was Ziggy. After he saw the struggle going on between Bob and me he hollered for his grandmother, shouting to her: 'Don and Daddy fighting!'

When Bob heard that he calmed down. He respected his mother, despite their differences, and he would do anything not to upset her. So I left, but not without noticing that Bob's moods seemed to be becoming more and more unpredictable.

I knew then that it was over: my relationship with Bob could never be the same again. We had both come too far from our humble beginnings to be able to retrace our steps. He had risen from the slums of Trench Town to become a worldwide superstar and an icon of liberation movements all over the globe. I, too, had undertaken an odyssey of my own since my thirteen-year-old mother had gone into labour in Jamaica's Victoria Jubilee Hospital...

Beginnings

1 Growing Up in Jamaica – Waterfront Version

It was a typical cloudless azure blue Jamaican sky and bright sun that welcomed my birth on February 10th, 1943. I arrived at about the time that the morning newspaper, the *Gleaner*, was being delivered to the uptown homes.

I'm told that it was the kind of day the tourist brochures would advertise and plead that the good Lord would always bless Jamaica with; it was the kind of day that Bob Marley would best be able to depict:

> *Sun is shining, the weather is sweet*
> *Make you want to move your dancing feet*
> *When the morning gather the rainbow*
> *Want you to know, I'm a rainbow too*
> ('Sun is Shining')

My thirteen-year-old mother Cynthia Llewellyn, a maid, had given birth to me at the Victoria Jubilee Hospital. Statistically, I was one of some twenty such children born at that hospital on that day.

The Victoria Jubilee Hospital, with its four wards and one hundred beds, was situated in the west central end of Kingston on a large sprawling acreage of neglected lawns, on which only the hardiest of plants survived; plants such as ram goat roses (periwinkle) and uncared for bougainvillaea bloomed in profusion as if in defiance of the neglectful collaboration between man and nature.

Built to commemorate the reign of Queen Victoria on the throne of England (a period often referred to as the age of 'Rule Britannia'), the hospital was intended by the colonial masters to serve the needs of a colony suffering from an exploding birth rate. And the pretentious colonial-style building reflected the British intention to impress the nation with their generosity. A historic detail which was part of our curriculum at school.

Impressive as the building was, it did not take long before its capacity was far exceeded by the demand for beds. The hospital had suffered from an increasing overcrowding of the maternity ward, and a rapidly decreasing comfort level.

Kingston, my birth place, had seen many changes since its founding in 1692, when the island's original capital, Port Royal, was destroyed in an earthquake. It had barely survived another major earthquake in 1907 and the fire which followed, which had all but destroyed the town.

The city, however, still retained its original seventeenth-century grid-like physical layout, with its main boundaries on three sides being North, East and West Streets and the southern one being the harbour; its main arteries were called, in true colonial style, King, Queen, Duke and Hanover Streets.

The area I lived in, Franklin Town, was located in the eastern end of the city. It was an area of dimly-lit small narrow streets, which intersected each other in the planned grid-like fashion. Streets bearing such names as Victoria Street, Albert and Cumberland Avenues stood as testimony to the character of its earlier residents, residents who had obviously still been proud of their British heritage.

It was an area with small but spacious Victorian-type houses, houses now occupied by rental tenants rather than the owners, well-off merchants and businessmen who had moved out of Kingston into the foothills of St Andrew to escape the influx of poor Jamaicans from the countryside.

Here then is where I spent the first ten years of my life as Donald Kidd.

My mother, whom I never really knew either then or in

later years, was at the time of my birth living with a gardener called Taylor, a black Jamaican. She had a brief relationship with a white man named Vernal Kidd, a British soldier, stationed at Up Park Camp, which was locally referred to as Duppy Gate, and still remains as the home of the Jamaica Defence Force.

At that time, however, Jamaica as a colony of Great Britain had a battalion of British soldiers stationed there.

As the story goes, on the day I was born, Mr Taylor remarked to my mother on my fair complexion, but somehow my mother convinced him that in time I would become as dark as both of them.

When after nine months this did not happen, and Mr Taylor started to ask questions again, my mother promptly took me to Up Park Camp and deposited me on the desk of Mr Vernal Kidd. Mr Kidd, or 'Kidd' as everyone in Franklin Town knew him, now began to look around for somewhere to leave me. This search for someone whom I could be left with permanently continued throughout the first ten years of my life. I remember one incident in his search for such a person. I recall quite vividly, perhaps because of its hypocrisy and its racial undertones, how he took me to the home of Mrs Minnie Malabre, who apparently had no children. I remember how Mrs Malabre took me by the hand to the back verandah (a common feature of many of the houses at the time), giving me the decided feeling that the front verandah or sitting room was too good for me. She obviously felt very strongly about my black parentage, and about my mother being a maid.

My newly-found father, who had obviously sired me, was of Scottish descent, and in charge of the motor pool of his regiment. He was never close to me, and after the first ten years I didn't see him again until 1969. Having failed with Mrs Malabre, he left me with Aunt Daisy Belizario who resided at Cambridge Street. Aunt Daisy was one of that rare breed of 'brown' Jamaican ladies of English descent and good breeding who had fallen on hard times. She stood some four feet eleven inches in height, with a petite form and shape, which she carried with dignity and pride. She was a kind, soft-spoken, gentle person not much given to histrionics.

Aunt Daisy also looked after four other children in similar circumstances, so her day-to-day living was built on the theme of 'God will provide', and God did provide, because certainly my Mr Kidd didn't.

Many were the times Aunt Daisy would scribble a note, stick it in my hand, and send me off to Mr Dudley HoSang who had an import business store on Orange Street in downtown Kingston. I would return with an envelope with money; it never failed and to this day I have never been able to figure out the connection.

By the time I was eleven, however, Aunt Daisy had just about given up on me. She could not keep me in school, no matter how she tried, and all my days were spent on the waterfront. For me this bustling stretch had all the attraction and reward I needed, and I had decided that the waterfront in Kingston was where the action and the future lay for an almost abandoned brown boy. I had learnt very early in life, from the Mrs Malabres of this world, that to be brown, poor and a bastard offered a very limited future in Jamaica.

Kingston's waterfront was a hive of continuous activity. Not a week would pass when there was not a US or British naval ship in port. In addition, unlike today, there were the tourist cruise ships, and the United Fruit Company banana boats which came to offload cargo for Kingston's merchants and traders before moving on to the outports of Port Antonio, Oracabessa and Montego Bay to pick up the large banana exports destined for the markets of Britain and the USA.

It was quite a sight for me, a boy of eleven, to see all these ships sailing into one of the world's finest natural harbours –

the port of Kingston – whose backdrop was framed by the Blue Mountain range, at its highest point over eight thousand feet.

It was along this Kingston waterfront strip that Jamaica's first major hotel, the Myrtle Bank, was located.

Built by the United Fruit Company, the Myrtle Bank was not far from Pier One, and certainly on my route from Franklin Town. This route would take me along Windward Road, down Elletson Road to Tower Street and on past the General Penitentiary to turn left on Gold Street where I would arrive to face this magnificent edifice known as Myrtle Bank, the grand entrance to the waterfront. At this point I would turn right down Harbour Street, and begin my patrol, looking for tourists and the dollars I could make from them.

Awestruck, I would pass the magnificent colonial-style edifice almost daily, with its elaborate iron fence protecting the expanse of green manicured lawns from the passing native feet, lawns overlooked by the swaying arms of the royal palms lining its driveway. This was forbidden territory to all but the rich brown Jamaicans and the white tourists. This serenity would be shattered one day by the late Evon Blake, author and journalist, who, exposing his black skin, dived head first into the swimming pool. Consternation and newspaper headlines would follow. But a change was in the making.

At that time it was the Myrtle Bank Hotel which with the Titchfield Hotel and the Ethelhart in Port Antonio and the Casa Blanca in Montego Bay together formed the core of the budding tourist trade.

These hotels were very important to the likes of the United Fruit Company, the banana giant of the Latin America region, and it was they who had developed the hotels into world-renowned inns. For they would, in addition to transporting bananas in the holds of ships, also bring visitors. It was also quite common for Jamaicans to take the ships from Kingston for a round-the-island cruise, leaving Kingston for Port Antonio and going on to Oracabessa and Montego Bay for an interesting local shipboard holiday.

In its heyday the Myrtle Bank Hotel had been the social centre of Kingston, but by my day, it was on the wane. World War II had had its effect on the hotel, as the United Fruit Company lost its banana operation due to the war, and the tourists stopped coming, all of which led to the company putting the hotel up for sale.

This move was to be significant for Jamaica's future, as it led to an Arab-Jamaican, Abe Issa, godfather of the tourist industry, buying the Myrtle Bank Hotel, a very bold and visionary step for those war days, but a step that began his fantastically successful career in tourism. He moved on to buy Tower Isle (now Couples), in St Mary, and finally some five more hotels worldwide, leaving a legacy and a family business that is still being developed by his family, and an industry which today is one of Jamaica's largest foreign exchange earners.

In my day the Myrtle Bank Hotel, although still the rendezvous for well-to-do brown Jamaicans, had to share its clientele with the Jamaica Arms, located some two blocks away and the first air-conditioned bar to be opened in Kingston. The opening of the Jamaica Arms reflected the changing tempo of the times, and the class and colour barriers began to break down. And although the celebrities did still come – Errol Flynn himself was not an uncommon habitué of the Myrtle Bank – the doors began to open wide.

Not wide enough to admit street urchins like myself, however. Many were the days when I would stand outside gawking, having brought the most recent ship arrivals to the portals of the Myrtle Bank.

It did not take me long to realize that the streets of downtown Kingston, running parallel and perpendicular to the waterfront, formed the pulse of the city, for herein lay the premier commercial shopping areas of Harbour Street and King Street, then the home of the leading Arab and Jewish merchants; these were streets which boasted some of the best and most exciting stores to be found anywhere in the then developed world. Along these streets were the businesses of the Issas, the Morins, the Duries and the Hannas, operating such stores as Nathans, Morins, Times Store and E.A. Issa & Brothers, stocked with the finest merchandise from the UK and USA. They competed cheek by jowl with Indian merchants, like the Dadlanis and Chatanis, with their exquisite jewellery and silk; there was also the occasional itinerant vendor hawking his camphor balls, hair curlers, clothes pins and sweets from the sidewalks.

Duke Street, some two blocks away and running parallel to King Street from north to south, was the home of all the major legal firms, much as it is today. Here were located the offices of the Ashenheims, Judah and Desnoes, Dunn, Cox and Orrett, Myers, Fletcher and Gordon and all the other leading giants of law in Jamaica.

I wasn't really interested in any of this. It was when the city offices and stores closed, and the Kingston lights were switched on and the action began, that my world really came alive.

The bars and clubs I frequented were scattered among the dimly-lit streets of downtown Kingston, from east to west and north to south. West Street housed the renowned Fats Waller All American Bar, which had recently relocated itself from Hanover Street, so that it was the first bar that visiting sailors would stumble upon.

But it was Hanover Street which boasted the most bars and clubs; for along this street was located Ma Chung's, Captain's Corner and Sailor's Rest, to name a few that I frequented, and with all of whom I had my own special money-making arrangements.

All these clubs were much of a kind. They all had a wooden

bar, with stools of varying heights, sizes and styles. They all had juke boxes with the latest overseas hits and the outside walls were festooned with the talent of numerous untrained artists, colourfully recording the name of the club in the most delightful and interesting way.

The inside walls were invariably decorated with photographs cut from the pages of US magazines or naughty nude calendars, and, not to be outdone, the sign painter would invariably record the wisest of sayings, such as 'Cash is alive, Credit is dead.'

Almost all boasted backrooms fitted out with the basic essentials, supposedly meant to provide for a good home away from home, but actually offering only short-term personal gratification.

The stock in trade of the bar was Jamaican white rum of the highest proof, a rum which could scorch the most experienced alcoholic throat. Red rum brands such as Black Seal, Gold Seal and Appleton were offered, alongside the inimitable Jamaican Red Stripe Beer as well as foreign beer brands such as Pabst Blue Ribbon, Budweiser and Heineken.

The bars all but exclusively catered to the ordinary sailor, soldier and lower-class Jamaican, although intermittently they saw upper-class Jamaicans who would occasionally stop by on their way home from their offices, or on their way to and from the more upper-class brothels and whorehouses located in many of these areas of Kingston.

Kingston at this time boasted such exclusive brothels as Strolley's, Dewdney's Paradise Club and Maidman's Bamboo Bar, a bar which was run by an Englishman, who thanks to his very uncommon position was always referred to as Mister. Many of today's businessmen, politicians and columnists were frequent visitors to these brothels, and one or two of the live-in girls have gone on to fame and fortune. There was, as usual, a distinction between the street whores and the live-in ladies.

In fact, I very rarely visited any of these upper-class clubs and whorehouses, as they offered very few economic benefits for me. The bars, on the other hand, did not carry the rigid rules of brothels, and since they were open to the public, it was quite in order for these uptowners to visit and partake when visiting east or west late at night. In those days, Kingston had not yet become segregated by wealth and class and all of its citizens moved freely without fear for their safety. This was the fifties.

The city, however, was slowly starting to show signs of decay, so that as the more successful residents moved out of Kingston and migrated to the hills of St Andrew, the city was taken over by people moving in from the rural areas; and as one moved westward, such areas as Jones Town, Denham Town and Trench Town were now increasingly becoming the base for the newly-arrived downtrodden and the oppressed, about whom Bob Marley would sing in his song 'Trench Town Rock'.

But the waterfront of Kingston is where my exposure to life began, and this is where I flourished. One of the first things you learnt in this environment was to be sharp, quick, smart and ready for any break, and to be ready for any break usually meant escaping from the island. This in turn meant that another of the first things you learnt was that you needed a passport, which you always kept nearby, as you had to be prepared for the first opportunity to get away from Kingston, Jamaica to the great big world.

It was this ambition to move on which led me to seek out my birth certificate, finally and fatefully bringing me into contact with my registered name – Donald Delroy Taylor – and bringing back to me the reality of my birth.

My mother had in fact registered me after her live-in man; I had his name, but not his colour.

By the time I turned thirteen, in 1956, I was four feet tall, and confident enough to face life with a smile. Given the rules of the game, I was learning fast. I was hustling day and night.

It did not take me long to be accepted within the ranks of the waterfront's slickest hustlers. There were such people as Benjie Howard, the top waterfront pimp, noted by his peers for his mode of dress – always in the latest American style and fashion. We all had what I would call a 'foreign mind', maybe because our minds were always on the next US buck, and our hearts were always yearning, seeking a way to reach out to the exciting worlds of New York and London. Many of the hustlers even spoke with a phony American accent, but this was one thing I never did adopt.

I can still visualize such professionals as Dutch, and the pier foreman, Mr Kirlew. Dutch always dressed like a naval officer, clean, fresh and upright. He was the kind of character who would arrive on board the ship and with military precision salute the captain and launch into his well-planned marketing spiel. It never failed to work. It was characters such as Dutch and Benjie who fine-tuned my antennae, preparing me to face the world with confidence and very few hang-ups.

There was never a dull moment for me on the waterfront, for as the sailors and the cruise passengers disembarked, I was all things to all persons. In the few hours they were on shore, I was tourist guide, pimp or hustler, depending on their needs and their search for action. I would, for a fee and a reward, guide them to whatever they wanted. I would take those of the cruise passengers who were touristically inclined to the Myrtle Bank Hotel or hustle them into a taxi to go uptown to the Hope Zoo and Gardens, or further on to Castleton Gardens, some twenty miles from the waterfront. I preferred, however, to persuade them to go with me to my favourite bars, where I had my private financial arrangement with both the bartenders and the girls.

By sixteen I had come up with a lot of ideas that seemed to make me stand out from the average hustler. I struck many and varied deals with the various club owners and waitresses.

One such deal was that any beer I ordered would be sold to me for two shillings, and I in turn would sell it for three or four shillings to unsuspecting sailors. In many cases, I would negotiate with the waiters to refuse to take the sailors' orders except through me. They had to support this deal as it was because of me that the sailors were there in the first place, and I could have taken them to any one of the other bars. In true hustler style, I got them to realize that they had to cater to me in order to keep the business.

On the days that the ships did not come in, I had to find other ways and means to earn a living. On those days, I would wash the cars of leading businessmen. I remember washing cars in the open-air car park at Duke Street for such businessmen as Danny Williams, then working for North American Life Insurance Company; Roy Morin, owner of the best men's department store on King Street; Vivian Blake, leading lawyer and politician who challenged Michael Manley for leadership of the PNP after the retirement of Norman Manley. But all this I learnt later, as politics was the furthest thing from my mind in those days.

I was able to survive by being street-smart, and knowing how to hustle. I spent most of my nights in the clubs, which meant that I knew everybody in all of them. I knew the barmaids, the waitresses, the bartenders, the pimps, the prostitutes, the gamblers.

On looking back I still regard those days as some of my most enjoyable. I had known no other life, the waterfront had become my home, the inhabitants my friends and family. They replaced the mother and father I never had, and there was always Aunt Daisy in the background providing refuge when I needed it.

Another of my main means of income was to hustle Lucky Strike and Camel cigarettes from the US sailors and sell them at a good profit to the Chinese, Indian and Syrian merchants and the bars. To buy the cartons I would often dive for the money thrown overboard by the cruise ship visitors – a favourite pastime for us waterfront boys.

I used to frequent Mr Hill's kerosene shop on Hanover Street, between Laws and Barry Streets, where at times his son Micky Hill and I would exchange youthful thoughts. Uptown kids were always curious to know how we, the street people, lived.

I remember vividly my one and only brush with the law, when my friend, if I could call him that, Chiney Man, got me into a tricky situation. Over time I had developed this connection at Wray and Nephew which allowed me to buy rum at a good price. On this occasion, Chiney Man and I had taken some money from an American lady to buy white rum for her but instead he ran away with the money, and she reported the theft to policeman Gupte. Gupte was an Indian policeman who made no bones about sending thieves and pimps to jail, and he had become quite feared by the waterfront hustlers. He chased me and held me that Friday and locked me up over the weekend at the Central Police Station. The only reason I escaped going to prison like most other people was that a young lawyer, Noel Silvera, who used to play cricket at Kensington Cricket Club where I hung out in my younger days, saw me in the Sutton Street Court. Because he knew that I was not a totally bad boy, he took up my case and made an agreement for the money to be paid by him personally, thus causing the case to be dismissed, and eternally placing me in his debt.

My first taste of and experience with show business and its personnel came through the Ward Theatre, a few blocks from the waterfront, and immediately overlooking the Queen Victoria Park.

Ward Theatre was, and still is, Jamaica's premier theatre. This impressive concert hall was a gift to the people of Jamaica from Colonel Ward.

One day I was on the waterfront close to the Queen

Victoria Pier, with very little to do, as it was not a cruise or war ship day. I was looking for action and as fate would have it, I met Lloyd Price, the American singer. Lloyd had broken big in Jamaica following his massive hit 'Personality' which brought him to Jamaica. I knew all about him because transistor radios were just becoming popular, and being on the waterfront, I had been able to hustle many of these. They helped to introduce many of my friends and myself to the world of music; we played them constantly and looked on them as status symbols.

Lloyd Price and I got talking and immediately struck up a friendship during which he told me he was staying at the Flamingo Hotel in Cross Roads. As this was an uptown area, it was not my beat. In fact, I had very rarely ventured uptown, so that when he asked me to accompany him to the hotel, I jumped at the invitation – but more because it offered me the opportunity to conclude our conversation on the world of entertainment, which I had found fascinating.

As Lloyd Price and I talked, the world of entertainment seemed more and more attractive and it was during this encounter that I first heard the name Stephen Hill, because it was he who had brought Lloyd Price to Jamaica.

It was the late fifties then, and Stephen Hill had built up a considerable reputation as Jamaica's leading impresario. Hill was a brown Jamaican like myself, a medium-height, sharp-featured man who had, with his wife Dorothy, pioneered the business of show promotions. As I would later learn, Hill had from the early forties to the sixties brought to the island a range of artistes such as Artur Rubinstein, Marian Anderson, and Todd Duncan in the classical field, and in the popular field, Nat King Cole, Billy Eckstine, and Cab Calloway, to name but a few – a truly remarkable achievement.

This encounter with Lloyd Price now led me to begin hanging out at some of the Kingston theatres, and led to my first venture into the world of show biz. On many occasions

I would be chased away by Stephen Hill himself, whom I admired from a distance, and whom in many instances I wished to emulate. But he would always shoo me away, calling me a 'dirty little hanger-on'.

My waterfront hustling skills, however, were soon to come in handy, for while hanging around the Ward and other show spots such as the Carib Theatre and the Regal and Tropical Cinemas in Cross Roads, I began to hear complaints from the performers and managers of these artistes that they could not get their stage clothes properly cleaned.

I was struck by the opportunity this offered me, so I immediately went and checked out the clothes cleaning scene. I spent one whole week visiting the dry cleaners in the area, before I decided that I would offer a professional valet service for artistes when they came to Jamaica.

I set up my machinery so as to keep a check on the comings and goings of all visiting artistes, as I had decided to work it out by directly hustling their managers for their valet business. I felt that by this method I would be cutting out all middlemen, and would specifically bypass Mr Hill, who I felt would inevitably try to block me.

In no time I had built my valet service into a kind of full-scale personal service for the artistes, as in addition to my valet service I now also ran errands and picked up the things they needed, and saw to it that everybody was on stage on time in their professionally cleaned performing clothes. And before anyone was fully aware of what was happening, I had also extended my service to protecting their valuables, such as money and jewellery, from any light fingers that may have been close to the dressing rooms during their performances. I carried out all this despite the objections and much to the continued annoyance of Stephen Hill.

Even in those early days I earned the respect of the people I dealt with, whether it was the businessman whose car I washed, the sailor whom I showed around Kingston, the lawyer, the trickster, the whore, or the general street person; respect given, respect returned was the hallmark of my associations.

So it was that my valet and personal service grew, boasting such clients as Fats Domino, Ben E. King, Chuck Jackson (who in time would come under my managerial wing), and Little Anthony and the Imperials; and as time passed my prestigious list grew in leaps and bounds to include Patti LaBelle and the Blue Belles and Jerry Butler. All these artistes have, over time, expressed their appreciation to me for my professionalism, whether I was offering them my personal Jamaican valet service or in later years acting for some as their manager.

It was through my valet service that in 1959 I got my first chance to travel. The time had finally come to venture forth, something I had always looked forward to and the reason why I always had my passport with me.

After all, although until now I had spent my life on the waterfront, I had met people from all over the world, and somehow I had begun to feel I belonged to the world.

And as fate would have it, it was during my valeting for Little Anthony and the Imperials that I struck up a relationship with a friend of theirs, Phillip Bowe, who had come over from Nassau and who did basically the same thing in the Bahamas as I did in Jamaica. It was not surprising then that after the visit of the Imperials ended, Phillip invited me to visit the Bahamas.

As the Bahamas was also a British territory, you needed no visa to visit, but as I later learnt, you certainly needed a work permit to stay there and work, even if you were only sixteen years old, as I was at the time.

I arrived in Nassau with some ten US dollars in my pocket, and immediately began to hang out at such clubs as Jonkanoo and Black Beard's Tavern, which I felt were the logical places to continue my valet service to the stars; and where I figured

I would probably find some talent to manage, as my ambitions were now moving in this direction. So I began to make friends with most of the entertainers, including such persons as Richie Delmore and the Kemp Brothers, Jonathan and David. It was David Kemp who put me up in a wooden house he owned on Taylor Street which he only used intermittently or more specifically when he had a girlfriend he wanted to spend time with. In order for me to survive he got me a job as a bus boy at the Dolphin Hotel, which exists to this date without a name change.

My life in Nassau contrasted quite markedly from Jamaica and must have prepared me for my US days. For during this time, Nassau was openly racist, with most if not all of the black Bahamians confined to over the hill and the stores on Bay Street, all owned by the white Bahamians; a scenario which gave rise to black consciousness and later led to the long reign of Sir Lynden Pindling and the PLP.

This, of course, left only menial or service jobs open to the black Bahamians and indeed even if you were Bahamian, you were required to identify yourself to security if you were found on the Cable Beach or the tourist side of the island after dark. This meant that entertainment was virtually one's only escape.

The nature of the music business was such that the transition from valet to manager was usually one short step. People like me, by the very nature of our exposure to those who were stars, would attract the interest of newer stars seeking a break, and so I took on the management of the Bahamian calypso singers Tony Seymour and Rusty, with great success.

But I felt increasingly uncomfortable in Nassau. I was becoming aware that I had to play it cautiously, if ever I was to obtain a Bahamian work permit. Especially as there always seemed to be this fear by Bahamians that the increasing flow of Jamaicans was threatening their well-being. I was always looking over my shoulder, and having to play it very safe.

At the same time I was growing in experience in the entertainment business, and adding confidence to my management style, as I was doing this in another country and doing it successfully, even if it was for little or no real return.

As I had feared, the dreaded day came when, four to five months after I first arrived in Nassau, I was advised that Immigration was looking for me. This was all the excuse I needed. I immediately packed what little I had and headed back to Jamaica.

This first trip, however, had opened my eyes to the future possibilities of the entertainment world and I resolved to make it my career.

As it turned out, Immigration had done me a favour, because I arrived back in Jamaica at the time Jackie Wilson was visiting. I immediately revived my business operations and offered my valet services to him. I provided Jackie Wilson with such excellent service that he offered to buy me a ticket to the USA – Miami to be exact.

Things moved very quickly after this as Jackie gave me sixty US dollars for my air ticket, as he wanted me to join him in the USA. But now I needed a visa. It was then that I remembered this military attaché from my hustling days, who worked at the US Embassy located on Duke Street, and who would visit the downtown bars after work. I recalled that he had promised me that if I ever got a ticket, he would grant me a visa.

Having some idea of the visa requirements, which included a recommendation letter, I immediately went to Mr Nari Chatani who owned a shop located on Harbour Street known as the East Indian Bazaar and with whom I used to do business. I usually got a commission from him on all sailors brought there to shop. Without any hesitation he gave me the recommendation letter, which I hurriedly took to the attaché, with the ticket, and I got the visa stamped in my passport. After that with much glee and excitement I headed straight for 10 Kensington Road, where I had hung out ever since my return from Nassau.

Ten Kensington Road was a well-known whorehouse and club owned and run by a friend, Billy Farnum. Billy was a slick, slim, sharp, tall brown Jamaican. His club, the High Hat, and his racehorse, Sir Alec, gave him an aura of flair and style. He would cruise around Kingston in his white Cadillac visiting such friends as Freddie Chin, who owned the Club Havana, where Carlos Malcolm and his Afro-Caribbean music – forerunners of the ska music of the sixties – held sway.

I hurriedly explained to Billy that I was leaving that day with Jackie, and as if by magic the word spread through the house, and indeed through the neighbourhood: 'Don T' was on his way to the USA, and leaving with Jackie Wilson, no less.

Dumping my limited possessions into one small bag, and with a certain sense of importance, amid cheers and best wishes, I jumped into Billy's car and waved goodbye to my friends and neighbours.

Thus it was that in 1960 my longed-for dream of reaching the USA seemed only a few hours away. I had for the time being washed my hands of Jamaica and was now moving ahead into the sixties, excited by the prospect of the good life.

2 Bob's Early Life – Concrete Jungle Version

The Jamaica I left behind in the fifties was not the Jamaica I later returned to, nor was it the Jamaica that Bob Marley was experiencing through the fifties and into the sixties. For despite my hardships I had been fortunate enough to live in east Kingston and to be able to leave, and migrate to the USA. But meanwhile the rot had set in: the major flood of migration from village to town had begun and the deterioration of the city was showing, especially in the west.

My side of Kingston, the east side, was to me a place of gentle breeding and courtesy, which it seems left those of us who lived there more tolerant and aware of each other, and of our common needs. For in those days, perhaps as a carry-over from colonialism, and due to the advent of self-government, it seemed to me we were much more aware of the need to live in harmony. Not for me, then, the violent, divided city, riven by politics and poverty which ultimately placed us in armed camps, with an ever-increasing rate of crime and violence.

In my time, on my side of town, we would walk the streets and acknowledge each other with a smile and a greeting. The house doors would remain unlocked and the church doors open and no matter what your station in life, there was a certain civility that transcended such classifications. In fact, nowhere was out of bounds to anyone; the city was yours from east to west, from north to south, from one bar to the next, from one cinema to the next, whether it was the Majestic in the west or the Rialto in the east.

The nights as always were noisy, resounding with the barking of dogs, and the early-morning hours were still at times punctuated by the clip-clopping of the horse-drawn carts delivering milk and bread door-to-door. And all this against the background of the whistling toads. The early evening was heralded by the whistle of the peanut vendor stridently announcing his arrival. This was Jamaica in the fifties.

But unnoticed during this time the underdevelopment of the rural areas was leading to more and more persons from the country swelling the ranks of the city's unemployable. The city, unable to absorb them, or to provide housing and facilities for them, deteriorated into the ghettoes of today, and the existence of wealth and poverty on a cheek-by-jowl basis was seen for the first time.

Cold ground was my bed last night
And rock was my pillow too
('Talkin' Blues')

Meanwhile, the more aspiring new middle class and the well-to-do had begun to move out of the area of Jones Pen subsequently called Denham Town, and Trench Town, all in the west, and Franklin Town and Vineyard Town in the east.

New areas of development began in such areas as Mona. And the pretentious homes which were being constructed in the locally renowned Beverly Hills stood in stark contrast to the ghetto areas only a stone's throw away.

In addition to these developments, the years since my departure had seen the decline of colonialism worldwide, and Jamaica had itself moved rapidly towards Independence.

In my youthful days of hustling, trying to make a living in Jamaica, I had not been aware of the underlying political and social needs of the people. Nor was I aware of the outside world's pressures which were beginning to attract the attention of the politicians and the populace at large.

Years later, then, I would always find it interesting to

compare notes with Bob about our parallel lifestyles, growing up in different parts of Jamaica during the same period. For while I was experiencing the pain, pleasure and anguish of the Jamaican city boy, Bob Marley, also the descendant of a white man, was growing up, so to speak, on the other side of the hill, first in the hills of St Ann and then on the other side of the city, in West Kingston.

Whereas I knew my father, and the people of Franklin Town knew him, and whereas I could actually approach him on his sober days, and people knew me as Mr Kidd's son, this was not the case with Bob Marley.

Bob never knew his father, nor did he ever meet him in his lifetime but, like me, he was virtually abandoned by his mother, Cedella, who left him to be raised by his Granny Yaya and his grandfather, Omeriah.

Bob's father, Norval, being a descendant of a supposedly respectable white Jamaican family, would not have been allowed by the social mores of the time to acknowledge a bastard child by a black country woman and a peasant at that. And the only contact Bob ever had with the Marley family, he told me, was when in later years he visited his uncle, a lawyer on Duke Street, to borrow some £300 for the production of a record. He was unceremoniously thrown out of his office without a greeting or a smile. His uncle, one Cecil Marley, not only ejected him but also called the police.

Bob was a rural child, raised in the hills of Nine Miles in St Ann. His grandfather, a farmer, lived a typical Jamaican peasant's life, full of hardship, but one which was spiced with Anancy stories, riddles, Blackheart stories and African proverbs of great wisdom. His grandparents were able to trace their ancestry from the Coromantee slaves of the tribe of Akan, a tribe noted for their resilience and prophetic powers.

Bob's mother had left him at an early age to move to Spanish Town to live with a Chinese man. She left Bob in St

Ann, where he attended Stepney School. He often told me that he would never forget the day he went to visit her at the shop. He had been sent by Granny to look for his mother, and when he arrived at the shop and called her name, 'Mama', she asked him, 'Who yu a call Mama?' This, he said, left an indelible mark on him, and it was a story he often repeated.

In recounting stories of his early life he always emphasized the fact that Granny was the person he was closest to. She saw to his every need as he moved about Nine Miles, attending school but increasingly being attracted to the city. To get a true picture of Nine Miles, one must appreciate that St Ann is a parish historically steeped in the plantocracy and its way of life. One of its main towns, Brown's Town, boasted one of the best upper-class girls' schools, St Hilda's – a school which literally lived up to the town's name as black girls were hardly ever admitted. Although Bob himself had the right tint, he lacked the right upbringing.

As soon as Bob realized that St Ann did not hold much for him, like many other rural boys, and encouraged by his equally curious 'cousin' Bunny Livingston, later known as Bunny Wailer (with whom he shared an early interest in music), he decided to move to Kingston where his mother was now living with Bunny's father, Thaddeus, in Trench Town.

Trench Town and the rest of West Kingston were beginning to experience a flare-up of the ghetto problem which had started to become noticeable in the early fifties: there were large tracts of wasteland crammed with the makeshift houses of the itinerant rural squatters who captured every square inch of living space, as they moved from country to town.

The shacks were built cheek-by-jowl and unaccountably the politicians thought that the way to solve the problem was simply to bulldoze them all down and build large concrete structures, of which Rema and Tivoli were the most outstanding examples. This was where Bob ended up, in the area the country would later call 'Concrete Jungle'.

It was here that Bob was to begin his association with Peter Tosh. Bunny had already joined him and their interest in music brought the three together.

Many idle days were spent by the majority of young ghetto dwellers in a world without regular work and opportunities. This was a world where the only escape seemed to be in the learning of a trade for the boys and the cleaning of white people's houses for the girls, or in migration to 'foreign' by first the mother and finally the family.

For recreation, cards, dominoes and early sexual experience were the order of the day and the night and any woman who had not had a child by fifteen was considered a mule.

The only relief from tension were the blues dances featuring the sound systems of the likes of Sir Coxsone Downbeat held at Love Lane and Beeston Street and at Cho Co Mo Lawn. Here the sharply-dressed youth would move to the beat of Fats Domino and Louis Jordan and his Tympany Five, while blissfully inhaling the ganja which heightened their appreciation of the local kings of toasting such as King Sporty, King Stitt and Count Machub, the real forerunners of Dee Jaying, rapping and hip hop.

The only other outlet of escape was the creative talent of the individual, and with the increasing availability of the transistor radio, thousands of which were now finding their way into Jamaica, it was not surprising that the world of music would attract many adherents and dreamers from among the ranks of the sufferers in the ghettoes. Like me, Bob was one of those who found the music irresistible.

It was to Vincent 'Tata' Ford that Bob told me he turned for guidance and comfort in this era of his life and with whom he virtually lived. He slept in Tata's kitchen, where he met Rita and where they first consummated their sexual life.

Over the years Bob continually expressed to me his deep love, appreciation and trust of Tata Ford, whose name he subsequently used as the writer of 'No Woman No Cry', the song which was set in Tata's government yard and spoke of people Bob actually knew, like Georgie.

I remember when we used to sit
In a government yard in Trench Town.

Trench Town was filled with concrete structures and a myriad network of unpaved footpaths, with few trees and little or no grass, where only the cacti and the acacia withstood the neglect of man and nature. The disposal of human waste was carried out in the open and the night was lit by the flickering glow of kerosene lanterns and kitchen bitches. Running water was limited to the government tenement yards, or the odd standpipe. Thank God for the transistor radio which needed no electricity, and allowed an escape to the wide world of music.

As Bob said in 1975, 'We used to sing in the back of Trench Town and rehearse plenty until the Drifters came 'pon the scene, and mi group singing, so me just say, well me 'ave fe go look a group.'

Now that Bob was living in closer proximity to his mother Cedella, who had by this time become very church-conscious, he was finding it increasingly difficult to deal with her; she was pushing him to choose a trade as a way out of the ghetto and Bob finally enrolled to learn the trade of welding. But he was far more interested in the field of music and more attracted to the Rastafarian religion, which was becoming increasingly popular in Trench Town. Bob was intrigued by Rastafarianism's haughty rejection of the material world and the injustices being heaped on the people by 'Babylon', or the establishment. His differences with his mother increased, especially as he seemed to be becoming quite a proponent and admirer, in the eyes of his mother, of the rude boy culture which was beginning to impact on Jamaican society.

In the ghetto world one had to subscribe to the motto of dog eat dog, kill or be killed. And it was necessary to fight in defence of one's territory and rights, for survival. And one's political grouping was becoming increasingly important as the divisions between Labourite community and PNP community took shape, especially as the youthful socialist Tony Spaulding tried to wrest away from E.C.L. Parkinson and Wilton Hill of the JLP the whole area known as Trench Town. The rude boy culture reflected this new aggression and divisiveness.

Now the fire is burning . . .
Ride natty ride
Go deh dready, go deh
('Ride Natty Ride')

All around the area the political culture grew, noticed and unnoticed. But the other cultures with the most impact were sound system music and the Rastafarian religion. The music world expanded and exploded, embracing the likes of Count P, Duke Reid and his Treasure Isle label and Clement Dodd, a cabinet maker turned DJ who hired Prince Buster and selector Lee Perry to expand the impact of his sound system. The music attracted and enveloped the youth who themselves mirrored in increasing numbers the rude boy image of the time, as the systems each established their home turf, which needed protection.

Coxsone's Musik City which opened in 1959 was where Bob spent many hours and where he eventually got up enough courage to show his songs to Dodd. But as fate would have it, first he ran into Leslie Kong at Federal Records, for whom he recorded his first ever songs, 'Judge Not' and 'Do You Still Love Me', for which he was paid twenty pounds.

Meanwhile it was Mortimer Planno of the Divine

Theocratic Temple that Bob turned to for guidance and explanation of the Rastafarian religion.

Planno took Bob through the stages of Rastafarianism, taking him to the settlements deep in the interior of the country where he learnt about the grounation ceremonies, and the all-night convocations which meant feasting on coconut meat, rice and peas (ital cooking). It was here that he listened to the chants of the traditional Bongo Man and the Humba and Nyabinghi chants, while hundreds of Rastas sat on their haunches passing the sacred chillum pipe.

The Rasta women, contrastingly, would sit separately, especially if they were menstruating – an unclean state for a Rasta. In the Rasta world women play a very restricted role and make-up and perfumes are not permitted. They are required to dress modestly.

It was during one of these exchanges with Planno that the spirituality of Bob manifested itself as he told Planno of a dream he had had. An old man attired in khaki had come to him in his dream, described himself as an emissary of the deceased Norval Marley (Bob's father) and presented Bob with a ring set with a curious black jewel. Bob then told Planno that on telling his mother of this dream, she had produced the very ring in the dream and slipped it on Bob's finger, but it had made him extremely uncomfortable to wear it. Planno told Bob that his dream had a double meaning: he would either grow in spirituality through his experiences or he would 'Ketch a fire' (catch hell) – which would later be the name of one of Bob's albums.

Needless to say welding did not hold Bob for long and an unfortunate accident where a steel sliver damaged his eye forced him to stop. This accident, however, heightened the tension between Bob and his mother. She objected strongly to his Rastafarian leanings and his smoking of ganja and she virtually banned him from the home, which is why he ended up sleeping in Tata's kitchen.

In later years Bob would lose some respect for his mother when she herself took up the Rasta faith in the face of his rising worldwide recognition. To see her come full circle, smoking the weed and calling him Brother Bob, never sat comfortably with him, and on one occasion when I raised some personal business matters his response was: 'Don Taylor, you don't know my mother?'

Bob had broken with Kong following his recording of some five more songs including 'One Cup of Coffee'. And his musical strength and confidence were already showing. The group had by now become known as the Wailers, and with the addition of two Rema girls to sing back-up and Junior Braithwaite to share the vocals the scene was complete.

Somewhere around this time the first Wailers album, *Simmer Down*, done with Coxsone Dodd, was released.

Forming the political backdrop to this was the failure of the Norman Manley PNP government to take Jamaica into a Federation of the Caribbean States. This had resulted in the JLP government of Alexander Bustamante taking the country into Independence on August 3, 1962.

The dawn of the Independence era brought to the fore the hopes and aspirations of the people, and given the racial and economic make-up of the society, some 80 per cent of the population saw Independence as the road to greater opportunity for wealth and success. Hard work was not preached. The celebrations and all the great expectations that led up to Independence further aggravated the situation, and saw an even greater influx of persons from the country into the city. People were in search of the new opportunities that everyone was talking about.

The area of West Kingston from which the musical Marley emerged had always been the centre of violent political swings, but somehow always remained the cultural centre of the country.

One good thing about music
When it hits you, you feel no pain.
('Trench Town Rock')

By coincidence the political representative of the West was none other than Edward Seaga, who was himself steeped in the history of the development of Jamaica's music. It was the same Edward Seaga who had become the first record producer on the WIRL (West Indies Recording Limited) label. He formed part of the original small body of producers which included Leslie Kong, Coxsone Dodd and Duke Reid.

A Harvard-trained anthropologist, Seaga, after receiving his degree in 1952, had proceeded to study the history and development of revivalist cults and the indigenous music forms of Kumina, Pocomania, and Obeah practices in Jamaica, out of which came his 1955 album of cult music recorded for the Ethnic Folkways label. In those pre-political days he set out to develop in the ghettoes of West Kingston an opportunity through music that had been long awaited by the area's residents.

Seaga moved the music into more commercial territory and from his base in Cho Co Mo Lawn began to record sessions at JBC and Federal Records, signing such Trench Town or West Kingston groups as Joe Higgs and Roy Wilson to the WIRL label. Out of this came the Higgs and Wilson 1959 ska track called 'Manny O', which realized an unprecedented sales return of thirty thousand copies; perhaps even more startling, however, was the fact that for the first time a producer made sure that the actual talent of the artiste was suitably recompensed with real money. Seaga then went on to sign up such additional talent as Slim Smith and Byron Lee.

Joe Higgs himself had long ago been influenced by the Rasta faith, through which he retained the kind of black dignity that was becoming admired in the ghettoes. He now brought his influence to bear on the music coming out of the ghetto.

As soon as Higgs knew he had the attention of the creative youth of the area known as Rema, he started a music clinic. Using his knowledge and skill and access to the records of such stars as Nat King Cole, Billy Eckstine and Lord Kitchener, he imparted to his pupils the rudiments of music. Among these pupils were Bob Marley, Bunny Wailer and Peter Tosh.

It was around this period that Bob met up with Danny Sims and Johnny Nash and the whole story which has become linked to Cayman Music and Sims Publishing Company was born.

It was shortly after Bunny Wailer was sent to prison for smoking ganja that Bob, having returned to St Ann, was approached by Johnny Nash, his personal manager Danny Sims, and Arthur Jenkins, all of whom were visiting Jamaica. They persuaded Marley to sign to the US JAD (Johnny, Arthur and Danny) label.

Johnny Nash subsequently paid for Bob to go to Europe to make an album, and a film scene. In the end only one single came out of the album and the film scene has never seen daylight.

Johnny Nash, however, struck gold with his cover version 'Guava Jelly', coming out of his *I Can See Clearly Now* album.

Bob complained about not being paid what he was due, and said, 'Me don't want to say nothing "bad" 'bout them, but still me no have nothin' much good to say.' Needless to say he had learnt his lesson.

All that time, I learnt later, Bob was also recording with the Wailers for Lee Perry, producing such tracks as 'Soul Rebel', 'It's All Right', and 'Duppy Conqueror'. I would later learn that all that Bob knew about laying music came from Lee Perry. I discovered this when for the first time I had to produce Martha Valez's 'Disco Nights' which was written by Bob for Sire Records, the independent arm of Time/ Warner. We discussed how we would do it and without any hesitation Bob called Lee Perry to work with him. I recall Bob saying that Lee 'Scratch' Perry was the best at laying rhythms. We did this at Harry J's studios.

It was also during this period that Arnett Gardens was bull-dozed to clear the area for a new development. This was the PNP politicians' attempt at providing some facilities for the downtrodden, but it also increased political divisions and tensions as the old residents were pushed out and PNP supporters brought in to create a new constituency. Concrete Jungle was created. Meanwhile, *Soul Revolution*, the second Wailers album, was kicking up a storm.

The studios of Perry and Kong were themselves frequently releasing the Wailers' tunes, but not to the liking of Bunny, Peter and Bob. Leslie Kong died at thirty-eight of a heart attack. Kong had no previous trace of heart trouble, but died immediately following a curse wished upon him by the Wailers who, like all recording artistes of the time, knew they were being exploited.

The story about Bob's deadly curse went the rounds, and coupled with Planno's interpretation of the dream and the ring began to create the aura of mysticism which would later surround his life.

The political temperature was rising, continuously raised by the sounds of the ghetto, and as many of the musical stars in the ska scene, the emerging dance craze of the rude boys, were Rastas, a natural national identity developed.

Seaga had by now forsaken the musical world for the hallowed halls of political representation and made his first major political speech as Senator about the haves and the have nots, steeped in his knowledge of the ghetto. Bustamante had appointed him to the Senate in 1954, and made him Minister of Development and Welfare.

The early divisiveness of the political scene with its two-party rivalries had continued to worsen, with Seaga charging that the police were hired guns for the PNP and Manley retaliating with verbal accusations of Seaga's thuggery. The stage for confrontation had been set and would continue into the future. For indeed what was this white Lebanese doing trying to carve out a stake in the black-controlled ghettoes of the west, and even winning a seat in the 1962 elections against none other than the 'Burning Spear', Dudley Thompson, who had just returned from Africa after defending no less a person than Jomo Kenyatta?

All this was too much for Bob's mother and she took off for Delaware in the USA, unable to understand Bob's attraction to the ghetto and his unusual approach to life. Perhaps, however, it all lay in Granny's famous saying which Bob would often repeat to me, 'When the root is strong the fruit is sweet.'

Bob plunged deeper into the music world in the absence of his mother. And as the opportunities increased with the opening of new studios, so did the impact of his music, the music of the ghetto which still failed to be accepted by the upper-class Jamaicans, who saw it as an insult to the culture of the brown upper class.

One person who did not see it this way was the innovative and creative Byron Lee, a Jamaican of Chinese descent, who had himself now joined the ranks of record producers, having bought out Seaga's WIRL label and worked out a deal with Atlantic Records to launch ska commercially. This coincided with Millie Small's 1964 world hit of 'My Boy Lollipop' which followed her arrival in England where she recorded it on the Island label owned by one Chris Blackwell. Offspring of the plantocracy, he had now discovered a niche from which he could make big money.

The music itself was changing from ska to rock steady and had begun to produce some major successes. It was the period during which the likes of the Blues Busters, Millie Small, Desmond Dekker and the Aces all made their mark, and the music world was beginning to take note.

Not surprisingly it was Seaga who capitalized on the new craze and decided as Minister of Development and Welfare to send a ska delegation to the 1964 New York World's Fair to exploit for tourism the potential of this Jamaican music. He also earned the respect of the Rastafarians when he brought Marcus Garvey's body back to Jamaica that year.

Back on the home front the sound systems grew in appeal and intensity and Coxsone now passed on special duties to Bob by asking him to develop material for the Soulettes, Rita Marley's group.

Rita was born in Cuba and brought to Jamaica by her parents, who then migrated to England and all but abandoned her in Jamaica. She knew her father Roy Anderson was somewhere in Europe. She had had a child, Sharon, at the age of nineteen, and if only for this reason the person who raised her, Auntie Viola, was very strict and demanding.

Bob never really liked Auntie and would always say that she was a practitioner of obeah; he expressed great fear of her to me. The relationship with Rita, however, developed despite Auntie, and they ended up living together and producing some four children during this period.

Bob's mother Cedella never stopped trying to bring him to the USA, but he stoutly refused to go, showing little or no desire to leave his roots and the attraction of the ghetto, where by now he had earned the reputation of 'Gong', a descriptive word for the toughest.

The island's continuing economic problems however had not eased, and as they continued, they had their greatest impact in the neglect of the youth, heightening the attraction of the rude boy culture which expanded in equal proportion to the neglect of the masses. The promise of Independence had not brought prosperity but only further neglect. Cedella continued to pursue her goal of getting Bob to come to the USA and finally achieved this in 1965, after pointing out that it would help Rita and the children; and as Rita was corresponding directly with Cedella she agreed that Bob should go. And so it was, Bob told me, that to facilitate the family's entry to the USA he got married to Rita.

Bob never liked America and missed Jamaica. The music business was developing in Jamaica and now saw Jamaican acts beginning to open for such visiting stars as Betty Everett and Ben E. King. Bob was always bitter about how his sojourn in the USA made him miss the most important event in the life of Jamaica, and what would have been the event of his life, when the Emperor, His Imperial Majesty Haile Selassie, touched down at Palisadoes on April 21, 1966. This was a visit which Bob very much wanted to be a part of but which he had to hear about second-hand from Rita, who would regale him with her own experiences.

This visit saw a crowd of some 100,000 people turn up at the airport, exceeding even the most optimistic of expectations. Mortimer Planno had to ascend the steps, at the request of the officials, and quieten the crowd so that His Majesty could attend to state duties.

By August 1966 Rita got her wish and arrived in Delaware with Sharon, but as Bob did not intend to stay in America he sent her back. He lost his job very shortly after this and since he was now being considered for draft to the US Army, he left the USA for Jamaica.

3 Making It in the Land of Opportunity – USA Version

Unlike Bob's short sojourn with his mother in the USA, my escape to the good life took me to the gateway of music. On my arrival I picked up on the contacts I had made from my Bahamas and Jamaica days. One of the first such persons I got in touch with was Dizzy Jones. I had actually met Dizzy Jones in Jamaica along with his group, which consisted of two guys called Sam and Dave. They had been left stranded in Jamaica by Stephen Hill following a failed concert and had been staying at Mrs Enid Bruce's guest house. Mrs Bruce was a friend of Stephen Hill and this is where he would put his second-rate stars, stars who did not warrant being put up at a major hotel.

Sam and Dave were trying to earn enough money to pay their fare back to Miami. In what could be regarded as my first booking anywhere, I contacted Freddie Chin, who, like his friend Billy Farnum, drove a big white fishtail Cadillac and put on a lot of foreign shows, though his main occupation was to bring in a lot of female dancers from the Dominican Republic. I took Sam, Dave and Dizzy to meet Freddie one evening at the Club Havana, and Freddie decided that he would hire them for a week so that they could earn their fare back home. By this time Sam, Dave, Dizzy and I had become close and they told me that if I ever got to Miami they would not forget my friendship.

We kept in touch after they left, so on my arrival in Miami I decided to head straight for the Mary Elizabeth Hotel on 2nd Street, off 7th Avenue where they lived. Miami was still fairly segregated, with the black population herded into the overtown area.

As soon as I cleared Customs I got on a bus and headed for overtown where I went to the hotel and checked in. The Mary Elizabeth had three prices for rooms per week: eight dollars with the bathroom down the hall, ten dollars with toilet and no shower, and fifteen dollars for a room with toilet and shower.

The Mary Elizabeth Hotel was a hang-out for hustlers, prostitutes, drinkers and party people, with the lounges open all night. The hotel was owned by a light-brown blind man whose name now escapes me, but whose family had a lot of money. and was involved in politics.

The Mary Elizabeth was clearly a hotel with efficiency apartments in which a number of people lived permanently.

As a matter of fact it was at the Mary Elizabeth Hotel that one of Miami's biggest disc jockeys, Butter Ball, lived. Butter Ball was like a legend in Miami, as he would very often host a cookout for the kids. He worked at a radio station called WMBM, which was the number-one station in Miami and made him famous in his time.

One block from the hotel was a club, which though owned by white people, was located in a black neighbourhood. This was not atypical. The club was called Sir John's Nite Beat, and was the number-one club in Miami.

Also located a couple of blocks away was the Cargo Hotel, which with the Mary Elizabeth Hotel and the Nite Beat Club formed the core of the exciting nightlife of the Miami area. In fact everything happened in a radius of about eight blocks starting around 8th Street, and going all the way down 2nd Avenue and 7th Street to about 12th Street and up back to 3rd Avenue. The Cargo Hotel was a little more quiet than the Mary Elizabeth, while the action at Sir John's Nite Beat Club went on all night.

I did not see Dizzy, Sam or Dave until the next morning, and they were all happy to see me. Dizzy asked what I would be doing and I told him I was here to try to make it. He said he had a club in Liberty City and he could give me a job as a waiter there at nights. After that meeting I went and had breakfast. In those days you could get eggs, grits and coffee for thirty-nine cents.

For the first two days I just hung around during the days and Dizzy would pick me up at nights and take me to his club to do my waiting. I earned sixty dollars for the week, and would hustle up to eight dollars a night in tips.

After the first week I had sixty-five dollars in my pocket after paying rent. A few days after I arrived in Miami I had met a girl and we went about a lot together. One day while we were doing our usual thing, she turned to me and asked if I could lend her forty dollars because she had left her purse at home. I never saw her again, nor my forty dollars, and I record it here for posterity only to show that Don Taylor, super-hustler, was himself once hustled. I found out later she was a heroin addict.

I now had to find something additional to do during the days to pay the rent. So I went to the employment agency and got a few days' work at a bagel bakery. By the following week, however, I was sent to Denny's Restaurant on the beach to work, washing dishes at a minimum wage of one dollar and forty cents per hour.

This brought my first direct experience with racism. It happened on my way to Denny's Restaurant (interestingly, Denny's recently achieved some infamy in the media after an incident in which the restaurant refused to serve some black federal agents). I had unsuspectingly got on the bus, which on its way to the beach stopped by the bridge at the police station, where the driver ordered, 'All negroes and coloured people off the bus.' I could not figure out why at the time, but later learnt that there was a pass system, and that you had to check in with the police. If you were coloured you had to tell them where you were going and what you were going there for and how long you thought it would take, and if you were caught on the beach after that time they would arrest you, usually on the charge that you were loitering around to steal something.

After we got our passes and went back on the bus, another shock was awaiting me when we were told that all coloureds should be in the back of the bus. I complied and went to the back of the bus until we reached Miami Beach.

During my third week in Miami, Dominic Schiffoni, Jackie Wilson's manager, who had been with him in Jamaica, and who himself owned an interest in Brunswick Records, told me that their organization had a hotel on Miami Beach called the Crown Hotel. He sent me over there and I got a job carrying bags.

It was about a week later, however, that fortune seemed to smile on me again. Jerry Butler came to the Sir John's Nite Beat Club to work for the weekend, and upon seeing me again, immediately offered me forty dollars a week plus room and food if I would join his tour as his valet.

Little did I realize at the time that this would be the beginning of my entry into show business and the tremendous success which I have achieved up to today.

Once we left Miami our first stop was in Tampa, Florida, where we stayed at the Sheraton Hotel. The following morning I ventured out on the road looking for something to eat. Because I was not very familiar with American food, I stuck mostly to eating hamburgers or tuna fish sandwiches. When I entered this restaurant to order tuna fish on toast the man in the restaurant took my order and ordered one tuna fish to go. Politely and innocently I said to him that I wanted to eat my sandwich there, whereupon he turned to me and said, 'Boy don't you know we don't allow niggers to eat in our restaurant.' He then handed me my sandwich in a paper bag.

Jerry worked his way up to the next city in Florida, Jacksonville, which had a much larger black population and where we were to meet up with another tour which would be starting there and would include the likes of Sam Cooke, Chuck Jackson, the Drifters, the Shirelles, Patti LaBelle and the Blue Belles and a host of other unknowns like Gladys Knight and the Pips.

The tour was being promoted by Henry Wynn, an extraordinary black man whom I consider to be a legend. He represented what I thought I wanted to be at that time, if for no other reason than that he was everything to everybody. He owned a liquor store on Auburn Avenue in Atlanta, but also had an interest in the Forest Arms Hotel, which was the only hotel that blacks could stay in at that time. He also was the number-one numbers man in Atlanta.

It was to this location and his clubs that the growing body of black consciousness leaders flocked, and where the likes of Martin Luther King, Andrew Young and Jesse Jackson gained their resolve to refer to it as sweet Auburn Avenue.

In my opinion Henry Wynn was single-handedly responsible for the growth of black music and black companies such as Motown because he was, to my knowledge, the first person to have the vision to put a group of acts on a bus to travel through the USA. Needless to say this met with a lot of rebellion and hostility because most of the acts were black, a brave move which was later copied by Dick Clark who watered it down, by having a mixture of white and a few black acts. This appealed to the white audiences and met with great success, enabling him to build an empire from this humble start.

In contrast, Henry Wynn ended up dying in jail for tax evasion, for no other reason than because he was a black man in a white-controlled world.

The tour itself lasted thirty days and allowed me to see aspects of American life, especially in the South, that I had never imagined possible. I witnessed behaviour by white people that I could not have predicted, never having seen that side of them when I came in contact with them in Jamaica. Many a time we were refused lodgings after having the proper reservations, simply because we were black. We would arrive at auditoriums and not be allowed to perform because we were black. I saw blacks and whites sitting in the same auditorium divided by chicken wire.

When the tour ended, Jerry set out for Chicago, his home town, and because I did not have a home base he took me along. On arriving in Chicago, Jerry placed me in a hotel close to his home. We had two weeks off between tours and Jerry was using this opportunity to move into a new townhouse which he had just purchased, and which to this day he still occupies.

The experience I obtained from this tour, both by my exposure to these future greats, and the exposure to the management style of the likes of Henry Wynn and others, contributed greatly to my later development. I did not miss the opportunity to learn from them. By observing and absorbing all that the experience had to offer, I was able to become a successful manager.

I spent the next two weeks helping Jerry move into his house and at the same time getting ready for our next stop, which was to be New York City at the Apollo Theatre. I looked forward to this with great excitement as anyone would who was visiting this musical centre for the first time. Because of Jerry's success, he had his personal Cadillac El Dorado and a station wagon in which we travelled from Chicago to New York. Mere mention of Jerry's Cadillac reminds me of the time just after my arrival in the US, when while touring Jerry entrusted the driving to me. He did this forgetting that I as a Jamaican was accustomed to driving on the left, or do I say the wrong side of the road; suffice it to say that Jerry opened his tired eyes to see that I was madly scrambling and weaving the car and cursing all the other drivers for seeking to come at me on my side of the road.

With some expletives, Jerry quickly grabbed the wheel, brought us to safety, and as he would relate it later, never ever trusted my driving skills again.

On arriving in New York we checked into the Gorham Hotel on 55th Street between 6th and 7th Avenue where we would be located for the duration of the performances.

During the week at the Apollo I got into some arguments with Jerry's percussionist and bandleader Jamo Thomas, about what I don't remember, but it bothered Jamo enough that he asked Jerry Butler to dismiss me. The way he presented the story to him Jerry was forced to sacrifice me, if for no other reason than that I was the least important person in the scenario at that time. So Jerry advised me that he would have to terminate my services at the end of the week, and I would thus be left in New York.

This experience increased my resolve to heighten my importance in all future roles.

Even though I had just come to New York, I had already met and made many show business friends, including the charming Tammi Montgomery. It was still a jungle of confusion to me, however, so that after a few days I called a friend of Jerry B's, Charles McMillan, a schoolteacher in a small town in Pennsylvania called Chesterville, and asked him if I could spend some time with him. He told me I was welcome to stay with him and his mother. Chesterville was a seaport town like Kingston, which helped to make me feel at home. I made friends quickly with people from the street who were not unlike the street people in Jamaica: pimps, hustlers and prostitutes.

During my four-month stay in Chesterville, I kept in close contact with Tammi, who would later become famous as Tammi Terrell. Tammi was being managed by the young heirs to the Gimbels Department Store, whom she asked to give me a job. So I was now employed at the Gimbels Store, in an area called German Town, as a stock boy for a salary of forty-two US dollars. It was during one of my treks from Chesterville to German Town that I saw posters advertising that Little Anthony and the Imperials were coming to town with Joe Tex, the Supremes and the Temptations to appear at the Uptown Theatre.

Now anxious to return to show business, I decided to contact Little Anthony and ask for the job I had had before as his valet, when they toured the Bahamas with the now famous Hubert Laws. I was given back the job which I had held with them some two years before.

The tour, as planned, culminated in New York City with the final performance being in Brooklyn where the Imperials were born and raised.

After the tour, with nothing else to do and nowhere else to go, I took to the streets of Brooklyn to learn more street games. The engagements of the Imperials were now so organized that we only worked three days per week, so that I had three to four days free, during which I found out that life in the ghetto in Brooklyn was no different from street life anywhere else, as everybody survived by gambling and hustling.

I started out hustling numbers, which was similar to 'drop pan' in Jamaica. I would use the returns from hustling numbers to go to the poker games held by ordinary working people and called rent parties because all the players used whatever money they made to subsidize their rent. This was how I met a guy called Pete, whom I saw setting a deck of cards in one of these games.

I knew from my knowledge of the streets that it was not in my interests to wise up the squares in the game, but to do what was necessary for him to know that I was hip to what was going on. Because of this we became friends and gambling partners. Our scam was that we would go to some games pretending not to know each other. Whenever one of us had a winning hand the other would raise the pot so as to get as much money as possible from the other players, who had no idea of what was happening to them. As our association developed I learnt that Pete had just got out of prison in North Carolina for hijacking a cigarette truck, which was big business because of the high duties on cigarettes in New York at the time.

All of this began to bring home some hard truths to me, so that I became aware that time was passing and that I had been in the US for some four to five years illegally. I started to become concerned about my status. I realized that there were two ways that an immigrant could get into the mainstream. One of these was to get an a honourable discharge from the military, but supposedly the only way one could get into the military was to be a resident American or a US citizen. The other was to get married to a US citizen. I confided all of this in another friend called Brown whom I used to hang around with on Pacific Street between Nostrand and Bedford Avenue and who confirmed that I had no other choice: I would either have to get married to an American citizen or go to some country town and register for the draft. He told me that when registering I should play at being illiterate, claiming that my father was a US sailor, and hope that because of the increasing problem in Vietnam at that time, they would not check it out thoroughly. This is what I did and it worked. In August 1965 I received a letter from the draft board ordering me to report for US Military Service in Philadelphia at 9.00 a.m. on October 25, 1965.

This of course led to my becoming not only a legal US resident, but eventually a US citizen. I had fulfilled my childhood dream: while watching the many US ships leaving the port of Kingston, I would quietly ask God why was I so 'bad lucky' as to be born in Jamaica and not in the USA so that I could be on one of those ships.

I never realized that my two years' service in the US Army would be like finding my mother and father all in one organization. It was the first time in my life that I would have supervision plus three meals a day, and clothes to wear, with free dental care and everything else that most middle-class children were born with. I was twenty-one years old before I realized that.

As I look back on my time in the US Army, I do so not as Don Taylor, but as US 52-652-558, a number which acted as a symbol that gave me the necessary respect for myself and imparted to me the self-discipline that I needed to embark on the road of life I now know.

I did my basic training at Fort Jackson, South Carolina, then went to Fort Benning, Georgia and to Airborne School and then I was stationed in Fort Ord, California for the remainder of my time. It was during this time that I got married to my first wife, Monica. I did it because I had the security of the US Army behind me.

During my two years' stint in the Army I made sure to stay in touch with show business and whenever possible I would make trips with the likes of the Drifters, as valet. I would do this during my vacation time. In addition I was also assigned to the Special Services Branch of the Army, which was the office responsible for providing entertainment for the Armed Forces.

On my discharge from the US Army on October 25, 1967, I immediately headed for New York City, to be exact 1228 Pacific Street, Brooklyn, which was between Nostrand and Bedford Avenues and the original area of my hustling in those days. And it was from that location that I charted the course which would enable me to renew my acquaintance with the likes of Chuck Jackson, and Little Anthony and the Imperials, this time as manager not valet. This allowed me to achieve a lifestyle beyond my previous expectations, and the respect of all my musical peers and those whom I steered through my management to greater heights and major successes.

How I became the manager of Little Anthony and the

Imperials is the kind of story that dreams are made on.

The Imperials were the clients of the William Morris booking agency, then run by Lee Solomon who had himself discovered Peggy Lee, and who had the power and the control to affect the career of black performers who were seeking to cross over from the black music world to that of the white charts.

We were at the time appearing at the Newport Beach Hotel in Miami. A difference developed between the Imperials and the agency and they all requested their manager Phil Strasberg to have a meeting with Lee Solomon so that they could discuss it. I myself was the road manager at the time. It was obvious to me that Phil did not really want this meeting, perhaps because he felt it could reflect badly on his ability to handle problems.

On the day of the meeting he made this even more obvious by first sitting on the ledge beside Lee Solomon instead of our side of the table and then to add insult to injury opening the conversation with, 'Well, we are here because the boys have a problem.'

I could immediately feel a charge run through all of us, and I saw Sammy Strain – one of the Imperials – look at Lee and I knew the matter would not end there.

As soon as we left the meeting and were going downstairs Sammy told Phil he was fired. When Phil recovered and asked why a chorus of voices brought home to him the simple truth that as manager any problem the boys had was expected to be his problem too.

This then presented me with the opportunity to act in the capacity of manager while the Imperials and I looked for a new manager. One person they contacted was J.W. Alexander, who was also managing Sam Cooke and Lou Rawls at the time. He came to listen to the group and to receive a report as to the group's plans and what had been taking place. The boys explained to him how they were managing and how much of the work I had been handling.

After it had been explained to J.W. he said to them, 'You guys don't need a manager, you have a manager,' and he said to me, 'Don, you are a manager, you are their manager.' He then turned to them and said, 'Give Don the money and the position.'

So I rose to the challenge and actually took the Imperials' career to greater heights, giving them such hits as 'Going Out of My Mind' and 'Hurt So Bad'. And when there were no hits, I did what very few managers have done. I kept them working Las Vegas for twelve years.

This experience further exposed me to the intricacies of the music scene, and I gained access to the world of the Mafia, with whom, like all managers, I became closely associated, and with many of whom I developed a lasting friendship.

Some years later in Las Vegas when I met J.W. again he was with Colonel Parker who was there because Elvis Presley was appearing as the main attraction, and we were discussing how I was getting on. At the time I had just returned from Jamaica and was wearing a straw hat. J.W. was telling Colonel Parker how I had got started when the Colonel reached over, took the hat off my head and placed it on his own and said, 'From all I have heard from J.W., you have started a brilliant career and you are going to be big.' Come to think of it, I never saw the hat again.

But this was not to be my last meeting with the Colonel; indeed as Little Anthony worked the hotel for those number of years, and Elvis would frequently return to Vegas, I developed a good relationship both with Elvis and his manager.

I learned a lot from the Colonel. I admired him. He was very shrewd. He was to my mind basically a hustler too – just a different kind of hustler, an uptown hustler, a hustler on a different scale. He looked after Elvis well and always made sure that he was well dressed and in style. And, from the very early days, he always made sure that every Elvis concert was full – even if he had to give away the tickets himself!

I liked Elvis a lot too. He seemed for real to me. Even when he was big he never acted the big star – I never got that from him.

One day we were at the house Little Anthony had rented and at eight o'clock in the evening the doorbell rang. I answered it and there was Elvis – and his four bodyguards. He was dressed in a jumpsuit – not the fancy kind he wore on stage but smart.

He came in and he sat on the sofa talking to Little Anthony. What amused us was that when he got up to go to the bathroom all four bodyguards automatically got up too and followed him. They didn't actually go in there with him, but waited outside the door. Elvis didn't seem to find this strange. Then we all went over to the Sahara Hotel in Las Vegas and the guys ordered something to eat – burgers I think – for dinner in the dressing room.

Anthony and Elvis got on well, they were very relaxed with each other. They went way back and they talked about music, about good times in the old days. Elvis laughed about the first time they met. It was on the 'Ed Sullivan Show' in 1958 and he was telling us about how he sang this song and as soon as he started the camera moved from his body to his head. It didn't show anything beneath the neck until he'd finished!

I respected Elvis – and the Colonel. And when the Colonel told me I'd make it big I guess I knew deep down that my love and respect for the industry would result in me respecting those words and making every effort to prove them correct. Little did I know that this self-realization would ultimately come through Bob Marley.

The Man

4 Marley and Me – First Encounters

I was at home in Los Angeles taking care of Little Anthony and the Imperials when I got a call from Stephen Hill Snr, telling me that he was in Los Angeles, and had been told about me and the help I could give and that because of his son's involvement with Member of Parliament Anthony Spaulding, he and Spaulding were looking for a singer interested in doing a benefit for the Trench Town Sports Complex in Jamaica. He then invited me to the Hyatt House Hotel on Sunset Boulevard where he was staying, to assist him in going over the names of the various artistes he considered suitable.

Recent visits to Jamaica had exposed me to the developing political culture under Michael Manley, the recently-elected Prime Minister. In fact, I had become quite impressed by and committed to the approach of Michael Manley. The exposure of all, visitors or Jamaicans, to Jamaican politics is unavoidable, as Jamaican society eats, sleeps, and breathes politics.

Manley's articulation of the needs of the poor and his emphasis on the urgency of seeking the upward mobility of the disenfranchised appealed to my inner instincts and indeed related to my own achievements.

His cabinet appointments involved people I had come to know, people who seemed more in tune with the needs of the poor, persons whose rise to recognition seemed to mirror the hopes and aspirations of the underprivileged. One such person was the aforementioned Tony Spaulding, the

Minister of Housing and the son of Frank Spaulding.

I actually became quite passionately committed to Michael Manley and his PNP government. If Manley or Spaulding had asked me to jump, I would not have asked 'Why?' but 'How high?' I later learnt that in this I was no different from Bob, who had himself come out of Trench Town, an area which formed part of Tony Spaulding's constituency; indeed he ultimately won the battle for this area by defeating his own father-in-law E.C.L. Parkinson who ran for the Jamaica Labour Party (JLP).

Manley's approach contrasted quite strongly with that of the previous Shearer/JLP government, which seemed to react badly to the rising tide of black consciousness.

The black Hugh Shearer had succeeded Sangster as Prime Minister and leader of the JLP in 1967. His government placed travel bans and immigration restrictions on such persons as Walter Rodney, a Guyanese lecturer at the University of the West Indies, who was a strong black power advocate. This kind of decision and policy gave rise to general unrest and led to demonstrations and rioting. In addition, the Shearer government extended the ban to include a list of books and periodicals. They also sought to suppress the publication of a radical local newspaper, *Abeng*. They published a list of banned books, almost all of which consisted of so-called black consciousness literature. Even people like Julian Bond, a respected supporter of the Civil Rights Movement in the USA, were required to have special clearance to visit Jamaica. Names such as Stokely Carmichael and Malcolm X sent tremors through this government.

It was against this background that Michael Manley came to power and rose to such commanding heights.

I now realize that he was given to flights of rhetoric, which, on analysis, went way beyond what he was willing or able to do. Rhetoric and myth became entangled with fact and reality as he became absorbed in his cult of words. On reflection I think that this may have skewed the thinking of the Jamaica I knew and grew up in, giving rise to the problems of today. The politicians of my boyhood days, Bustamante and Norman Manley, although taking somewhat dissimilar routes, never preached the politics of division; in fact, the message I got as a youth would be 'Busta' saying, 'The whole a we must come together,' while Norman Manley would preach the virtues of education, convinced that it was education that would bring power. To my mind, the rhetorical and divisive political approach of Manley produced conditions not dissimilar from those in the USA, where the Reagan/Bush era in the eighties created the highest level of recession, and reintroduced the kind of racism I never thought I would see again in the USA. And so it is with the Jamaica of the nineties; the rhetoric of the seventies produced a scorn for the poor, not the scorn and anger of racism, but a kind of harshness and violence never seen before.

By the time Michael Manley had been in power for a year Rastafarianism seemed to gain acceptability. It had by now permeated the middle and upper classes, whose children were adopting its beliefs in unprecedented numbers. Long gone were the days when Rastas were in danger of having their heads shaved.

Homage was now being paid to Mother Africa and Michael Manley boasted in his speeches that the 'Rod of Correction' had been handed to him by Haile Selassie, God to all Rastafarians. 'Jah Rastafari' was the cry, and it took on more and more significance as it became embedded in the evolving cultural and musical expression of the people.

Getting back to Stephen Hill Snr and the singer that he and Anthony Spaulding were looking for to do the Trench Town Sports Complex benefit, I suggested asking Marvin Gaye, with whom I was still in touch, to do the benefit. Hill agreed and I then put him in touch with Yvonne Fair, whom I had known from my days of being a valet for Chuck Jackson, and who was now a solo artiste with Motown Records. She deserves the credit for getting the wheels turning for that Marvin Gaye performance in Jamaica.

Stephen Hill then informed me that he needed me to pick up his hotel bill and pay whatever expenses were necessary to get Marvin Gaye and myself on an introductory trip to Jamaica. He convinced me that I would be reimbursed later for the twenty thousand US dollars that it would cost. As the concert was for a worthy cause, I agreed to upfront the costs, but to this day I have never received full reimbursement, and as far as I can determine I am still out of pocket some ten thousand US dollars.

I had met Marvin way back in the mid-sixties, when he was a part-time chauffeur for Berry Gordy, and trying to break into show business. With Yvonne's help it was not difficult for me to convince him to fly with me to Jamaica to support the Jamaican government's effort to raise funds for this project of development for the people of the depressed areas of Trench Town. In fact, Marvin would be performing technically for free, or in reality at my expense. Once again, I was combining business and my own interests, as I had every faith in the project and it gave me a chance to be a part of the developing trends which I had identified.

And so, Marvin having agreed to be the star attraction, I accompanied him to the concert. Bob Marley was to be the opening act. I did not know much about Marley at the time. I knew that he had written songs for the likes of Barbra Streisand, and Eric Clapton, who had had a major hit with his 'I Shot the Sheriff'. At the time Bob was contracted to Danny Sims and Cayman Music, following Danny's visit to Jamaica with Johnny Nash.

During the trip Marvin was overwhelmed by the freedom

with which Jamaicans and Jamaican performers used ganja and he was impressed by the purity and strength of the Jamaican homegrown variety which Bob, of course, used freely and openly.

It was during this trip that Hill and Marvin developed a liking for each other, so much so that Hill eventually became Marvin's manager. The rest is history – a history which records the rise and fall of Marvin's career until his sad and untimely death by his own father's gun on April 1, 1984. He was still being managed by Stephen Hill at this time.

I remember Marvin with affection. He was an understanding man and very generous. I remember on one of our travels to Jamaica for the Trench Town concert, when I was working as a valet and he was a struggling singer. Someone cheated him but he didn't get mad.

He said: 'They can cheat me but they can't cheat God.'

He was a kind man. But in many ways I think he was his own worst enemy. He supported everyone and he shouldered everyone else's burdens as well as his own, not unlike Bob. I remember he started a company and then gave it to his sister and millions of dollars just ran through her fingers.

It was during this trip also that I was forced to speak to Stephen Hill regarding Marley. I saw Bob and his representative at the Sheraton Hotel in New Kingston looking for Stephen Hill so they could be paid for the concert appearance. They felt Hill was giving them the runaround. I spoke to Hill about this, advising him that this was no way to treat a performer. I was later led to understand that Bob was impressed by my approach to the matter. I had taken this stand also because earlier that week Tony Spaulding had sent Jean Barnes to a meeting at my home where I was told that Bob would be part of the show and that she, Jean, was to see that he was treated properly.

I clearly remember meeting Bob again later that day. He turned to me and said, 'Yu really is a Jamaican?' I said, 'Yes,' and Bob then said, 'How yuh learn the business so?' I told him that it was because I had been in the USA since I was a youth and had been around the theatre all my life and had learned the trade through experience. To which he replied, 'Then nuh a man like yuh me a look for, because with a man like yuh around and with your knowledge, when mi chat me nuh have fi repeat miself.'

For about a year following this meeting in 1973, Bob and I made intermittent telephone calls, holding brief discussions as to how we could get together, leaving messages, and always trying to get together as promised; but the vagaries of the music business, and my own sometimes bad habit of long periods of non-responsive silence, had us missing each other, sometimes by hours, both in the USA and Jamaica. But we still never gave up hope of getting together.

I was not then aware of the behind-the-scenes pressure on Bob from people like Chris Blackwell, who would continually send different agents under various guises and with various excuses to 'inveigle' him into signing a new contract, since the first one was no longer valid as a result of the break-up of the original Wailers in 1974. Bob, using his uncanny, natural ability to avoid obvious pitfalls, was secretly searching for someone to handle these problems, someone with whom he could feel a certain 'vibe' or affinity. I only discovered later how anxious Bob was over the original Island contract which also existed at the time, which he had entered into after the Danny Sims/Cayman Music contract expired.

In reality our busy careers conspired to keep us apart. By then, in addition to managing Little Anthony, I had also started to handle Martha Reeves of the Vandellas, who came to me having just signed with Island Records, Bob's recording company. This was some time in 1974.

Island had given Martha an advance against a recording contract. However, while the contract was being prepared for signature, Martha was approached with a new and better recording contract by Clive Davis, President of Arista Records, who had recently signed Barry Manilow.

Martha told me that she wanted to pursue the new deal with Arista rather than the Island deal, especially as Island had not yet created any waves. So I set up a meeting with Island Records, to try and opt out of the deal by returning their initial advance. It was the kind of deal I could easily handle.

The meeting between the then President of Island Records, Charlie Nuccio, Martha and myself was set to be held at Island's office at Sunset Boulevard in Hollywood. I collected Martha and drove her to the meeting. Charlie Nuccio, whom I had known from before, was Italian, and had just moved to Island as President. We shared a mutual respect for each other's abilities and know-how, and this, and our known connections to the music business, made us dispense with the usual foreplay and proceed to the matter at hand. Charlie was not aware of my Jamaican background and history, but knew that I would come straight to the point. So it was not difficult for us to conclude the deal in the interest of all concerned.

It was either during the meeting or in its aftermath that Charlie told me that he had an artiste on the label who could be a mega-mega star, if he could get only him to work. But somehow he could not get the singer to work and co-operate with them.

I asked him who the artiste was and he said 'Bob Marley.' I seemed to be hearing Marley's name more and more often. It was frequently being referred to in music circles, as 'the next big thing'. People were starting to talk about Bob Marley and reggae music.

In fact, reggae interpretations by the likes of Paul Simon, Stevie Wonder, Paul McCartney, the Rolling Stones, Boney M and Abba – to name a few – were becoming commonplace. Reggae was also beginning to be seen as a music which dealt with social issues, politically arousing and giving voice to the oppressed both in Jamaica and the world at large.

Charlie told me that Island Records had recently released an album by Bob entitled *Natty Dread*, his third release. The album was doing OK, but Island needed Bob to come on the road and support it. I said to Charlie, 'Damn, this is the guy who wants to work with me.'

I then gave Charlie the background to my relationship with Bob, how we had met, and how Bob and I were currently trying to hook up, and had been trying to meet over the past year as Bob wanted me to represent him.

Charlie told me that he would do anything for anyone who could get Bob to work.

The discussion renewed my interest, so I hurried home from Charlie's office, bundling Martha into my car. I dropped Martha off at her home rather hurriedly and headed to my office, which was then located at Sunset and Vine – 6290 Sunset Boulevard to be exact.

My office housed my company – Judant Music Corporation, jointly owned by Little Anthony (Anthony Gourdine), Avco and myself. Some might say it was elaborately furnished. I had had it furnished some time in 1971 by a professional decorator. As President of the company I was paid the impressive salary of US$743.52 per week, or US$40,000 per year, plus expenses of car, house and complete entertainment. It was a good start in those days, especially for a hustler from humble Jamaican beginnings, and it didn't include my other earnings in management.

I caught the next plane to Kingston. During the flight I considered my plan of action, and decided I would go directly by taxi from the Norman Manley Airport at Palisadoes to Bob's home at 56 Hope Road, which was the address given to me by Charlie.

It was between 2.30 and 3.00 in the afternoon when my plane got into Kingston. When I arrived at 56 Hope Road about an hour later, I was struck by the impressive old colonial-style house. It was not far from my own apartment and no more than a block from the Governor General's residence, King's House, which had itself housed visiting kings, queens and presidents. Further along was the Prime Minister's office, the Police Officers' Club, and the Priory School, one of Jamaica's most exclusive schools. Finally there was Devon House, the home of the earliest black Jamaican millionaire, Thomas Stiebel.

That Bob Marley, Rastafarian, reggae musician and marijuana smoker, should actually reside in this area was a mark of the new era being ushered in for Jamaicans. It was a sign of the gradual acceptance by Jamaicans of their African ancestry, arising from the impact and the influence of Garvey, black consciousness and Rastafarianism.

I later learnt that the house had been loaned to Bob by Chris Blackwell, who felt that he could have more control over Bob by keeping him where he could be reached. Also, if the truth be told, Chris and many of his bearers and representatives were afraid of Trench Town, and of the obviously shady characters who hung around Bob daily in the ghettoes of East and West Kingston. The Hope Road location eliminated this fear and also made Bob more accessible to the overseas press and the local media.

On my way to the house I saw three or four people, all Rastafarians, sitting down and reasoning. I discovered that this was a typical scene, and a daily pattern in Bob's life. The Rastafarians looked at me with mild suspicion when I asked for Bob, as if convinced that I was another hustler. I was told that Bob was sleeping. I later learnt that it was considered unwise to disturb Bob while he was asleep. I paid no attention and ignoring the suspicious looks headed upstairs. The first thing I noticed on entering Bob's room was a pair of soccer shoes on the floor close by the bed, as if they awaited only a whistle to leap into action. On the wall behind the bed, I saw a guitar leaning on the wall below an imposing portrait of Haile Selassie. Bob was lying on his bed. As I stepped into the room it appeared that Bob felt my presence, because he moved. I touched him and said, 'Bob, Don Taylor. I come to manage you now.' He sat up rather lazily and almost nonchalantly looked at me and said, 'Yea Don Taylor, what deal you want?' I said, 'Twenty per cent.' He said, 'Wait 'til Allan come dis evening, an' you can come back an' we will discuss it.' I did not know who Allan was, but I told him I would be back.

I went back down, jumped in my taxi and headed for my Jamaican home, knowing somehow it was going to be OK.

I had always maintained a residence in Jamaica as I do today. At that time, I owned an apartment at Worthington Towers on Worthington Avenue, some three miles from Bob's Hope Road premises. I relaxed as best I could, waiting for evening to come.

When I returned to Hope Road, Bob had just finished playing soccer. After showering, he came downstairs, touched me and said, 'Don Taylor, mek we discuss dis deal.' And so he and I and Allan Cole, whom I was meeting for the first time, met in the yard under a tree. I instantly detected a very close personal relationship between them. They seemed to be kindred souls, the tall, lanky, dreadlocked, athletic-looking Allan Cole and the shorter but not physically dissimilar Marley. It was clear how close they were from Bob's negotiations. He said, 'You can get ten per cent, not twenty per cent, and as it grow, it cyaan be on everything.' I responded that it had to be on everything. He looked at me, then turned and looked at Cole. Allan listened and seemed to impart his thoughts to Bob without speaking, and after a short pause Bob said, 'Blood claat Don Taylor, mi wi work wid yu.' In the subsequent discussion, he made it plain to me that he was not interested in signing any long-term agreement, but that as long as I did the job to his satisfaction, I would maintain my position, and this was how it remained up until his death, when Rita took over the estate. We arranged to meet the next day at eleven o'clock at my apartment. I had begun my first lesson on how Bob Marley did business, and his unique and somewhat uncanny way of arriving at a decision.

After leaving Bob, I headed back to my apartment. As soon as I got there I called Stu Weintraub of Associated Booking. I did not intend to let the grass grow under my feet. I had been told that it was his agency that wanted to book the upcoming Marley tour. I told Stu that I had already met with Bob at his home, and that we would be meeting again the following morning at eleven o'clock to finalize getting this thing on the road. After that I called Charlie Nuccio, who had been increasingly anxious and frustrated at not being able to get Bob's co-operation, and also advised him of the developments.

Both Stu and Charlie, and everyone else I spoke with, reacted with obvious scepticism, all saying, 'OK. We've heard that before.' They obviously don't know DT, I said to myself.

The following morning I had just finished my coffee when I heard a knock at the door. When I opened it, I saw Bob standing there with a brown-skinned woman. She had sharp, clean, attractive features, but to me was somewhat incongruously dressed in a long white cotton creation and locks, reflecting, I suppose, her pride in her religion. Bob introduced her as Diane Jobson, his attorney.

Bob, Diane and I sat down and discussed the proposed arrangement. I repeated what Bob and I had discussed the evening before, and my proposal to be his manager. It did not take long to confirm the agreements made in the earlier discussion and move on to finalize arrangements. We agreed with a handshake to draw up the details of our association and my management later. This was never really done; the only written confirmation of my managerial position was contained in a simple letter from Bob to a booking agent, a copy of which I would receive only years later, in November 1976 to be exact.

When my discussions with Diane and Bob were almost concluded, I picked up the phone and called Stu Weintraub and then handed the phone to Bob, who confirmed to him that I was now his manager. He confirmed that he was prepared to go on tour, and that he would do anything I said, including going on tour immediately, if that was what I wanted him to do.

I then called Charlie at Island Records. I told him of the deal, and that Bob and I would be in New York one week later to finalize and verify all attendant details. Everyone agreed, but I still had the distinct feeling that nobody really expected things to happen. Apparently they had been down this path before.

Although Stu and Charlie still felt that Bob would not be co-operative, I had up to then (and always after) found Bob very co-operative. For obvious reasons he was cautious and careful, and he would often say to me (then and throughout our relationship), 'Blood claat Don Taylor, dem waan trick mi,' and I had repeatedly to assure him that I would make sure that this did not happen.

Bob's co-operation, to the surprise of the others, manifested itself almost immediately, as we proceeded to plan a tour which would take us from summer 1975 to the end of that year. I realized that this first tour had to be planned carefully, taking into account the fact that I was fully aware that Bob's career had great potential, although at the moment it seemed to be on hold.

I recalled the 1973 tour with Sly Stone and how I had heard that Bob had walked off the show. I found out later that this was because Bob felt he had outperformed the others and yet was not given enough time on stage, but I was reminded of Charlie Nuccio's words. Still, the vibe between Bob and me was right. So we decided to start out in Canada and then move on to the rest of North America before taking a break and continuing in Europe, which would include the UK, France and Spain.

The first objective of starting a working relationship had been achieved, and the real work and the real world now lay ahead. I knew that Bob Marley could do it. I knew he would make the world get up and recognize him, and I had very little doubt about how I would direct his career. From here on in, it would be Marley and me.

5 Our First Tour and My First Meeting with Chris Blackwell

The tour started out in Canada with our first concert scheduled for Massey Hall in Toronto. The promoter was Michael Cole, who was later to become the partner and co-owner of the Toronto Maple Leafs. We arrived the day before the concert to good publicity as I had ensured that the press releases were well prepared, and I grew in confidence as we approached the performance.

When the concert night arrived I just knew, as I drove up to this old-style English concert hall, that this was it – the vibes seemed just right. And as I entered I saw that the hall was already almost packed to capacity. As was my custom, I arrived alone and well in advance of the group so as to use the spare time to check out the arrangements for the concert. This time around, however, the whole ritual was even more important for me, as this was my first Marley concert, and I wanted to make extra sure that everything was just right. Also, this would be my first opportunity to see Bob Marley live and the first chance to see if all my plans could work. It would in fact be my first chance to assess the real talent I would now be managing.

While I awaited the arrival of Bob and the group I stood watching the other acts from the wings with road manager Tony Garnett and the I-Threes – Rita Marley, Judy Mowatt and Marcia Griffiths, who was pregnant at the time. It always seemed as if, because of pregnancy, we only had the I-Twos. When it came time for Bob to take the stage I purposely decided to move to the back of the hall, as I wanted to be alone to absorb the performance fully.

From my new vantage point I watched fascinated as Bob

walked on to the stage in what I would later recognize as his inimitable saunter. It was awesome to watch him immediately make contact with the crowd, who seemed to be mesmerized by his presence. With his guitar slung over his shoulder, and his Rasta locks flowing in unrestricted freedom, one could feel the raw power of his personality enveloping his worshippers. He immediately sounded his refrain 'Hail Jah Rastafari!' and without speaking any further, moved into his opening song, 'Concrete Jungle', which brought the crowd to its feet. For my part, I paid little attention to them, keeping my eyes riveted on Bob as he moved smoothly into his follow-up song, 'I Shot the Sheriff'.

When he was about halfway through his performance, he stopped, and while the audience seemed to hang momentarily in the air, began to introduce the brothers in the band. The band at the time had Family Man Barrett on bass, 'Touter' Harvey on keyboards, Carlton Barrett on drums, Al Anderson on lead guitar, Alvin 'Seco' Patterson on percussion and Lee Jaffe, who was a kind of gofer, on harmonica.

After he completed his introduction of the band, I watched as Bob took a side bow and with his finger pointing to his temple, said 'My name is' – pause – the audience seemed to hang in the air – 'some call me natty, some call me dread, some call me natty dread', and as he said this, while still holding the finger to his temple, he leaped some six feet in the air as the voices of the thousands roared in thunderous response 'Bob Marley', and in one continuous movement on landing he went into performing 'Natty Dread'.

I knew then and there that a superstar was born. Even though the magic continued and grew to immense proportions, I never saw Bob use that introduction again. But he never changed from his trademark introduction of 'Hail Jah Rastafari!' which I could only describe as a prayer to Jah.

From Canada we worked our way down to New York; I had planned it this way, knowing we would get maximum media coverage before our New York arrival. And as I planned it so did it work out. The reviews poured in from all the majors and the interviews grew in depth and exposure.

It was against this background of increasing media interest that we arrived in New York City, to much acclaim as I had skilfully sent the releases and the reviews ahead of us through my publicist. The machinery was working and my plans were falling into place.

In fact, my sights had been carefully and cautiously set on our New York arrival. As a planned strategy I had arranged for Bob to play in Central Park, in a show promoted by Ron Delsner and sponsored by Michelob beer as part of the New York summer series in the park. The show, the first such summer concert ever held, charged a mere two dollars for entrance, which was exactly what I wanted as I knew it would widen Bob's audience appeal and guarantee mass exposure. As I had expected, the park was jammed and the show unfolded like a revival. My musical antennae had told me that the underground piracy of reggae tapes in the US had in fact opened up the music; this was a fact that very few in the recorded music world seemed to have realized, and this well-timed public exposure seemed to be what the musical world was waiting for. It was also what Bob needed.

We followed up the concert in the park with another New York concert appearance and then moved on.

With New York conquered and its success behind us, we continued the tour by heading for Philadelphia, where we performed two shows before moving on to conquer Cleveland, Chicago, Detroit, Seattle, Portland and San Francisco and finally Los Angeles.

> 'Bob Marley and the Wailers... Reggae at its sinuously, sexily rocking best.'
>
> (John Rockwell, *NY Times*)

'Marley is fantastic, incredible, his lyrics should be printed on the front page of every newspaper.'

(Dr John)

'Best thing I have seen in ten years. I could watch the Wailers all night.'

(George Harrison)

'Marley's exceptional show generated the kind of emotional celebration – some called that kind of experience "magic" – that results when a performer not only meets the high expectancy level, but actually gives his audience new reasons to believe.'

(*LA Times*)

'His fans come for the music, but it's the message they take away.'

(Tom Bradshaw, *LA Times*)

It was in LA that I was to have my first face-to-face meeting with Chris Blackwell. Having proved that we could break into the difficult US market, which up until then had seemed immune to reggae as an important new musical form, I was ready for the whole world, but first I had to deal with Chris Blackwell.

We were playing at a club called Roxy on Sunset Boulevard in the heart of Hollywood, in which Jack Nicholson had an interest. I had specifically wanted these club appearances as part of my targeted plan for Bob's career, knowing that they would further enhance his reputation by exposing him to new and different audiences. They were major successes and formed part of my plan to establish a base to renegotiate the second Bob Marley–Island contract.

It was on this tour that I discovered the true professional that Bob Marley was: his disciplined approach to the business of music, his preparedness and sense of responsibility and his quick way of learning. As this would be my first meeting with Chris, and because I was negotiating Bob's recording contract with Island, I needed to have a serious discussion with Bob. I had, on assuming managership, reviewed the original contract and come to the conclusion that it was anything but a good contract, and it left no doubt in my mind that something had to be done about it if Bob was to get what was he was rightfully worth.

The contract called for Bob to get advances of £4,000 for the first album, £4,000 for the second album and US$12,000 for the third.

Considering that the first two albums were *Catch a Fire* and *Burnin'* and the third album was *Natty Dread*, I was more than startled to find that Bob had not up to now received any royalty payment for himself, either as artiste or as producer. This seemed indefensible to me.

He had in fact only got the US$12,000 for *Natty Dread* after hiring Ray Tisdale, head of business affairs for Capitol Records, and a well-known lawyer in the music business. But after his trip to London, and having been wined and dined, he could only himself come back with US$12,000, which to Bob's mind was still unacceptable.

To my mind, the break-up of the original Wailers – Bob, Peter and Bunny – meant that the existing contract was technically and legally binding only on the original Wailers, and certainly did not relate to Bob Marley as a single artiste. Bob felt the same way and I meant, if necessary, to make this a major part of my renegotiation.

In discussing the matter with Bob and Diane I discovered Bob's negotiating skills, which had previously been manifested in a masterly business manoeuvre. After the break-up, Bob had gone ahead and signed a new contract with Island as Bob Marley and the Wailers, naming Family Man Barrett and Carly as the new Wailers, upon the signing of which he received the above-mentioned US$12,000. At the time Bob had advised Ray Tisdale that Family Man and Carly would sign later. Bob then advised Family Man and Carly not to sign. They took his advice, so that in reality this new contract had questionable legality, as it was not yet completed by all the parties. Bob told me that he had done this so that he could take the money and not be committed. Years later this same manoeuvre would lead Junior Marvin to persuade Family Man and the other members of the Wailers to use it to claim ownership. They filed a lawsuit in the Supreme Court of Jamaica, even trying to get me to testify, so that they could take over the Wailers band. However it was obvious to me that Bob was convinced that he had acted in his own best interest, and that he was always wary of Chris Blackwell.

So, in the short time leading up to this meeting, I had become increasingly aware of Bob's feelings about Chris. I knew that there were forebodings on Bob's part which made him want to extricate himself from the present contract at the earliest date. Perhaps this was what had given Nuccio and Island the impression that Bob was unco-operative.

The meeting to renegotiate Bob's contract with Island was then set for some time in July or August of 1975, at the Island Records office in Los Angeles.

Bob and I went to the meeting, and although I had not yet met Chris Blackwell face to face, I had sent him advance notice that I felt Bob's contract was inadequate, and probably not legal under US laws. I took the attorney David Steinberg with me. At the time David was also acting legally for Thom Bell, one of the persons who originally brought David and me together.

I had quietly done some research on Chris myself, but only in a limited way as I was still feeling my way through the situation. I was beginning to sense that Blackwell was using various persons and things to try to control the situation; I just could not put my hand on it at the time, but it was there.

Later it became clear to me that what Chris was doing was feeling out the weak links in the chain, the people he could own either by employing them in his firms or hanging out the carrot of benefits and monetary reward.

Throughout the meeting, Chris kept looking at me suspiciously, and after we looked each other over, he asked me directly what it was I wanted.

I proceeded to lay out the terms, conditions and the financial compensation I wanted. I told him I wanted a one-million-US-dollar advance, for which we would give him Bob's next three albums. This when added to the earlier three would make a total of six albums. Chris countered with his own proposal that he wanted ten albums instead, and when Bob asked, 'Why do you want so many albums?' Chris replied that after ten albums, an artiste's career is usually finished. Bob looked at Chris and in his most serious voice said to him, 'I will give you your ten albums, but I will show you that my career is just beginning after ten albums.' Chris laughed, and how right he was, if only in the physical sense, as Bob died right after he delivered his tenth album to Chris. But as history records it, Bob was right after all, as indeed to date his career has only just begun. The sad part is that the only person to benefit has been Chris Blackwell.

We ended the meeting with nothing settled, as I refused to budge from my demands except to agree to the ten albums which Bob had given in on. Chris advised Bob, David and me that he was not in any way agreeing to my terms. He told me in quite unmistakable terms that there was no way my proposal could work; he was interested in doing a deal, but my proposal was not viable, so we left the meeting with the agreement up in the air. I, on the other hand, was more than confident I would win, as I knew exactly what I was doing, and I expressed no fear or doubt to Bob that I would win the battle. This was always difficult for me in those early stages, as Bob never said yes or no to anything and would in fact leave the final decision to you – if for no other reason than to hold you responsible. This approach itself created its own problems, as very often he would be approached by people seeking business participation from him, to which his usual response would be, 'Mi think it wi work.' Taking this as a serious commitment, they would then begin to harass me for the money, and very often end up blaming me as the person who stood in their way.

All this time, meanwhile, I was ensuring that Bob was growing in stature and recognition. He was playing the right places, and making all the right moves. For instance, Mick Jagger, who was also appearing in Los Angeles, was cutting short his concert to come to see Marley perform, and Bob was giving some of the best shows that anyone had given in LA.

I saw the future clearly, or as Bob would say, 'I can see clearly now.' Bob had told me, however, that he would like to tie up the deal with Blackwell and get it out of the way. He further confided to me that Chris had appealed to him in the capacity of a friend; as Bob put it, Chris had said to him, 'Bob, me and you is friend, whey yu bring this bwoy from to mash up our business.' Although I respected this, I was resolved to ensure that this would not be a one-sided contract with only Chris Blackwell and Island Records being the major beneficiaries.

I decided, however, as a precaution and an alternative, to generate interest in Bob from Clive Davis, head of Arista Records (the same person who had been interested in Martha Reeves). Arista at the time was being financed by Polygram Records from Germany and was looking for new talent. Clive over the years had developed the reputation of being one of the best record men in the business; in fact, he was regarded by many as the messiah of the modern-day music business.

Clive also used to be President of CBS Records and had a nose for the right musical trends. He was interested enough in signing Bob and advised me that if we got into a lawsuit with Island, he would give us the money to fight it. So I put my act in order and just played for time and sat it out, as I knew it would not be long before Blackwell realized that he could no longer exploit this situation to his benefit only.

It was about two or three days after this first meeting with Chris that Bob and I left LA for London to begin the European leg of the tour. We arrived in London in the early morning and were met by a young lady, Denise Mills, who worked with Chris Blackwell. She insisted that Bob and I go straight to Island as Chris wanted to meet with us.

I had already figured out that Chris, not knowing anything about me, had used the few days to see what I was about. I felt sure he would have tried to find out, for instance, if I could be wined and dined. In other words, if I could be bought out by the slick sharp companies. The apparent haste with which he wanted this next meeting made it clear to me that he had done as I had anticipated, and the anxiety to meet with us meant that he had in fact checked and found out that I knew enough about the music business, I knew the right people, and that it would be in his best interest to start to negotiate in good faith. I was not going to be a pushover and the days of less than favourable deals were over.

Bob and I had discussed the alternatives and he had taken his usual noncommittal position. On the other hand I entered the discussions with the full appreciation that Bob wanted to be free of Chris and his contractual commitments. I knew that what he really wanted was, for old times' sake, to give Chris his albums, and be free of him once and for all.

It was also becoming clear to Bob, and certainly to me, that Bob *was* Island. And I found it difficult to forget that this was the same Chris Blackwell who had earlier financed the pirating of Jamaican reggae music and Marley recordings through his dealings with Trojan Records and Lee Gopthals.

That was what came out of Bob's and Lee 'Scratch' Perry's trips to London before he signed with Island.

We arrived at Island's office in St Peter's Square, near Hammersmith. The office was a converted old English house not unlike 56 Hope Road; opposite it, I can clearly recall, was a big bingo parlour catering for what was the craze at the time in England. Denise escorted us to Chris's little office in the back which was cluttered with recording industry paraphernalia.

When we entered the office Chris was sitting there dressed in his usual unassuming fashion – tennis shoes and no socks. Without too many opening pleasantries, Chris said, 'OK, let's try and put something together.' I felt a great sense of gratification. I was right. It was as I thought. He had done his checking and learnt about Don Taylor and Don Taylor's knowledge and savvy of the music industry.

I then laid out to Chris what I wanted, which was merely a repetition of my earlier demands, but with a new request to purchase the premises at 56 Hope Road. In all of this I was supported by Bob.

I had been thinking about Hope Road for quite some time, and felt that the time was ripe for this move to be made, so I told Chris that Bob wanted to purchase it. Chris said that that was not necessary, because it was Bob's to use as he wanted. I felt an unease immediately; it sounded too much to me like the slave master giving accommodation to his slave. It came over as 'You can stay there as long as you are a good boy.' I emphatically told Chris I did not want Bob staying under that kind of understanding, and that we had to buy it. Chris must have seen the resolve in my position, which was supported by Bob, because I got him to agree to sell us the premises for US$125,000.

However, as would prove to be typical of Chris in his dealings with us, this was not the end of it, as two days later when we went to sign the contract Chris produced a statement claiming that Bob was indebted to his company to the tune of US$550,000. He said that this was what his accountants showed had been advanced to the Wailers. This alarming figure contrasted unbelievably with the money that Bob, Peter Tosh and Bunny Wailer could actually remember receiving, which they had repeatedly told me was only £8,000 and US$12,000 in total.

I asked Chris to pull me the account records on the figures, and was not really surprised to see that all the signatures for the money said to have been received on behalf of Bob Marley and the Wailers belonged to people employed by Chris Blackwell.

Needless to say, I found all this very unusual, because normally when a record company dispenses money, especially such large sums of money, they would want the signatures of the people on the contract, not representatives or known employees of the record company.

But in reality, Chris waited too long to begin to deal with me on the contract, for by then, thanks to shrewd management and teamwork, Bob was becoming big. Bob's stature was growing and the tour until then had been a huge success. Indeed, Bob's natural lifestyle, his unchoreographed moves and real raw talent were increasingly appealing to the world. And it was obvious that the depth of Bob's lyrics and the message they carried were capturing the heart and soul of the world. To use Bob's parlance, the world was beginning to 'overstand' his message.

I was steering his career carefully, with some really interesting propositions, not the least of which was the Arista deal. And in the record business, it is common knowledge that the more you have something going for you, the harder the bargain you drive – I guess it is the same in any business.

It was also apparent to me, especially from these meetings, that Chris had realized that Bob's best works were still ahead of him. I can recall Bob telling him, 'If yu give me a good deal you get good records, if you give me a bad deal I give you a bad record.' But Chris already knew he had given Bob a bad deal before, and had still got three great records, so he smiled at this.

Taking all of this into consideration and wishing to play my cards to the fullest extent, I refused outright to pay any share of the disputed debt, even though it would have been divided equally between the Wailers. Bunny by this time had left the Wailers, as had Peter Tosh, with each now seeking to develop his own career. I don't know if Chris ever made the same claim to Bunny and Peter, although my knowledge of them suggested that Chris would have had to accept the losses.

I, for my part, as Bob's manager, told Chris there was no way this could work, and finally got him to agree to waive the recoupability of Bob's share, close to US$175,000, a lot of money at the time in any currency (and the Jamaican dollar was then 80¢ to the US dollar).

Upon finalization of the million-dollar contract which called for a 25 per cent advance of US$250,000, I advised Chris to take out the $125,000 for Hope Road, and prepare us a cheque for the difference of $125,000. Everyone including Bob was pleased.

We then proceeded to complete the UK leg of the tour, which called for three shows at the Lyceum in London, resulting in Bob's first live recorded album: *Live!* These concerts helped really to launch the song 'No Woman No Cry', previously recorded on the *Natty Dread* album, Bob's debut as a solo artiste. Both the *Live!* album and 'No Woman No Cry' made the charts.

By this time the press releases and interviews had already had their impact on the rest of Europe, which was clamouring for Bob, so much so that we had to bring in the major press from all over Europe and hold a press conference at the Kensington Hotel, promising to visit the other countries in Europe the following year.

Following this we moved from London to complete the UK tour in Birmingham and Manchester, before returning home in triumph. During this time our association grew closer and closer, as Bob continued to express his satisfaction with my management style and confidence in my ability to direct his career to new heights.

6 Managing Bob

During the first years of my management, it became clear that Bob mistrusted everybody. It was my guess that this was based on his past experiences with the persons closest to him and also others in the music industry, and the recording business in Jamaica. He simply mistrusted everybody. I gained a little more trust, I guess, because I was the one who was making the deals and making all the money for him at the time. But Bob had his own way of checking up on people.

At the close of our first year, around the time of the signing of the new contract with Island, Bob's star was continuing to rise and I realized that the time had now come for us to re-examine our whole accounting structure. The contract with Island was a London-based one and thus subject to UK taxes. This meant that once our income had increased and the record sales started to climb, it placed Bob in the 70–80 per cent class of British taxpayers, the highest class.

I decided to discuss the matter with Marvin Zolt. I had originally met Marvin through Anthony Gourdine of Little Anthony and the Imperials, for whom Zolt acted as accountant, when I managed the Imperials. Over the years of my management of Little Anthony and the Imperials and my association with other stars I had used the services of both him and David Steinberg, both on my own and on the recommendation of different artistes who had been handled by them. So I now brought into my management orbit the later infamous team of David Steinberg and Marvin Zolt, as lawyer and accountant respectively. My exposure to the intricacies of the music business over the years had made me realize that you needed whites to deal with whites. I had a further meeting with Zolt and Steinberg as to how to proceed with Bob's tax situation. I was referred by David and Marvin to a contact person in DC who was an aide to a creditor and client of theirs.

I was told to contact this person for reference to a good tax lawyer and the aide in turn referred me to one Jerome Kurtz; this was in 1975.

I told Jerome Kurtz what I wanted and then went on to discuss his fees. Kurtz told me that he would come to New York to set up a tax plan and that the cost would be $7,000 per day, a lot of money. He felt sure that he could get it done in one day, going from Washington to New York to sit with the accountants and show them what to do.

I discussed all of this with Bob, saying that I felt this was the right approach, and then went ahead with it.

Jerome Kurtz came to New York and offered us the following advice. He told us that the island of Tortola in the British Virgin Islands had a treaty with the USA dating back to 1939, protected by a law in the US tax books.

The law, he further advised, allowed that any company registered in Tortola and owned and managed out of Tortola could treat all the monies earned by the company, in respect of commission or royalties, as exempt from taxes in the US and UK, and that this company could move all of the company's money out of the US or UK, tax-free. He advised me that Bob's company fell within these guidelines and that this law would suit us admirably in our situation.

He gave me the name of a contact attorney in Tortola, one Michael Regiles, who could form the company. In fact with the continued renegotiating of the Island contract this company was urgently needed. I had a feeling that Chris's company was not doing too well, as none of his other recording artistes was selling any records. His other potential star, Steve Winwood from Traffic, wasn't doing well; he wouldn't work and things seemed chaotic. In fact, Bob was his biggest seller.

Armed with this kind of knowledge I used the opportunity to dictate the terms I needed and also to take risks I would not normally take. For instance, during our London tour we had recorded *Live!*, but because it was a live recording it was not covered by the contract. I tried to get Island to accept it as part of the deal, but Chris refused, so we now needed a name for the company that would own it. I had demanded a lot of money from Island for distribution rights for the album, which Chris did not want to pay, and this created an impasse between us. Despite this impasse Chris took the risk of having Island release the album in the UK only, which led to a confrontation.

I immediately demanded payment for the UK rights, as well as a further payment for the European rights separately from the UK rights, and we were paid a substantial sum – as I recall about $500,000. Needless to say this did not make Chris very happy. These and other developments, however, now called for another meeting between Chris, Bob, Steinberg and myself. I called the lawyer in Tortola who advised me that he had already formed a company called Media Aides which he would sell to us for US$1,000. I immediately sent him a cheque to pay for the cost of the company and for him to open the company account at Barclays Bank in Tortola.

This now gave me the opportunity I needed to try to correct the situation with not only Chris Blackwell and Island, but also Danny Sims and Bob's publishing rights which Danny had placed in Cayman Music.

In reality what had happened was that when Bob had been signed by Cayman Music, which was owned by Danny and 'Big' Paul Castellano, that contract gave Danny the control of management, recordings and publishing of Bob's music. Among the songs owned were 'Guava Jelly', later recorded by Barbra Streisand, and 'I Shot the Sheriff', an early Eric Clapton hit, and other Marley classics such as 'Get Up Stand Up' and 'Reggae on Broadway'.

The earnings from these records were to be accounted for by Copyright Service Bureau, which was run by a lawyer, Walter Hoffer. His actions created and compounded the problem and would later cause a confrontation between Danny, the Mafia and myself.

When Bob saw the earnings from 'I Shot the Sheriff', which were about nine million dollars from publishing rights only, he become more aware of the value of the publishing rights left with Cayman Music and started to suspect that Danny was keeping earnings from him. This was when he decided, with Allan Cole and Yvette Morris (then an employee and one-time girlfriend of Bob), to put other persons' names to his songs to escape Cayman's publishing ownership. They did this for all the songs on the *Natty Dread* album, including 'No Woman No Cry'. This aroused the concern of Danny and the Mafia as it eventually resulted in Cayman Music losing the rights to these songs.

In his characteristic way, by hanging around with Danny, Bob had begun to get the hang of the intricacies of the music business. He began to learn more about the difference between managing, publishing and recording, so that when the contract with Danny came up for renewal, Bob negotiated for Danny to extend the publishing rights for another year, but only on the basis that Danny would release the recording and management parts of the contract back to him.

Once again Bob had absorbed the goings-on until he learnt enough to make his own demands.

After Danny agreed to this, Bob then proceeded, with the help of Allan Cole and Yvette Morris, to form a series of companies using the name Tuff Gong (which was the original company he had formed with Bunny Wailer and Peter Tosh and which they owned jointly). This then gave birth to Tuff Gong Music USA, which they registered in the USA. (This company should not be confused with Tuff Gong Distributions Jamaica, Tuff Gong Music, also registered in Jamaica, or Tuff Gong Records and Tuff Gong Productions, formed by me and registered in Tortola.) It was to this company that he, Allan and Yvette assigned the earnings of the new songs.

Having inherited this scenario I realized on investigation that there were two glaring errors: first they should not have registered the company in the USA as it would be taxable; and second Yvette had registered the company showing herself with 99 per cent ownership with only 1 per cent for Bob.

I advised Bob of both of these factors, and proceeded to correct them.

Knowing that the real power in the music business lies with the person who collects the money, I proceeded to register a new company, Bob Marley Music, in Tortola, and assign all earnings to this company, which made the earnings non-taxable. I also corrected the ownership of the company so that Yvette Morris no longer owned 99 per cent.

We had just completed the *Rastaman Vibration* album, which came out at the same time that the contract with Danny Sims expired. Bob and I decided to put some of the new songs under fictitious writers' names so as to escape Danny Sims's ownership.

But because we needed to keep Bob's visibility as a song-writer going, I carefully selected the songs that I would put under the names of others. In fact I myself placed such names as Allan Cole, Carlton Barrett, Family Man Barrett and Rita Marley on the songs which we had recorded for the *Rastaman Vibration* album, the jacket of which would show the following:

Bob Marley & The Wailers
Rastaman Vibration
Bob Marley Music
(Media Aides Ltd Tortola)

Songs	*Writers*
Positive Vibration	V. Ford
Roots, Rock, Reggae	V. Ford
Johnny Was	R. Marley
Cry to Me	R. Marley
Want More	A. Barrett
Crazy Baldhead	R. Marley, V. Ford
Who the Cap Fit	A. Barrett, C. Barrett
Night Shift	Bob Marley
War	A. Cole, C. Barrett
Rat Race	R. Marley

Changing the songwriters' names did not make much difference to the collection of revenue, as in all cases Bob's company or Bob was the publisher, and we were using the same address for all the songwriters. The cheques in their names would come to the same address and we would just endorse them and place them in the Tortola account without anyone being the wiser. This arrangement was further perfected by frequently putting on the album 'R. Marley, writer'. This served a two-fold purpose as R. Marley could be interpreted either as Robert Marley or Rita Marley, in whose names many of the songs were also registered. In this way I kept up Bob's visibility as a songwriter and at the same time was able to show the source of income and earnings as not being Bob's and therefore not subject to other company claims as to payment of royalties and expenses.

This kind of management of a performer's business is one of the more important roles for a manager to play, and I felt proud of the way I was overseeing Bob's earnings and his career growth. Until I took over as manager it had been mainly Island Records that was profiting.

By this time we operated some five bank accounts and the incoming earnings were substantial. In fact we had up to ten million US dollars in the Tortola account at that time.

Bob in relaxed mood at the house in Kingston where we were both later shot.

pposite: The laid back stage performer hid the personality of the "tuff gong" street
ghter *(above)*.

Top: Meet the gang – Bob and the team take a rare break from touring.
Below: Bob in pensive mood.

ɜob was a formidable soccer player, who was more than good enough to have turned rofessional.

The rising star. Bob with The Wailers in their early days together. (© Rex Features).

20
22
26

The Lion in his element.

Predictably, this spectacular success created enemies, so that I was constantly coming under pressure from all sides. Bob was continuously growing in stature and fame and was being pressured from every angle to get rid of me. There were apparently any number of persons who could do the job better than I could and the way to get such an opportunity was to tell Bob how much he was being robbed by me.

I had to deal with constant newcomers appearing almost out of nowhere, while trying at the same time to cope with the old hands at the game. I refer of course to the likes of Danny Sims. Danny never gave up trying to get back into the driver's saddle or to prove that he was being cheated. He was always using someone to front for him; it could be man or woman, and whichever it was, he would try to set them up to influence Bob. I remember the time during a tour when he sent the Zimbabwean, Joe Stebleski, who appeared out of the blue one day claiming that he was an accountant with Danny Sims. He insisted on meeting with our accountant in New York, Marvin Zolt, with the sole intention of proving to Bob and all concerned that I was stealing from him. This charge was a two-edged sword, as inherent in it was the songwriters' scam which Bob knew about, along with the veiled accusation of me personally. They seemed to know that we were registering the songs to fictitious songwriters.

Then there was the continuous pressure from Chris Blackwell: his method was to keep two or three people continuously purveying rumour and carrying news. Although many associates of Bob claimed that there was a genuine friendship between Bob and Chris, this was never apparent in all the discussions, conversations and exchanges that I had with Bob, nor did I ever see it for myself. In fact, without any fear of contradiction, I can categorically state that no such friendship existed. What Chris and Bob did have was mutual respect for each other's professional and creative abilities, but friends: no! In fact, from what I had observed, Bob never liked Chris.

Chris's management reflected the classic method of money making, where he sought to manage, publish and record his artistes in such a manner that he was publisher for the record company as well as manager for the group. This was what he wanted to do with Bob, but Bob was smarter than he was and certainly smarter than all the others.

They were from very different cultures, although Chris also grew up in Jamaica. He represented all that Bob was against. Under the tutelage of his mother Blanche Blackwell, one of the heirs of the Crosse & Blackwell fortune, Chris had formed Island Records (spawned in name, some would say, by Alec Waugh's novel *Island in the Sun*) in 1959 and opened its London office in 1962.

Chris had seen Bob's first two albums, *Catch a Fire* (1973) and *Burnin'*, which boasted such tracks as 'Get Up Stand Up' and 'I Shot the Sheriff', get a strong response from the music world. Chris had an ear which was very responsive to and supportive of anything that was not mainstream. In fact, he was a person who shied away from the traditional; if it was mainstream Chris did not want to touch it.

This trait had a dual advantage, as it allowed Chris to exploit ignorant artistes and pay them only what he wished. This was possible because no one knew what value was to be placed on the new, innovative music. So it was left to Chris himself, as there was no one else to turn to, no other guiding light or historic precedent. And as most of this non-traditional and non-mainstream music was coming from the so-called Third World, where such things as music publishing and copyright were not understood by the lawyers, much less the musicians, Chris was able to get the best out of these musicians before they themselves became mainstream.

In fact, Chris would get them at a very low cost and get the best out of them before they knew what was happening.

This was a typical independent music company approach and practice, and was a classic way of behaving in the music world.

It wasn't surprising then that the talent in Chris's stable achieved financial success usually when they left him; one has only to look at the experience of people like Steve Winwood, Robert Palmer, Joe Cocker, Jimmy Cliff, and Cat Stevens, to name a few artistes who formed part of his Island Anglo Rock era from 1969 to 1972, to realize how true this is.

Chris's personal life was another reason Marley could never be close to him. Chris had many gay and bisexual friends, which Bob, like most Jamaican macho men, abhorred. This, along with Bob's realization that Chris had not given him a fair deal on his first two albums, did not help the relationship.

Take *Catch a Fire*, which is still selling today. By any standards this album achieved great sales but neither Bob, Bunny nor anyone else ever received their fair portion of these sales. By my own reckoning this record must have sold well over two million copies to date, yet for all three albums, as far as I know, the Wailers received only £8,000 and US$12,000 from Chris.

As Bob said in June 1975, 'Wasn't because of no connection that we go to England [for a recording contract]. The guys we used to deal with in England was some big pirates. Them guys kill off reggae music, kill rock steady and kill ska. Them guys for reggae music like some people is for rock, y'know, suck out the artist and sometimes them kill them.'

One of the things Bob told me he resented about Chris, was that Chris was always trying to put his own name on to Bob's work. He tried to do this by putting his name on the record as producer, which was not accurate as he never produced any of Bob's work. He may occasionally have given the idea – he did this from time to time – but he never produced.

Just for the record – no pun intended – on the first contract

Bob had with Chris, Chris was paying Bob only 8 per cent while paying himself 2 per cent as producer, although he was not the producer. But then this is pretty much what happens to the unsuspecting and the ignorant in the music world.

Take for instance the case of Trojan Records. This company was putting out all the early Bob Marley records in England without authorization, but try as we did neither Bob nor I could get royalty statements or indeed any royalty payments. We tried to investigate the source of the organization and distribution of these records, but all to no avail; eventually, however, we were able to track down the source, only to discover that Chris was in fact a shareholder in Trojan. We discovered that Chris had formed the company with Lee Gopthals, an Indian from Delhi, so that in reality Chris was a major part of the wholesale piracy.

My research revealed that it was in 1968 or thereabouts that Chris merged his business with a company called B&C Records which he used to handle all the releases generated by the leading Jamaican labels and producers, including the Upsetters, Duke Reid, Harry J, Treasure Isle, Leslie Kong and Coxsone Dodd. At my estimate it included some fifty labels in all – little short of piracy.

Chris's business was so structured that no one could figure out who was doing what. Deals were signed on top of deals and no one knew who was selling, who was producing, who was licensing or who was distributing what. If ever there was a hydra-headed monster this was it. And this only served to show me the extent of Chris's deceit, teaching me to be ever more cautious when dealing with Chris Blackwell, and in fact, increasing our resolve to regain ownership of all that was rightfully Bob's.

I guess that is why Bob said in 1976, 'Yes, people rob me and try fe trick me, but now I have experience. Now I know and I see and I don't get tricked. Used to make recordings and not get royalties. Still happen sometime. All Wailers records made here [Jamaica] but then pirated to England. All them English companies rob man. Everybody that deals with West Indian music – thieves.'

I really have no deep resentment for Chris; he played his part. And as a distributor he opened up his cheque book and finally allowed me to run the show. But he made more than his fair share, and he is not the creative genius that everybody tries to make him out to be. If he is a genius it is as a smart businessman; and Bob recognized this. He was always anxious to finish the contracted albums and would often say to me, 'Don Taylor when we a go finish these albums and get rid of this man.'

In fact a number of things created an atmosphere around Chris that was not to Bob's liking and these manifested themselves more and more with each passing day. Indeed it must have begun to become clear to Chris that Bob was becoming more independent of him, especially financially. Take for instance the 1975/76 period when we were due some $2.2 million in royalties. At that time things were bad for Chris and Island, and they were in a tight cash position. On his request Bob and I agreed that we would not take the royalties due. And so he assisted Chris by leaving the money in the form of a loan to Island so as to keep the company going.

In reality, then, Bob had reduced Chris's power almost to that of a distributor and I always felt that Chris resented this. Chris was the type of person who, if he could not have things his way, would rather see you off the scene.

All this reminds me of how much Bob really wanted to be rid of Chris. He wanted to own himself totally, so as to harness his creativity for his children and not for Chris Blackwell. It was a position which he never stopped emphasizing to me.

When I realized how very important this position was to Bob, I decided that I would work towards his wish and speed up the delivery of the albums to Island.

But in the meantime, I had to deal with the unhurried Jamaican scene, which was my first day-to-day exposure to Bob's way of life. This was a way of life which was unpretentious and slow-moving, in total contrast to the hectic touring days, and very much unlike the after-tour pace I had learnt to live with in LA.

7 The Jamaican Scene

Despite the unprecedentedly high level of political friction and confrontation produced by the ideological passions of Jamaican politics in the seventies Bob was resoundingly welcomed on his return to Jamaica in late 1975. His musical achievements and his remarkable lyrics had hit a responsive chord in his country, and it could already be seen that he was becoming a living legend.

On our return Bob settled into a normal routine, or as normal as possible for Bob Marley. And with Bob being the new owner of 56 Hope Road, things took on a more personal note there. It was not easy for the world to understand Bob's laid-back attitude and unpretentious and open Jamaican life-style; it always tended to baffle and surprise the unsuspecting megastars from the UK and USA.

On what could be called a normal day, Bob would wake early, almost always before anyone else, no matter what the night before had entailed.

On waking, he would almost instantly begin rehearsing – alone. He would break for breakfast, which would be prepared by his personal hired cook, Gillie. Bob never expressed any particular likes or dislikes regarding his food, his main concerns being that it was ital (cooked without salt), and that it did not include pork or any other meat, as he was virtually a vegetarian, eating meat only occasionally, a regime which had a good effect when Bob was placed on a rigid diet following the discovery of his cancer.

He would religiously start his day with a mug of porridge, usually cornmeal, which he would sip while reading his Bible, something he did daily. He also kept it nearby while he was rehearsing.

As the day wore on the entourage of visitors would increase, from the members of the band to other musical associates such as Tommy Cowan and business associates like Colin Leslie and Diane Jobson.

Diane was a typical case of an upper-class woman who was completely controlled by Bob Marley. She was a real uptown girl, whom he had taken and bred into the Rasta faith in the early seventies and to whom, after he got bored, he merely gave the day-to-day task of acting out a lawyer's role.

She must have resented my arrival on the scene and my relationship with Bob, because I assumed full control of Bob's accounts and transactions. Bob made sure that I knew everything about his business, to the extent that if he wrote a cheque the bank would call me to OK it. I expected that this would cause some enmity and bitter blood among those who were with Bob before I arrived, and it probably accounted for a lot of the rumours and stories that were spread about me and which still linger in the minds of many. Basically the rumours were along the lines that I cheated Bob. It was nonsense, of course, but that's the kind of rumour any manager can expect when he manages any successful artist.

There was also a continuous stream of hangers-on, with open and outstretched hands, who never seemed to be satisfied. They would begin arriving around ten in the morning, when the endless round of cooking and eating and the smoking of weed would begin, to last all day until three or four in the afternoon when they would all play football, either on the front lawn of Hope Road, or at a playing field nearby.

These people came from far and wide, and included adherents to the Rasta religion, ghetto strongmen, political enforcers and plain hustlers. It was as if Santa Claus had been reincarnated for them. Bob had become a soft touch for everyone. And every attempt I made to change this would be ignored by Bob until suddenly one day he realized that this could not be the way to do things. When he realized that he had given away one million dollars in two months, he decided to come to his senses. Finally, at one stage, he walked around with his trousers' pockets turned out, as a signal that the end of the give-away was at hand.

It was after this that he said to me one day that he wanted to expand the Tuff Gong Group of Companies, and wanted me to form a recording and manufacturing record company. I proceeded to do this, registering Tuff Gong Distributors (Jamaica), and Tuff Gong Recording (Jamaica).

I was very pleased, both at this and the fact that Bob seemed to have seriously decided that instead of giving away money, he would provide work instead, at least for those who wanted it.

Without a doubt Bob was unique in every way. He was unique in the way he approached life, how he approached his music and how he became a star, which he did in an era when there were no super videos, satellite dishes or CDs.

One of his most precious moments, he always told me, was the time in 1975 when we were flying by private plane into Philadelphia for our concert at the same time that the Pope was arriving. The tower held up the Pope's plane to allow us to land, and when Bob heard this he turned to me and with seriousness said, 'Don Taylor, you see who is God pickney, see how them hold up the man for I.'

Babylon system is the vampire
Sucking the blood of the sufferers...
('Babylon System')

Bob was close to the edge, but until then, the only known criminal thing that Bob could be accused of was the smoking of weed. And this to Bob was not an offence as it was part of his religion, and he smoked his weed before the highest representatives of law and order, even before prime ministers and church leaders, without a single charge being brought against him in Jamaica.

Bob was probably one of the few persons in the entertainment world who had the provision and supply of marijuana written into his contracts. Indeed his 'normal' use of marijuana, especially in the context of his clean, clear, and honest political beliefs, was probably why his ganja smoking was accepted.

Eventually he even had me, unknown to him, trying to ensure his supply personally. I remember an occasion when I myself bought some and smuggled it through Customs in my boots. This was on the Japan tour. When I think of it now, I marvel at my taking such a chance, but then it was obvious that he was not called 'Gong' for nothing, which in ghetto terms meant 'Tough Shit'.

This period in Jamaica also allowed me to get to know the original Wailers, as well as the later shifting band of musicians.

In getting to know the original Wailers I came to understand the reasons for the break-up. I could identify with and appreciate Peter Tosh's negative feelings towards Blackwell, especially since the albums *Burnin'* and *Catch a Fire* had only brought in four thousand US dollars despite their obvious success. As I have pointed out already Chris Blackwell was not really up front with his different deals and his attempts to control Bob's creativity. At the same time the crowd reaction to the music was increasingly aimed at Bob and not the Wailers in general, and it seemed quite normal and logical to Bob that the group should go their individual ways, if only to keep the vibes on the same wavelength. For how else could they cater to Peter's deep radicalism and ambivalence towards Blackwell, and Bunny's strong individualism?

On the other hand Bob never felt he had ever left the Wailers, and he made it clear that Tuff Gong was still all three of them: himself, Bunny and Peter. I recall the time that Diane

Jobson wanted to remove Peter's and Bunny's names from the company, and Bob replied, saying, 'We are still Tuff Gong, it started with me, Peter and Bunny, and we no split.'

Although Bob felt pretty much as Peter Tosh did about Chris Blackwell, unlike Peter he was always conscious of the need to pick the right moment to deal with a situation. In fact it became quite clear to me that he would deal with this once he felt Blackwell and himself were on even ground, and that time came after the *Natty Dread* album, when we renegotiated his original contract.

Bob's personal relationship with the later Wailers was usually based on the depth of their own ability to be involved, and their ability to exchange musical ideas with him.

> 'If you play music, or listen to music and you don't know why you're playing or listening except for money and pleasure, you can be in serious trouble. Reggae say something if it mean something to the people who make it and the people who listen to it.'
>
> (June 1975)

There was Willie Lindo, who would flit in and out, and even at one stage left to tour with Taj Mahal, which really pissed Bob off.

On the other hand, Bob liked Tyrone Downie. It was Tyrone who would gather music from all over the globe and bring it to Bob. Bob felt a great affinity with him, and considered Tyrone 'a young and progressive musician' compared with Family Man and Carlton, whom he felt were both trapped in the 'one drop' concept of reggae music.

I continually marvelled at Bob's uncanny ability to predict the trends and modes he needed to code into his music and how careful he was about not trying to change anyone who was unwilling to change, although he was always looking for those who wished to expand their own musical horizons. This became manifest when Bob got interested in punk rock and wanted to 'mesh' it with reggae to record 'Punky Reggae Party'. He found great resistance from many in the band, especially Family Man, and so Bob went directly to London with Lee Perry and ended up recording it with Rico Rodriguez's band. And much to everyone's amazement the success of 'Punky Reggae Party' locked Bob into the mass musical movement of the time. This created a closeness between Bob and Tyrone Downie, because Tyrone had fully supported his experimentation.

> 'Soul, jazz, reggae, calypso, blues – I like plenty good music. Jazz, that's a complete music. Music with feeling . . . don't like music or anything that deals with the wrong things of life, because I only want to deal with the truth.'
>
> (June 1976)

In fact, it was quite common to hear Family Man say that if it was not 'rockers' he would not play. On the other hand, Carlton would say very little, the only difference being that he invariably tried to do whatever Bob wanted. And what Bob wanted was clear in his description of how he saw reggae music:

> 'You get to appreciate [recognize] the foolish ones, the guys play reggae skanop, skanop, skanop. Not my type of reggae that. My reggae unncha cha, unncha cha, unncha cha, more rootsie.'
>
> (June 1976)

In the case of Al Anderson, he was not really a Wailer but a hired musician, a hired guitar player who was almost always available when Bob needed him. He had toured with us on the first tour in 1975. Al, however, was always wanting more and more money, definitely more than Bob was willing to give. Eventually Bob and Al failed to see eye to eye on certain things. Also Al was an American. Al's habit of demanding more money was what forced us to bring in Donald Kinsey, who remained with us through 1976, until the time we were shot in that assassination attempt. In fact, Donald was rehearsing at the time of the shoot-up.

This attitude of Al's of wanting more and more was completely unjustified, as Bob almost always overpaid his musicians. He did so for the very reason that he wanted to make sure that his individual rights to his music were protected, so it was a calculated plan on his part to pay all his hired musicians top dollar.

I remember how Donald came to replace Al Anderson, a story which highlighted the shrewd and calculating business side of Bob Marley and which led some of Bob's immediate associates and friends to comment unfavourably on his loyalty to people.

Al Anderson was making all sorts of demands on Bob in terms of royalties; in fact, he wanted the moon, so Bob told him that he would send me to London where Al was touring at the time to negotiate with him. His actual words were, 'Listen man, everything yuh waan yuh will get, but I am going to sen' Donald Taylor there, an' yuh can work it out, an' when Donald Taylor gets there, Donald Taylor will hook up a call, an' I will work it out an' clear it up.'

So off I went to England. But before leaving, Bob said to me, 'Listen, when yuh get to England an' meet with Al, whatever yuh seh, yuh going to seh to me over the phone, an' I am going to say yes; but listen for a knocking sound on the phone,' and at this point Bob picked up the phone and knocked on the mouthpiece. 'When I knock twice, that means no. Even when I say yes. In the end you will advise Al dat yuh will get back to him.' Which of course we never did, leaving Al with the distinct impression that it was

I and not Bob who did not want to meet his demands.

Junior Marvin was not around at the time, as he was the last addition to the group in 1976, coming on board after the free concert. He too came in as a hired musician, which always makes me ask how it is that today Junior can have the gall to make claims against Bob's music and royalty earnings. I recall Bob once telling Junior, 'A bring yuh to Jamaica, tek de earring out a yuh ear, gi yuh a house an a woman. What more yuh waan?' Bob in fact saw Junior as one who, though nowhere nearly as talented as himself, was always seeking to upstage him.

In actuality, none of the musicians in the band ever knew how much they were going to be paid. Bob would just say, 'Dis man get dat, and dat man get dat.' But in each and every instance, it was clear that everyone was overpaid, and they knew it. In all that time I never heard Carly or Family Man ever ask for more, but this was not the case with Al and later on with Junior Marvin, who were considered outsiders anyway.

Bob would actually tell them that he had to protect them because they spent money so fast. This approach was what caused the conflict, especially with Al, and later on with Junior, as it led them to believe there was more. But no one had the guts to come up front and say anything to Bob; instead they took it out on me.

Bob was a very sensitive and funny man. He almost always gave people an opportunity to speak, listening to what they had to say, and then he would assess them.

Bob's closest friend was undoubtedly Allan 'Skill' Cole who has always been known for his thrifty ways. I recall how one day, shortly after he had won a large sum of money at the races, Skill came to Bob and asked him to lend him $10,000 on the spot. I can still see Bob's friendly reaction and hear the affection in his voice when he said, 'Rass claat, Skill, yuh mean yuh just win so much money and rather than use that yuh want borrow from me!'

It took me the first year, but specifically the combination of the first tour and this time spent in Jamaica, really to learn how Bob functioned. One rule I did learn was that only one man could speak for the Wailers and that man was Bob Marley. I also learned that Bob never said yes and he never said no; whatever you put to him, he would say, 'It sounds like it could work.' If you were waiting on him to say, 'It will definitely work,' that was never going to happen. It was left to you to take the step and go ahead so that if anything went wrong you had no one to blame but yourself and Bob was free of any blame. I also discovered that Bob liked to have money but only for the freedom it gave him to be Bob Marley, and to owe nothing to anyone, which was his cardinal principle of life.

Over the years, all these situations and revealing incidents contributed to the building of a very workable relationship between Bob and myself, despite the fact that Bob never trusted anybody, no one at all, as he always thought everybody was dishonest.

During all this, however, what came out most forcefully was Bob's desire to lead a revolutionary assault on the forces of Babylon. He felt that this assault had to come from giving voice to the downtrodden and the oppressed which had to begin with his mind and his music, music which he would now increasingly use as a means to assault the minds of Jamaica and the world.

From the outset Bob seemed to know that the forces to be united were almost exclusively linked to the political culture and to the Rastafarian religion. And it was clear to me by then that Bob Marley had become the leader and the focus of a disenfranchised army of dissidents, toughs, gunmen and political enforcers of both political parties – JLP and PNP. Leading the whole army was a general – Allan 'Skill' Cole – with Bob as the Chief of Staff who financed the operations, and who kept everyone in line, while he nursed the idea of when to move and how to ensure the defeat of Babylon's system.

Bob seemed to be obsessed with the challenge of bringing together not just the increasingly divided Rastafarian tribes into one unified organization, but the warring political activists whose constant violent confrontations were growing in intensity and viciousness. Bob wanted to demonstrate without question to the people of Jamaica, and indeed the world, that opposing parties could live together in peace and show respect for each other. 'God never made no difference between black, white, blue, pink or green. People is people, yuh know. That is the message we try to spread.'

When asked if politicians knew about him, he replied, 'Yeah man. They nuh like me 'cause I talk against de system. Some of dem seh, "Well Bob you're nice." They are looking for me like aluminium, Jamaica's main export, y'know, so I can bring back some money in. I'm not interested in that, I'm interested in what's happening to the people. I mean I really like to walk down the street, and everyone smile at me, instead of suffer. Guys suffer so much, they don't have time to smile. The politicians cause it.'

This was obviously what motivated him to take two ardent political supporters from opposing sides into his day-to-day life, and later, on the tours. Trying in a practical way to show them that by having to live, eat and sleep together while travelling with and being around Bob they could act in their own mutual interest, without the antagonisms and suspicions to which they were accustomed.

Because of this, we almost always had in residence two important generals of the street and political ghettoes, Claudie Massop and Tony Welch. They represented Bob's hopes that there could be unification, especially in this, the most divided time.

Claudie Massop was a noted front-line organizer for the leader of the Jamaica Labour Party and then leader of the opposition, Eddie Seaga. Athletically built and some six feet tall, with sharp appealing looks and a winning smile, Massop was the toughest of the tough, but still had a soft, gentle quality which endeared him to all those he met, although he was an enforcer of the highest order.

Tony Welch, on the other hand, was a leading fixer for the PNP. Five foot seven, slim and brown-skinned, he had been introduced to Bob by Tony Spaulding, for whom he was an equally efficient enforcer. These two guys mirrored the political behaviour of both sides and represented in many ways a challenge to Bob's hopes and desires. Through them Bob saw a way to deal with Babylon, the common enemy.

These guys could get anything and everything they wanted from Bob. For instance, on one trip to Miami I recall Bob buying Tony a BMW. Tony was supposed to pay him back, but as far as I recall, Bob was never repaid.

I guess Bob was what sociologists would interpret as a man trying to mobilize the masses into a revolution by using his money and the power it gave him. And if the mental revolution failed, one could always turn to the physical revolution. I think it also gave Bob a security blanket. He was playing it safe to a certain extent by maintaining his links with the ghetto – and with both sides.

Bob's attempts at social unification included the Rasta religion, whose members also played a significant role in Bob's way of life. The continued fight being waged against them by the Babylon system was a serious part of Bob's life. It was around this time that some eight Rastas were shorn forcibly in Kingston, increasing the tension and ultimately leading to the formation of 'Jah Rastafari Holy Theocratic Government'. This movement or government sought Bob's help and finally formed a thirteen-member delegation which called for a series of meetings with Prime Minister Manley to improve relationships between, as they would call it, 'yovernments'.

This move in itself, like so many others at the time, also

brought Bob into focus and seemed to emphasize to him that a greater effort was needed to heal all the wounds and the social and economic gaps that exposed themselves daily.

Following Bob's intervention the Rastas finally settled in Bull Bay, not far from Bob's other residence, which was a small government-built house. This was Bob's first house when he moved out of Trench Town, and had an interesting story behind it.

Bob had obtained the house through Tony Spaulding, the MP for Trench Town, who was close to Bob, close enough for him to be able later on in life to speak of the favours he had received from politicians. (And I later understood the underground stories of how in the early years it was political strong-arm payola that got your music played on the radio.) Until then Bob had not owned a house, so that his move to Bull Bay together with Skill Cole and Marcia Griffiths was a major one. He now spent his time between Trench Town, Bull Bay and 56 Hope Road.

I watched as Bob developed a good relationship with the group of Rastas he had helped move to Bull Bay, and they in turn influenced Bob's *Rastaman Vibration* album. That album also proclaimed his adoption of the Twelve Tribes beliefs – that he was of the tribe of Joseph, his colour was white, and his blessing would come from Genesis 49:22–24, and Deuteronomy 33:16: 'Joseph was a fruitful bough.'

At the other end of the scale the album also reflected the realities of the ghetto.

Woman hold her head and cry
'Cause her son had been shot down
On the street and died
('Johnny Was')

And most powerful of all was the political warning of the ranking reggae Rastamen:

That until there are no longer
First class and second class
Citizens of any nation
Everywhere is war
('War')

All of this only seemed to add fuel to the fire of the developing political culture, as the tension in the ghetto heightened and the ideological war of the seventies intensified.

For to the political reality of life in the Jamaican ghetto was now added the influence of the international ideological cold war, which began to add a new dimension to Jamaica's politics. Since it was the PNP and Manley in power, the JLP stronghold of Eddie Seaga – Tivoli – was coming under increasing police pressure. Tribalism was on the rise and there was indeed 'War' in the ghetto. As the so-called communist threat of Manley and Cuba escalated and the wider world began to take interest, the people, faced with all these pressures and the inability of the system to respond, began increasingly to express their antagonism. Random violence continued throughout Kingston, as we prepared for the *Rastaman Vibration* tour, exerting much pressure on Bob, as he was very close to the two main party enforcers and generals of the streets.

Then we had to deal with the problem of the 'Caymanas' scam and the horse race doping affair, which involved Skill Cole. Horse racing, an exciting feature of Jamaican life, had become exposed to political corruption, as party enforcers discovered how the racing industry could be manipulated to create quick earnings. Indeed the racing industry had been penetrated by thugs who would bribe groom, jockey and trainer and dope both horse and rider, not only to earn a living but also to finance political activity. And the control of the track and the race days was usually under the generalship of the supporters of whichever party was in power at the time.

And so Skill had become involved in what was later known as the doping affair.

For whatever reason, one such race failed to provide the desired results. The doped horses did not come in as anticipated and so many of the people in the scam were not paid what they considered their share, and as Skill Cole was very close to Bob, the feeling grew that Bob himself was involved in the gamble. It was also common knowledge that a lot of these events were linked to political ghetto leaders like Claudie and Tony. Bob felt obliged, because of his closeness to Cole, to help him in every way.

It was time, however, for us to go to Miami for the National Organization of Record Merchants (NORM) convention, which would be important in promoting the upcoming album. So off we went leaving the doping problems behind. We had decided that after the NORM convention, Bob would do some more work on the *Rastaman Vibration* album at the Criteria Recording Studio.

I had to round up a crew of engineers quickly, so I contacted King Sporty, whom I greatly respected. He had assisted in getting Neville Garrick bailed, through a Captain Curry, when Neville tried to smuggle ganja into Miami on his first trip with the Wailers in the summer of 1975. Sporty found Alex Sadkin for us, which was quite fortunate, as it was out of this meeting that Bob developed great professional respect for Alex, who did a remarkable job on the album, *Rastaman Vibration*. This finally led to Blackwell hiring him, as was usual with any of Bob's creative discoveries. Sadly, Alex was to die in a car crash in Nassau not long after Chris hired him. This gradually created for me, and I now believe for Bob, a sense of foreboding.

Rastaman Vibration hit the charts as soon as it was released, adding to Bob's success and his value as a musician.

But success or no success, Bob had not left his revolutionary plans behind. During the two weeks in Miami, he got

King Sporty to put him in touch with the Miami-based political dissidents who had fled Jamaica and were living in Miami, one of whom was 'Schoolboy' (Richard Morrison).

It was also during this trip that certain individuals were given all the finances required to buy what were referred to as 'arms'. I remember Bob telling me one day to give a cheque to a guy I knew only as Billy (now crippled). The cheque was for $40,000, and was to be picked up by Yvette Morris, as Bob did not wish me to be directly involved. Yvette also was meant to deliver the letter without knowing of its contents. I only realized what the cheque was used for later when, on going through the bank accounts, I saw that it had been cashed by a well-known arms-dealing company.

On completing the album, we returned to Jamaica, only to be confronted once again with the Skill Cole 'Caymanas' problem, which had escalated during our absence in Miami.

Skill was still in trouble, as it was felt that the payoff for the fixed double event in the Caymanas scam which he was supposed to have set up had not yet been carried out fairly, and one of the jockeys who had thrown the first two races had been kidnapped by the aggrieved parties.

As the deal had been struck at Hope Road, where the hangers-on were increasingly gathering, the unpaid gunmen and enforcer friends felt that Bob should pay Skill Cole's debt. This led to an attempt to extort funds from Bob, who was being asked to pay out some two thousand dollars per day. The first payment was extracted practically at gunpoint in the ghetto. Finally Skill left the island for the USA and ultimately Ethiopia.

As if that wasn't enough, Bob was also visited by a contingent of PNP bad men, who were questioning his political allegiance to democratic socialism and Michael Manley's cause. This was obviously the result of Bob playing both ends against the middle and using the situation for his own purposes, based on his philosophy that it was only through a united ghetto that the forces of Babylon could be defeated.

Because of Manley's charismatic appeal and his articulation of the needs of the poor, the people – especially the ghetto people – not fully understanding what Bob was up to, had begun to question the closeness of Bob and Skill Cole to the likes of Claudie Massop, Seaga's right-hand man. Very often Bob and Skill were seen hanging out with Massop and his crew at Dizzi Disco, Turntable, and other uptown clubs on Red Hills Road, or visiting the Caymanas Race Track, and it was well known that Skill had been part of the racing scam. The ghetto had obviously begun to feel that Bob was playing it both ways, just in case Manley did not defeat Seaga.

It was almost as if we should have seen these conflicts coming. In the four weeks that we had been away, the political tension had grown even stronger. All these tensions led to the announcement on June 19, 1976, by the Governor General, Sir Florizel Glasspole, of an island-wide State of Emergency. This was based on a charge by the PNP that Seaga and the JLP were fomenting a plot with the CIA to discredit the government and the PNP.

Once again the cauldron was beginning to boil and the widening political divisions meant that in true Jamaican tradition one had to choose a side. There could and should be no halfway house.

The declaration of the State of Emergency meant that the lines were being drawn even more finely and Bob, being from the PNP side of the ghetto, now had to choose in this arena.

The Women

8 Bob and Rita

The political and social tensions did not affect family affairs, however. Bob always had someone pick up his kids from school and bring them to Hope Road. Stevie, Ziggy and Cedella would arrive around two and stay until six or seven o'clock, watching their father play football and generally spending time with him. He would then put them in his VW van and send them off to his house in Bull Bay. After that he would sit around till eight or nine, and then venture out into the Kingston nightlife, very often to Dizzi Disco.

Dizzi was one of the pioneer disco clubs in Kingston, located in Liguanea some two miles from 56 Hope Road. It was a small club situated above a short, steep and narrow staircase in a cul de sac off Hope Road. It boasted flashing lights which blinked continuously against the background of mirrored walls, as well as an intimate dancefloor that was hidden behind beaded curtains. The real attraction for Bob, as I was later to learn, was Cindy Breakspeare. She worked at the club, but would not condescend to respond to any of Bob's attempts to woo her. Many a tale of these club exploits would be recounted the following day by Skill Cole, who was Bob's constant companion on the excursions.

For my part I was learning more and more about Bob Marley, and beginning to understand all the different political and personal things that happened to and surrounded him. I learned, for instance, that Rita Marley and Bob were wife and husband in name only. It was quite common for Bob, during the early period of his career, to tell people that Rita was his sister, as he always did when asked by the media who she was. In private, he went as far as telling Rita he did not want her to use his name. I knew about this because I once witnessed an argument between Bob and Rita over this very matter, when he reminded Rita that they were not married under normal circumstances. He said, 'Rita why you don't stop using my name.' She said, 'But I am married to you,' and he said, 'Rita, how you going on like you don't know how the marriage business go, that my mother was sending for me to come to America and because you have the children, I decided to marry you so that you could get a green card.' And very often he would say, 'Blood claat Rita, don't yuh know dat?'

It was also during one of these family arguments that Bob told me Rita could sign his signature better than he could. I found all this very strange but it taught me to be more cautious than usual.

Bob maintained an account at the Jamaica Citizens Bank at King Street, jointly with Skill Cole. One day some money couldn't be accounted for. Thinking that Allan had taken it out, Bob and I went down to the bank where Bob was shown the cheque. The cheque carried what appeared to be his signature, as far as anyone could see. It was then that he revealed his feelings about the matter: 'Blood claat, Don Taylor, Rita can sign mi name betta dan me!'

Rita was actually treated just like one of the workers. She was paid a salary separately from the allowance Bob gave her for the children and herself. Bob gave Rita no special treatment. When she went on tours she got paid just like everybody else; and when they were not touring she was merely there in the background.

Rita was raised by a woman called Auntie, of whom Bob would express his fear on several occasions. Auntie was a short black woman, standing only five feet tall, with a no-nonsense face and a certain way of looking at you that would dig deep into your mind.

I will never forget the time Rita brought Auntie along on

a trip to England. We were all comfortably ensconced in first class when the stewardess came by with hors d'oeuvres. Auntie refused to eat them, saying to me: 'A what dat foolishness dem a serve.' Whereupon she reached under her seat and opened a shut pan of doctor fish. In no time the smell of fish filled the first-class cabin and resulted in an abrupt exit of passengers. No amount of air freshener could get rid of that smell.

According to Bob, Auntie was an obeah woman. On many occasions he would tell me that he was sure she was a practitioner of this ancient Jamaican religion which, though legally banned, was still practised by a large percentage of the population. Auntie had continued to live with Rita through the years and did in fact take care of Rita's children by Bob, but she had very little to do with him. There seemed to have been a breakdown in their relationship before my arrival.

Bob would tell me very often that the reason why he could not make a clean break with Rita was because Auntie had obeahed him.

In spite of all of this, I was aware that a special bond still existed, and so I – and in fact all of us – learnt not to get into their relationship. You quickly learnt, especially while on tour, that although they stayed in separate worlds during the day, as soon as everybody had gone to sleep Bob would send for Rita. Most people do not know this. I know because I had access to his room at all times. That reinforced my decision to stay out of their business, and I never involved myself in it during Bob's lifetime.

I remember when Rita got pregnant with Stephanie between the first and second tour, and Bob accused her of seeing this other guy.

The result was that Bob never believed the child was his. Rita had, however, gone ahead and given the child Bob's surname. What was noticeable when the baby was born was that it had six fingers.

When Bob asked Rita about this she told him that her father, Papa Roy Anderson, also had six fingers and it was probably hereditary. At the time Anderson was living in Stockholm. It so happened that on the third world tour (Rita had missed the second tour due to pregnancy) we performed in Stockholm at Tivoli Gardens, and Rita's father came backstage to meet Bob. Bob noticed that his hands were quite normal and showed no signs of the extra sixth finger Rita had spoken about. Bob did not ask for any further explanation. Instead, reacting with great passion, he walked up to her and said, 'How yu so blood claat lie gal, yu want a blood claat kick.'

After this it was accepted that the child was not Bob's. I remember vividly the day when Bob went to Bull Bay to confront the man he thought was the baby's father. I could see the anger in this man's eyes and feel the passion bubbling, but after some very quick and heated exchanges he stopped Bob dead in his tracks when he said to him, 'Man, I man didn't know she was your wife, 'cause everytime I read something, and the I a talk 'bout her, the I seh she is "im sister".' The remark suddenly broke all the tension between them, and Bob started grinning. His own words had come back to haunt him. So he just picked up his feet and stepped and kept on stepping.

These episodes were typical of the confusing signals emanating from the relationship between Bob and Rita. There was little doubt that Bob's loyalty to Rita was almost completely due to the children she bore him. I remember another time when we were in Germany and one of Bob's baby-mothers who lived in Germany came to visit Bob in the Presidential Suite of the Hamburg Hilton where we always stayed. The very presence of Karen's mother (this was the name of the little girl who lived in Harbour View in Jamaica) obviously irked Rita, and she started to hassle Bob about the money he was spending on both the little girl and her mother. One particular day, the pressure got to be more than Bob could take and when Rita came up to the suite he proceeded to beat her mercilessly. In fact the fight wrecked the hotel room and we had to pay some large repair bills the following day. It was only the fact that we were regular guests who usually did not create trouble that allowed us to get away as lightly as we did.

When we reached the bus after settling the bill, Bob did not sit in his usual place at the back of the bus. Over the years, it had become Bob's habit to be the first person on the bus, where he would immediately occupy the back seat. Unlike other stars, Bob would always be checked out and ready to move as soon as the bus arrived. On boarding he would head straight for the back of the bus as it gave him more space to spread out and meditate. On this occasion, however, instead of heading to the back he came to the front, where I always sat. As manager I found this to be a strategic seat, finding it easier to communicate with everybody, especially the driver, who was perhaps the key person in this equation.

When Bob came and sat beside me, he told me that he wanted Rita off the tour, that her presence did not allow him to concentrate and he wanted her to be sent home right away. I had never seen this side of Bob before, nor did I ever see it again.

Realizing that this called for a different approach, I said to him, 'Bob! What is it yu want? Yu want a divorce from Rita? – If yu want a divorce I can handle it, I can get yu a lawyer. But if yu gonna divorce Rita yu got to cut it off clear! Yu can't be tiptoeing in and out of her room at night when everybody is asleep and gone to bed! Yu got to stop that.' Bob grinned in that special way of his, looked at me, and did an about face. He said, 'But yu know she is not a bad girl, 'cause I remember the days when she use fi carry mi records on her shoulder, and her shoulder use fi cut from the box of records which she use fi walk wit' through the hot Kingston sun and dirt.' We continued to discuss it and I told him that it did not look good for him to be beating up Rita in front of everyone on the tour. This discussion seemed to have an effect on Bob, who made every effort to control his temper where Rita was concerned. I never heard of any future incidents.

I learnt a lesson from this experience and decided to make sure that in future Rita and the girls would occupy a different floor from Bob, and I also saw to it that they had their own cook or that they would cook for themselves. I made sure that the rooms were not only on a different floor but also located at the furthest ends of the halls, and took the additional precaution of making sure that only I had access to Bob's room.

After that night we came to the agreement that if Bob needed Rita he would call her up after everything had quietened down. Most of the time they would either eat together quietly or she would come up to keep him company and often she would wash his locks and grease them. It is not commonly understood how important this is to Rastafarians, and how patiently they spend hours upon hours maintaining the level of cleanliness required of those who keep their hair in this style and to this length. This combing of his locks would continue into the late hours of the night, in fact into the early hours of the next day. The quite beautiful sight of them carrying out these tasks while lighting up their spliffs was one I will never forget.

The conflicting signals between Bob and Rita sometimes made life difficult for me, as did the cheque-signing business by Rita. Bob and I had already had a few run-ins with Rita which began exposing her dubious behaviour. On one occasion a cheque that was sent to Bob by Cayman Music for US$6,000 was signed and cashed by somebody with a signature just like Bob Marley's. This cast suspicion on a lot of people, but it later turned out it was Rita Marley who had cashed the cheque after signing as Bob.

Bob again repeated to me that 'Yu have to watch Rita Marley, you know, because she can sign my name even better than I can.' In London on our first tour her dishonesty was once again displayed. Bob had made some money on a publishing deal and he decided to divide the money from the tour with everybody, as a token of his appreciation. It was the kind of gesture he would make from time to time.

After all of us had been paid, Bob and I got a call from Rita and Judy to tell us that their money had been stolen by the maid. They claimed they had put it under the mattress and gone out and when they returned it was missing.

Bob and I proceeded to question the maid, only to realize to our great embarrassment that it was another Rita Marley scam to get more money. That she would actually involve an innocent person was my first indication of the kind of person Rita Marley was and of the extremes she would go to for money. I did not sit in judgment on her because I recognized that she had suffered a lot of mistreatment from Bob. He abused her a lot, both verbally and physically; it was almost a regular thing.

During all this time, nine out of ten times, any money that was distributed that had to do with Bob Marley came through me. No matter where I was, it still had to come through me. I was totally in charge of all his money; my signature was the only one on his now over thirty million US dollars.

This thirty million dollars was in the name of the three companies, Media Aides, Tuff Gong Records and Bob Marley Music. Allan Cole's name had once been on the account, but it was taken off and the only person who could authorize the movement of money was me, not even Bob, because in nearly all the cases the banks did not even know him. When he died my name was still on the accounts because we had a mutual understanding.

I remember the day he asked me to go with Rita to look at a house she wanted to buy. I will never forget the house Rita took me to. It was located up in Jacks Hill in St Andrew, some two thousand feet above sea level, with an exciting view of the city of Kingston and the Caribbean Sea. Jacks Hill was one of the newly-developed areas where the new rich lived cheek-by-jowl with the older established rich. I found the trip quite revealing, as I had not known that Jamaicans really built houses like this, especially as my intermittent visits to Jamaica kept me confined mostly to the gambling clubs and the recording studios located in the plains.

The contrast between Trench Town and what I was seeing up in these hills was quite remarkable.

The house was located on two acres of land; it had five bedrooms, a swimming pool and all the space needed for R&R (rest and recreation), and to top it off, all the bathrooms were equipped with gold faucets. Rita said this was the house she wanted.

I told her I could not agree without consulting Bob, and that she should take him to look at it.

I remember Bob saying to us after his visit, 'Rita Marley, what's wrong with you, how you like those kind of big life so – you don't realize that the money I have is not my money – is God money! And if you take God money and spend it wrongly and abuse it, God will take it away from yu!' Bob went on to tell her that he did not see himself in that kind of house and he went ahead and chose a more moderate place, located on Washington Drive, on the plains of St Andrew. It was an understated community, but prestigious, as living up the street was the Prime Minister, Michael Manley. The house boasted three units: Rita occupied one and a Mr Tseyaye of the Ethiopian Orthodox Church another. Bob obviously felt that this was more up his street. The mere concept of a communal yard seems to have appealed to his natural instincts.

Though he liked having money, Bob was never one to crave earthly possessions, and this was made even clearer when he toured. It was always a topic of conversation that he went on tour with one duffel bag and returned the same way.

Not for Bob the shopping sprees of the other members of the band and the touring party.

On the other hand, I recall how in the early days at a particular hotel I had to query the bill, which listed a large sum under 'miniatures', only to find out that Rita and the I-Threes had made it their business to empty out the courtesy bars provided in all the suites, on the quite innocent assumption that they came with the suites and were already paid for.

Bob was always conscious of where he was coming from and his faith, and he and Rita were true believers in the Rasta religion and completely dedicated to it. But although the Rasta religion may have demanded that the children grow locks, neither Bob nor Rita ever insisted on this. Maybe this was because he believed so much in education and there was still the problem of Rasta children being accepted in Jamaican schools, certainly in the schools with the best records of education.

Bob's children always went to the best private schools (at the time it was Vaz Prep), and like all, if not most uptowners, Bob's kids were always driven to and from school, even before I met him and before he had made a lot of money.

Despite having other homes in Jamaica, Bob would always be at Hope Road. He very rarely went to his house in Bull Bay or subsequently to Rita's home on Washington Drive. He was always at Hope Road in the daytime and at night he would either be at Cindy's or with any of the other women he was seeing at the time.

As he said in an interview in 1975, 'Me never believe in marriage that much. Marriage is a trap to control me; woman is a coward. Man is strong.'

He never hid any of this from Rita, and very often made it clear to her that she could not walk in the shoes of Cindy. Yet when asked in 1977 if he would marry Cindy he simply answered, 'She's one of my girlfriends.'

But though he never did live with Rita as man and wife,

for some reason he always kept his clothes at her house. I discovered that when I once had to come to Jamaica and go to Rita's house to pick up his stuff.

It seems that the deep-seated relationship between them was based on Rita's acceptance of the Rastafarian woman's role and her role as the mother of Bob's children. He was devoted to his children and would always remind me that it was for them that he was really working.

9 Bob and Cindy

It was open knowledge that Bob was not a one-woman man. He had converted many a highly educated 'uptown' woman to the ghetto, and made them into his maids-in-waiting. The list included lawyers, actresses, oilfield heiresses and top female entertainers, many of whom put their careers on hold so as to be next to Bob each day. At the top of the list was the former Miss World, Cindy Breakspeare.

I had met Cindy years before, during the time when I managed Little Anthony and the Imperials and brought them to Jamaica. We were staying at the Sheraton Kingston Hotel, now the Wyndham, in New Kingston. Cindy was a clerk there, and I remember her relationship with Harold Jenkins, a member of the group Little Anthony and the Imperials. She had dated Harold in Jamaica, and visited him in Miami while she was staying at Lucien Chen's apartment with her mother. She was clearly disappointed that Harold was just an employee of the Blue Notes and unlikely to be a high flier, and the relationship died.

As life and its coincidences would have it, Bob's purchase of the property on Hope Road had now made Cindy his tenant. Before that Bob, like Cindy, had been a tenant of Chris Blackwell, and had occupied one side of the house, and Cindy the other. I knew that Bob had made many passes at Cindy, but as far as I knew, he never got anywhere until he became famous and was the owner of 56 Hope Road.

Since Bob was now the owner I collected the rent from Cindy for the first few months, which was a minuscule amount of some four hundred dollars. Then one day, when I went to collect the rent, I was told by Cindy that she had already given it to Bob. I guess this should have given me some warning signals, but I really did not put much of a hook on it at the time. I did not ask Bob, or pay much attention to it, perhaps because the amount of money was so small. But after that I did notice that the relationship between Bob and Cindy was starting to develop.

It was then that I remembered the stories Skill used to tell of how he and Bob would go to visit her at Dizzi Disco at Northside Plaza where she worked when Bob was still trying to send his signals to her. This in spite of the fact that she was sharing the Hope Road premises as Chris Blackwell's tenant. I found it quite significant that these advances had borne no fruit until after Bob had bought the place from Blackwell.

I realized, however, that a serious relationship was developing between them when I happened to call Bob one night as I was taking my second wife, Apryl, to the movies. He said I should come and pick him up, and in what was totally out of character (Bob did not take women to movies), he brought Cindy with him. Even then I was still taken aback when she entered the Miss World contest and he asked me to give her the money to go to England, and to lay out certain things to make it easier for her in London.

At that time in Jamaica controversy surrounded the matter of beauty contests. Among the things abhorred by the socialist Manley government were the once government-endorsed beauty contests. Black power consciousness was the order of the day. This was no time for the marketing of female flesh, and the Jamaican government had actually taken a stand against beauty contests. Bob's support of Cindy could easily have proven embarrassing to him, as he was expected by his fans to be in sympathy with the trends of the time.

The absence of government support and the private sector's fear of going against the government's wishes had reduced the level of funding for Jamaica's attendance at the Miss World finals and it was only the Governor General, Sir

Florizel Glasspole, who seemed enthusiastic about the beauties. What this meant was that Cindy, Miss Jamaica, was scheduled to attend as Jamaica's representative but was in need of support – both monetary and otherwise.

Acting on Bob's instructions I arranged for the transfer of thousands of pounds and arranged for it to be paid out through our public-relations agency. (This would eventually lead to rumours that the payment had bought Cindy the crown.)

Although none of this was usual for him, I still did not take the relationship too seriously, maybe because at the same time Bob was openly going out with two other friends of Cindy, namely Virginia Burke and her sister, Nancy. In fact, I was told Bob was sleeping with them at the same time he was sleeping with Cindy; that was Bob.

When it came to Bob's personal life I only did what he asked, so that I never discussed with him his feelings on Cindy's pregnancy or the birth of their son Damien. It was obvious from Bob's life how happy he was to have children.

In fact, one of Bob's common practices while touring was to make impromptu stops, when he would get out of the car and mix with the people, especially the children. As he once said, 'Children are wonderful. It don't take plenty y'know. Just a nice girl who don't take birth control. Sexual intercourse is a lovely thing.'

I remember when we were working on the *Kaya* album and staying at 1 Harrington Gardens in London. Cindy came up to stay with Bob. On one particular night while Cindy and Bob were cooling out in his room, some ladies came to see Bob and he called me and told me to have them come to my room. I was on the first floor. About fifteen minutes later Bob came down, leaving Cindy in his apartment. Not surprisingly he stayed in my room longer than he had anticipated, which caused Cindy to come down and knock and enter, looking for him. She saw him sitting close to one of the ladies and showed her irritation by saying to Bob that if that was how he was going to behave then she was leaving, as she was not into that any more. (This took place after Bob's alleged affairs with Nancy Burke and her sister.) Bob's immediate reaction, as she turned and walked out, was to shout at me to go and catch Cindy, but I was too slow to follow and Bob pursued her himself. This was the first time I had ever seen Bob actually pursue anyone, and I found it quite significant.

I watched as he persuaded her to go back upstairs to his apartment. A few hours later when he did not return, I went to his apartment to find out what he was doing and seeing Cindy, said to her, 'Boy, Bob must really love you to chase after you so,' which made her somewhat irritated. But it was the first time I fully realized just how much Bob loved Cindy.

The following day when I saw Bob I took a 'jive' and said, 'Bob, I didn't know yuh got it so bad that yuh told Cindy how much yuh love her and would do anything for her,' whereupon he said to me, 'Don Taylor, what would you do in an intimate situation if while you are on the upstroke a woman look you in the eye and ask if you love her?'

This mild banter never really fooled me and I feel sincerely that if Bob loved any woman it was Cindy.

During my time with Bob it was clear that Cindy was the only woman he loved, and the only woman who had any kind of leverage over him, but as Cindy's skill at this grew so too did Bob's withdrawal. As Bob said to me once, 'When you money done you ain't got no friends' (he loved to hear Billie Holiday sing 'God Bless the Child', which contains this sentiment). 'If the money done, you may not have a woman either.'

It is my guess when I reflect further on the association, that Cindy, sensing Bob's wide involvement with many women and the fact of his marriage to Rita, probably decided it was in their best interest to get pregnant. I had always thought that Cindy felt she needed some stability to flow from the situation, which would protect her in a crisis. Whether this crisis would come from financial or physical things I was never sure, but the feeling seemed always to be there.

For instance, I remember when Cindy came up with the idea for her company, Ital Craft. Bob called me to transfer $100,000 from our account at National Commercial Bank to another one which I later found out was Cindy's account for the company, thus supplying the capital for her start-up. In fact, Cindy was even able to get Bob to buy some of the beads she needed for her business, while he was on tour in Australia, and Rita herself had to bring back the beads for Cindy.

After Cindy became pregnant, I received a call from Bob while I was in Miami. He told me that some insurance guy named Chunky Lopez was migrating and selling a house in Cherry Gardens, one of the more exclusive residential areas in Kingston, and as Cindy wanted a place for herself and the baby, he wanted me to pay the guy US$49,000 for the house. I did as he instructed, and had the house transfer completed so that Cindy could move in. In fact she continued living there until she married Tom Tavares Finson.

All these events reaffirmed my earlier belief that Cindy's relationship, and specifically the timing of that relationship, with Bob Marley was a planned move to better herself. It was very simple: Bob had become big and he would do anything for her.

I remember how when she won the Miss World beauty contest she took the opportunity to say that Bob was her man and that she wanted to hurry home to her Rasta. I still feel this was a deliberate strategy to let the world know, as until then nobody knew about their relationship. In fact, it created quite a stir among Bob's crowd. I can only see this as another opportunistic move. Right after that, I believe she realized that Bob was only going to give her so much money and no more, and she became pregnant, knowing that this would ensure a steady supply of money.

Before Bob bought her the house, Cindy had never lived like that in her life. Her family had fallen on hard times when she was very young. Bob might well have told Cindy that he was going to marry her and that he had only married Rita as a convenience. But to my mind, the very way in which she allowed Bob's intimate associations with her friends to continue, was significant as regarded her real intentions.

Cindy kind of shocked me. Maybe it's because I always thought that upper-class Jamaican women grew up with some morals, but when I found out that Cindy's friends were sleeping with Bob and also with his friends, and that Cindy closed her eyes to it, I lost respect for her. Virginia Burke, for instance, started going with Allan Cole, and it did not matter to her that he was also going with Judy Mowatt. That was when I realized that women from the upper class really had no class and they were just like any prostitute in New Kingston, the only difference being how much they got paid.

But none of this in any way affected the closeness between Bob and Cindy and their relationship continued as intensely after she had Damien as it had before his arrival.

It was about this time that Bob, as a result of this relationship, was accused of moving into uptown society. This certainly panicked all of us business people, because it created rumblings and objections in the very quarters from which the music had come. The ghetto was strongly opposed to what they saw as a Bob sellout, if for no other reason than that he was a militant black man talking about the unity of black people and Rasta. It was an accepted fact that the downtown people interpreted his protest music as speaking for all people. So when it came out that he was dating Cindy and others and that he had made his move into uptown society, the Rastas and the militant brethren started to question him about his association with these white girls, especially in Jamaica. Bob's answer to the Rasta community one day was, 'Wha happen to my brothers and sisters, yu no see me a carry Rasta uptown,' and with that reply they were silenced and he was never questioned again.

What the ghetto people failed to appreciate was that Bob, like any other successful businessman, had groomed himself and moved into another social level where each person looked out for his own best interest. He was continually being entertained by kings and queens and was dating princesses and being entertained by their fathers. They had started to expose him to what he considered their corrupt way of life.

I remember his first exposure to cocaine in Jamaica, one night after someone had introduced Bob to it at a party at Cindy's. This was the kind of crowd he got involved with as he moved up. And it happened in America too. When we were in America a number of people tried to introduce cocaine to him. At the end of Bob's career, at the time of his death, there was a scandal that he had used cocaine, but I never saw him use it, as close as I was to him.

One day Rita and I were talking about cocaine, saying that we did not think Bob had ever used it, when Ziggy said that one day he had seen his dad with this white powder he was putting up his nose and when he asked Bob what it was he said it was crushed aspirin. But I, Don Taylor, never saw him use it and as close as I was to him, I would have a hard time believing it. And if he did use it he had to be influenced by someone.

What I did come to realize, as a result of his relationship with Cindy, was that Bob Marley was three distinct persons in one.

There was Bob Marley the revolutionary – 'Tuff Gong'.

Then there was Robert Nesta Marley, the understanding, meek and kind human being who was in love with Cindy, who loved children and who would understand and listen to any problem you had.

Finally, there was Bob Marley, superstar and musical genius *par excellence*.

This, then, was the confusing scenario, both public and private, that was developing around Bob and Rita Marley as we approached the closing days of 1976.

Politricks

10 The Free Concert and the Assassination Attempt

During all this time I was between Miami and Kingston. Some time in November of 1976 I came down to Jamaica to deal with some of my own personal business, as well as Bob's management portfolio. At the same time I planned to hang out at two main gambling clubs, both of which offered me the rest and relaxation I desired in Jamaica. The clubs, Norman's and House of Chen, were themselves offshoots of a club that had existed close to Dizzi, the disco that Bob used to frequent.

It was not uncommon for the games, whether poker, craps or Mah Jong (at all of which I was pretty adept), to continue for days and nights non-stop, and it was also not uncommon for the sums won and lost to exceed millions. This was where the real Jamaican gamblers hung out, while they were plied with all the whisky and food they could desire.

Christmas was approaching. In Jamaica this carried even more magic than in many of the developed countries of the world. Jamaica traditionally began celebrating Christmas from as early as October. Nature itself saw to this, as November and December were ushered in against the backdrop of a profusion of red, pink and white poinsettias. It was also the time when the round of office and private parties began. It was quite normal for one to attend six parties all in one evening, invariably stretching into the wee hours of the morning.

In between these happenings and my own personal business rounds I visited Bob at Hope Road, and in the course of the visit tried to find out what he had in mind for the upcoming

Christmas. I felt this to be important, as Michael Manley had imposed a State of Emergency on the country.

There had been several warning signals before the situation deteriorated into a time of unprecedented violence and mayhem even by Jamaican standards. The country had experienced the Green Bay Massacre, which saw ten youths being lured to their death by the army and massacred in cold blood on the Hellshire hills. What the country later learnt was that an entire cadre of PNP bad men had been given false leads as to where they could pick up guns for an anti-JLP raid, only to find the army awaiting them in ambush. It was the kind of incident no one would have credited to Jamaica. The events of the time almost bordered on civil war.

The economy was deteriorating rapidly and the treasury was broke. We had really come a long way since the arrogant days of Independence.

The country had also seen the Orange Street fire. The ghettoes had become 'hot'. As Bob said in June of 1976, 'We trying to make things easier but y'know, the politics keep its teeth. You have two parties fighting each other so we come like nutten because them guys always fighting and claiming to be the big guys. Plenty people fight for jobs, so the only way to get a job is to be on one side or the other, otherwise you suffer, you suffer and they hurt you bad. They burn houses with people in it, babies in it, in Jamaica, you know. I don't really understand it bwoy, really can't understand that. And I know it is politicians doing it. It's the youth that catches the place afire, but it is the politicians' influence. That really not look good. Politics, man.'

The problem had now escalated beyond imagination as larger and larger areas became politically tribalized and were ruled by the leading gangs of either party. The very graffiti on the wall referred to the matter: 'PNP enter at own risk'; 'JLP keep out – or death.'

The Cuban Ambassador, Ulysses Estrada, was heard to

threaten Jamaicans that if they interfered with the 'revolution', they would have to bear the consequences. One did not really know whether he was referring to the Cuban or the Jamaican revolution.

Prime Minister Manley urged Jamaicans who desired riches to take one of the 'five flights a day to Miami' as there would no longer be any room in Jamaica for millionaires. The newly-emerged middle class and the business-trained, both of whom were indispensable to the country, now began to look towards the USA and UK. Many looked specifically at Miami, and literally took his advice, and Jamaica thus lost some of its best and most valued entrepreneurs and skilled workmen to the USA. Indeed many of these entrepreneurs sold their houses for whatever price they could get, in US dollars, and where the houses were tied to financial institutions, they merely handed the keys to the banks and insurance companies, in some instances while on their way to their airports, with their foreign exchange having been transferred illegally to Miami.

To say that a revolution of some sort was taking place would not have been to overstate the case. The ideological conflicts were reaching unprecedented heights. The Manley/Seaga confrontation was once again unfolding.

With the heightened ideological and political confrontation between the JLP and PNP one could feel the tension rising and see that the ghettoes were at boiling point.

It was against this background that Bob felt he wanted to put on a show in Jamaica for Christmas, a Christmas morning show to be exact. I saw this as a good money-earning proposition and a way to lift the spirits of the people, a show we could all smile at and with.

I guess I was influenced by the Jamaican habit of trying to make Christmas enjoyable. I was also capitalizing on the Jamaican tradition of celebrating Christmas with any number of shows. I could remember, from my boyhood, the Jamaican tradition of a Christmas morning concert followed by a visit to downtown King Street to Christmas Market dressed up in new Christmas clothes, and joining in the fun and frolic of streetside vending along King Street. This was before the neglect of Kingston and the violence had taken their toll.

I had assumed it would be a paying concert, but when I suggested this to Bob, he said that to do that would be like putting all the guys out of business. In his own words he said, 'Yu blood claat mad, yu would a mash up everybody business, yu woudda tek weh the little man food. We nuh need nuh more money out of we Jamaican people.' Bob refused to make money out of poor Jamaicans by making them buy tickets to the concert. This contrasted with the new trend of Christmas stage shows which were proliferating almost in proportion to the increase in the consumption of alcohol, the ubiquitous Jamaican plum pudding and sorrel. The variety of shows, beginning with the Jamaican pantomime, ranged from amateur to the slickest of professional performances and were put on everywhere from Negril to Morant Point.

He told me that Jamaicans had been good to him and in this time of turmoil and division he felt he needed to do something to relieve the pressure on the people. I saw no reason to argue with this, because basically I felt the same way. And the more so because Bob was perhaps the only really good news coming out of Jamaica at the time and perhaps the only symbol of hope and escape for the downtrodden.

We sat on the verandah and continued to kick the matter around and develop it until Bob came up with the idea of calling it a 'Smile Jamaica' concert.

As he watched the tension grow in the next few days, he made up his mind and showed me the penned words of 'Smile Jamaica'.

Help my people help them right
O Lord help us tonight

Cast away the evil spell
Pour some water in the well

Bob wanted the venue to be a place where the rich, the poor and the middle class would be able to mingle and relieve their tensions. I came up with the idea of holding it on the Jamaica House grounds, site of the office of the Prime Minister and only a stone's throw from Hope Road. Jamaica House was originally designed to be the official residence of the Prime Minister of Jamaica. It was built in 1963 and was to be to the Jamaican people what the White House is to the Americans and what 10 Downing Street is to the British. But this was not to be, as it was occupied as a residence only briefly by Sir Alexander Bustamante just before he retired as the first Prime Minister of independent Jamaica. And when Hugh Shearer took over as Prime Minister from Sir Donald Sangster (who died only a few weeks after winning the general elections of 1967), being a bachelor he did not put the large residence to the use for which it was built. This led Michael Manley when he assumed office in 1972 to comment (some said rather unfairly) that dignity would be restored to Jamaica House. It was not long after this, however, that Michael himself failed to follow his own words and officially changed the status of the house when he turned it into the office of the Prime Minister. And so Jamaica House was never really used for the purpose for which it was originally intended.

It seemed to me that Jamaica House, with its vast grounds, would be the ideal place for the concert as it offered a common ground that would appeal to all the people that Bob wanted to attract. Among other things, it was located midway between the haves and the have-nots, and people would certainly feel safe and protected there. Bob liked the idea, so he picked up the phone and called the Prime Minister. He was put through immediately – an indication of the power and magic of Marley. In fact he had developed a close relationship with the Prime Minister, who never hid his admiration for Marley's music and his achievements. Manley himself had written many pieces on reggae music and its cultural impact on the world.

In fact, since 1972, Bob had maintained a close relationship with the political hierarchy generally, but in particular with Anthony Spaulding, now the Minister of Housing and Member of Parliament for the Trench Town constituency of Kingston. I myself had developed a closeness with P.J. Patterson, then Minister of Foreign Affairs.

After Bob hung up, we drove to Jamaica House because the Prime Minister had responded with great enthusiasm and asked Bob to come there immediately. The guard at the gate guided us in without any hesitation and we drove up the impressive driveway past the expanse of lawn to the alcove where we alighted. We climbed the semi-circular staircase to the Prime Minister's office, which was guarded by some very charming secretaries, the Prime Minister's personal assistant, as well as the regular security men discreetly watching from safe distances.

We were immediately ushered into the Prime Minister's office by his secretary and I could see that Manley had been anxiously awaiting our arrival as he virtually greeted us at the door. He was his usual impressive self, oozing the kind of charm usually reserved for the acting stage. Dressed in his hallmark Kareeba suit, with his six-foot stature and his hair greying at the temples, he was an imposing sight. Self-possessed and confident, at times one could almost detect a sense of mischief in him and I was the focus of his disarming charm as he was meeting me for the first time. This must be what they call charisma, I thought to myself as he proceeded to greet us like long-lost brothers.

He asked Bob how his career was going, and spoke briefly of the problems of the country and how he felt that this gesture by Bob was very important to the country at that time. Bob then proceeded to explain that he did not want the concert to be politicized in any way, and he emphasized this more than once, making sure that he was fully understood.

The Prime Minister then asked his secretary to call his Minister of State, Senator Arnold Bertram. I had only heard of this brother through the press but had some idea of his likes and dislikes. When he arrived and was introduced to us we laid out our proposal again, and were then invited by the Senator to his office, located across the lawn. In fact, his office was located in a trailer-like building, which had been hastily put together to facilitate the hasty decision that had changed Jamaica House into an office complex. Bertram's office was not very pretentious and as we sat down and began the discussion, Bob and I again emphasized the non-political intention of the concert and our wish that all of Jamaica should reverberate with enthusiasm for the show just as the office of the Prime Minister was doing.

When Bob and I left we decided then and there to call a press conference and announce the concert. We did this, holding the press conference at Hope Road and informing the public that it was a joint government and Bob Marley promotion.

I can still remember how I felt when, immediately after our press conference, the government announced the general election date. This aroused our suspicions to say the least, as the timing seemed hurried and contrived.

Once the elections were publicly announced the die was cast. One could almost see and feel the vibes take on sinister proportions. It was as if a cloud descended. The people around Bob became more and more concerned.

Little did we realize that the world's cold war had arrived in Jamaica, much less that our small island had become a focal point of this war, and the extent to which we were being exploited and manipulated to further the ends of opposing world powers.

In Jamaica, then, wider divisions began to emerge between the political sides. The political tribalization had gone far deeper than even Bob thought and the outside influences were increasing. It was no longer a game between JLP and PNP but equally between East and West (Russia, Cuba vs USA, as symbolized by East Kingston vs West Kingston).

Now that we have seen the Noriega scenario and the role Panama played in the region, it makes the whole issue take on the most sinister appearance. For who would have thought that the CIA could be used to traffic drugs in the cause of democracy and that they would actually aid their import into Jamaica?

Those around Bob who had JLP leanings and sympathies – I refer to such persons as Claudie Massop and Tommy Cowan, Harry J and Tek Life – all told Bob that the JLP did not want the concert to take place. In fact Claudie, who was in prison at the time, sent Bob a message clearly stating this.

As the JLP saw it, the concert was an endorsement of Michael Manley and his socialist policies. But more importantly, they saw it as a slap in the face for the JLP, especially because it was felt that the whole State of Emergency was a trumped-up affair. This view was later accepted when an independent inquiry exonerated all concerned and proved that the whole affair was a contrived plot to discredit the JLP.

Out of all of this came a compromise agreement to move the concert from Jamaica House to National Heroes Circle, as the holding of it at Jamaica House would in itself seem to imply support for the PNP, whose 'bad men', through Tony Welch, had already made their feelings in support of the concert known to Bob.

Interestingly enough, National Heroes Circle had been established by a previous JLP government as the burial place for the remains of the National Heroes. It was on this site that all the monuments to the National Heroes were erected, including that to Marcus Mosiah Garvey, and so it was felt that it represented neutral ground.

Originally the site had been known as Edelweiss Park. It had provided the setting for many of Marcus Garvey's historic speeches, as he espoused the struggle for black rights. This was a historical fact that would in itself appeal to Bob.

The cauldron, however, continued to boil, especially as the PNP guys thought the concert was a great gesture and strongly voiced this opinion. So the political pressure continued to increase.

Even among our immediate circle there was resentment. I clearly remember that Judy Mowatt did not want to do the concert because she did not want to be affiliated with any political group, even by implication.

All this time I was trying to keep the boat upright, while trying to steer us through the obvious difficulties ahead.

We had begun rehearsing for the concert with the sparks still flying in many quarters, and while the feverish tension mounted and the pressure was building up, we continued daily, if not hourly, to discover how deep these feelings went. I kept trying to convince Judy to participate, arranging meetings with her to discuss this, but always coming away convinced that I would not win her over.

We still were receiving feedback from both sides. The JLP kept sending us messages that 'Seaga say this' and 'Seaga say that'. But Bob didn't seem really to care, nor did he appear to take them as seriously as he should have. In most cases he treated them as mere hearsay. His usual answer was that he did not take messages from any messenger boy, so if Seaga had something to say, 'Him have to say it to me direct.'

Ignoring all this, I started to release the funds to meet the costs of the concert, as Bob was funding everything. It was becoming increasingly clear to me that Bob wanted this concert to be his thing and his thing only. It was about then that I went to the USA to hire a crew to film the concert, as we intended to do everything professionally. And as was customary with Bob, there would be no shortchanging the Jamaican people.

When I returned from New York, I went to see Bob, who described something important that had happened during my absence. He told me, 'Don Taylor, when you were not here, the other day a white boy came here and told me that if I do not tone down my blood claat lyrics and if me no stop tek weh the white people them from America them a go tek weh me visa and me can't go to America again.' I asked Bob what he had said to the man. He said, 'I told him tek yu blood claat out of my yard, before me lick yu up.' Bob had had his men around him with their guns. He said, 'You should see the white man run out of Hope Road like a madman into his car and speed away.' It seemed patently obvious to me that whoever it was had been given instructions from the US Embassy.

At the time the US Embassy was clearly backing Seaga and the JLP, and they clearly saw Bob Marley as being associated with Michael Manley (whose close friendship with Fidel Castro disturbed them). What was worse, at the same time, Bob was capturing the hearts of white youths in the US. All of this combined to cause them great concern.

During our discussions of the incident, I reminded Bob that I had been in the US Army during the 1965 to 1967 Vietnam crisis, and that I had experienced the workings of the US Army. So I knew that whenever they sent a military attaché to any little man it was CIA business.

All of this, however, still did not deter Bob and his resolve to hold the concert, so I wired my crew in America, confirming the arrangements we had discussed in New York.

On the other hand, outside of the tense inner circle of the Wailers some semblance of normal life continued, so I continued to pursue my personal relaxation and enjoyment in the gambling clubs. As I said earlier, it was not uncommon for these games to last for days on end, and so in between the arguments for or against the concert, I would steal away to the House of Chen and Norman's.

I was in the middle of a game when I had to leave to go to Miami to pick up a US$143,000 cheque for Bob which had just come in. I also had to meet with Chris Blackwell, who was in Jamaica at the Sheraton in New Kingston. In fact I had arranged to pick Chris up and take him to the concert rehearsals at Hope Road. So I relinquished my hand to a friend, Dynamite Lyn, who was to play for me while I flew off to Miami that morning to return the following day. Since it was a short trip I drove myself to the airport and parked the rental car at the terminal.

On my return the following day, I collected the car and headed out to Kingston. I went straight from the airport to the club to see how Dynamite was doing. He was in fact even, which was considerably better than the sixty thousand dollars I had been losing when I left. I then went over to the House of Chen on Knutsford Boulevard, a stone's throw from the Sheraton. While waiting I ate my fill of curry goat, and then I left the club and drove to the Sheraton Hotel where I was to pick up Chris. But Chris was not there.

I returned to the car and proceeded to 56 Hope Road. I still had in the car a couple of cases of whisky that I had bought earlier and a briefcase that I had brought back from Miami for a friend who worked at Lascelles. I also had in my possession the royalty cheque for US$143,000 that I had brought back for Bob.

I turned into 56 Hope Road and parked the car as usual under the driving alcove and entered the house from the front door which led from the verandah into the hall. As I entered I could hear the rehearsal going on, so I looked in the music room located downstairs next to the kitchen. The full band was at work, but I did not see Bob. So I proceeded to the kitchen and saw Bob standing in the corner cutting a grapefruit. I told him I wanted to speak with him, and that I would also eat a piece of the grapefruit. He beckoned me to come for it and as I reached out for the grapefruit I heard a sound like a firecracker. As it was Christmas I paid little attention and Bob himself asked me, 'Who the blood claat a bus fire-cracker in mi yard.' But before he could finish the sentence we both clearly heard a repetitious 'rat-ta-tat, rat-ta-tat' sound. I suddenly felt a burning sensation I had never felt before, but I didn't realize that I had been shot. What I did feel was my body going limp as I fell forward on to Bob, whose only exclamation was, 'Selassie I Jah Rastafari.'

I recall Bob holding me up in front of him while they kept shooting. As soon as the shooting stopped, Bob let go of me and I sank into unconsciousness. It all happened so fast it seemed unreal.

When I regained consciousness I was still lying in the kitchen. There was dead silence, then gradually I could hear voices and I heard Bob say, 'They shoot up Don Taylor, Don Taylor dead or something.' Amid the cross talk between them, I picked up the refusal of the Rastafarians to lift me up, as they objected to picking up 'deaders'. I tried to say some-thing but no words came, and although I could hear every-thing I was unable to speak. A great sense of shock, but also of amusing reality, hit me.

I did not know at the time that my main artery was broken and that I was losing a great deal of blood.

I was hearing everything clearly all the time; in fact it was almost as if I was two people, one outside my body hearing everything and detached from the pain and suffering of the body lying inert on the kitchen floor. Meanwhile the body lying on the kitchen floor was feeling a great weight of blood running down its thigh and was struggling through the mist of consciousness to find out how badly it was hurt – and the voice on the outside was actually telling it that maybe they had shot off my 'joint' (penis). So the body on the floor slowly pushed its hand into the waist of the pants and once the message was clear that my joint was still intact, the inert body relaxed again into unconsciousness.

The police and Bob lifted me up from the floor and placed me in a police car, and as they rested mc on the back seat I could hear the policemen say, 'Damn, you know mi siren don't work.' Somehow I found this quite amusing.

I also heard the policemen say that I had been shot in the abdomen and that we needed to move quickly, almost immediately. Then another police vehicle with a siren arrived and escorted us to the hospital.

I was taken to the University Hospital, which was not far from 56 Hope Road. I still wasn't able to see or speak but I could hear, and I heard the nurses asking for two stretchers as there was one dead person. I did not relate this in any way to myself as my mind was functioning quite clearly.

When the stretchers arrived, however, I remember the nurse checking me and saying, 'This one is dead, put him in the metal stretcher, and take that one over there' – she was referring to Bob. I was still hearing all of this, and my outside body and the inert one both wanted to scream: 'No, I am alive!' But try as I might the body lying on the stretcher could not respond.

The body on the inside was talking to the one on the outside, recounting how he had heard of people being buried alive and how real it was going to be for me.

I heard the nurse tell the orderly to take me to the morgue and leave me by the door, maybe so that the doctor could pronounce me dead before they tagged me. They began to push me down the corridor to the morgue, when I heard a voice in the distance asking who or what this was. It turned out to be a doctor and the voice outside of me pleaded for him to take a look, and wished to cry out but couldn't. The orderly told him he would leave me by the door for him to check. To my relief the doctor said, 'Let me check him first before you take him to the morgue.' I recognized the

Bahamian lilt in the voice, which I later learnt belonged to an intern, Dr Phillip Thompson. My outside voice reacted with urgent anticipation while the inside voice urged the doctor on. I heard the doctor approach the stretcher and begin to check me, and to my relief I suddenly heard him say, 'This man is not dead, he is alive.'

The excitement was like an electric charge to the air. He sent me back to the emergency room immediately and ordered blood to stabilize me, as I had lost so much. As was becoming typical of Jamaica in the seventies, however, and also because it was Christmas, the lady with the key to the blood bank was at a party. She turned out to be a Mrs Trought, wife of the Deputy Commissioner of Police, Larry Trought, who had himself played an important part in the State of Emergency and was the Prime Minister's chief man. He was also someone I had known from my youth and whom I called 'godfather', a name used in Jamaica to refer to an older person you respected, who may have assisted you in your youth.

The mind of the body in the stretcher smiled at the unfolding scenario, for I had heard tales of this kind about the University Hospital and indeed all Jamaican hospitals. This was the result of the Manley experimental years and the economy was in serious decline. Hospital supplies and services had reached rock bottom, and patients had to provide their own blankets and food. And here was I experiencing some of it first-hand.

Finally the doctor was able to get me stabilized and I regained consciousness, to the point where I could open my eyes. As soon as I opened them both body and mind connected, and I could feel the constant burning almost as if someone had opened me up and placed pepper in my wounds. I looked up and saw standing over me Prime Minister Michael Manley and his wife Beverly, who I could see was crying. I do not recall what they might have said, but I could see the concern on their faces.

It was only then that I was able to inquire after Bob. I was told that he had been shot through his arm and that a bullet had grazed his chest. I then discovered that Rita had been shot in the front yard, in her head, between scalp and skull.

Rita underwent surgery for the removal of the bullet and was treated and released. I was actually the most seriously hurt and needed an immediate operation, so as to assess the extent of the damage and determine what needed to be done internally.

When it was time to operate on me, I was still so excited at being pronounced alive that I forgot to tell the doctor or the nurses (nor did they remember to ask) that I had eaten earlier at the House of Chen before I had been shot.

Blissfully unaware, the doctor opened me up and proceeded to operate. The operation was as successful as it could have been and I was left on the recovery table. But then I started to suffocate from all the food I had eaten, which was now coming up, as a result of the anaesthesia and the fact that my stomach had not been pumped. But once again fate played its hand, as the doctor had forgotten his bag in the recovery room and on his return to the room discovered my state and took the proper corrective action.

The next morning I woke to find myself in the recovery room of the University Hospital. I had had an emergency operation on my leg but a bullet was still lodged in my spine, and my left and right sides were both paralysed. I could not move. I asked Doctor Thompson why they did not operate, and he said that it was a miracle that I was still alive and if my only immediate problem was the loss of feeling in my sides, then I should consider myself lucky and not be impatient. To me it sounded more like an excuse for a hospital which apparently was not equipped to treat my type of gunshot wound.

I pumped him for information, and was finally told what I could do, but I got the distinct feeling that the doctor seemed to feel that I should be grateful they had saved my life and that I should expect nothing more.

By this time my friends had got in touch with my second wife. I was then married to Apryl Beckford-Taylor, who was nine months pregnant with my son Christopher. She flew down from Miami as soon as she was told of the incident.

I asked her to get in touch with the US Veterans' Administration and inform them of my service in the military, and to get from them the names of doctors who were accustomed to working with bullets and bullet wounds; and so it was that we got in touch with Dr William Bacon through the Veterans' Administration in Miami.

Arrangements were then made for me to be transferred to Miami by private chartered medical plane; Chris Blackwell arranged and paid for it. And so I went to Miami, where they performed a two-hour operation on my spine at the Cedars of Lebanon Hospital; by the next morning I was able to walk around.

I then remained in Miami at my house, located in the southwest area, a far cry from overtown where I had lived when I first arrived from Jamaica.

But the show had to go on, and many persons, including the Prime Minister, urged Bob to perform. The concert would now feature Third World, and I later learned that a constant report by two-way radio was relayed to Bob, who listened to the tributes while he still wavered about whether or not to attend. It was at this time that Tony Spaulding arrived and pep-talked Bob into performing.

The word that Bob was going to perform spread like wildfire – the band members Kinsey, Downie and Carly were located, and Cat Coore filled in for Family Man, who could not be found.

Bob bounced on to the stage and by all reports gave a performance of unequalled excellence. He spoke to the crowd in his usual way, saying, 'When mi decide to do dis ya concert two an a half months ago, me was told dere was no politics, I just wanted to play fe de love of the people,' and then broke into 'War':

> *That until the basic human rights*
> *are equally guaranteed to all*
> *Everywhere is war.*

After the concert Bob went to his house in Nassau to rest and took Rita and the kids, both his and hers. We constantly kept in touch by telephone, using this means to discuss business and inquire after each other's health.

One of the things we discussed was the invitation to go to Cuba to recuperate. This invitation had come to us, through Tony Spaulding, directly from Fidel Castro, who felt we would be safer there.

I would later find out that one of the crew members who came to Jamaica was the son of a prominent CIA official, but that he had been landed under a different name. When I learnt of this it left very little doubt in my mind that there had been a CIA plot and that its one intention was to kill Bob Marley. No doubt they wanted Bob dead because of his importance and his possible influence on the Jamaican political scene and perhaps on that of the wider world.

During these conversations with Bob I also learnt that about fifty-six bullets had been fired at Bob but, except for the crease, none had really hit him. I still vividly recall his only response as the bullets flew at and around us, 'Selassie I Jah Rastafari.'

I also learnt from him that he had told the police that he could prove who shot him. He also prophesied that this person would himself die from the same number of bullets that were fired at him.

Street fable has it that when Claudie Massop was shot and killed by the police, his body contained fifty-six bullets. Since some of the suspicion had fallen on the Massop camp, it gave rise to speculation as to the extent of his involvement. It was during such a conversation that I recalled how Stewbert, one of Tony Welch's accomplices, had in fact visited Hope Road a few days before the assassination attempt. He had come there hoping to speak to Bob, and had a serious look on his face when he tackled me on the verandah at Hope Road asking if I had a gun. I asked why I would need a gun when Bob and I had someone like him around. We would later learn that Stewbert had in fact recently come out of prison. Did he have any instructions to warn us?

I later heard that the gunmen thought they had killed Bob, and that it was probably my own body that saved Bob's life. I didn't see the gunmen. I had my back to the door. All my experience was of feeling and hearing. But, of course, I'll never forget it.

I still have a bullet lodged in my left thigh and when the weather is cold or I'm very tired, I limp from it.

11 The Aftermath

It was about two weeks after my Miami operation, while I was still walking with the assistance of a cane, that Bob asked me to come down to the Bahamas. We had to pick up his career and start planning our visit to London to complete some albums in keeping with our contract. I confirmed my Bahamas arrival with him, and asked him to pick me up at the airport, but when I arrived he wasn't there. The airline gave me a message from him that I should take a cab to the house. I knew that he was staying at a scheme of townhouses called West One, owned by Chris Blackwell and located on the western side of Nassau.

When I arrived Bob was not even at the house. In fact I had to wait for him to come back because he had gone to Joe Stebleski's hotel. When he came he explained to me that he had been unable to pick me up because he was upset over the loss of four thousand dollars which had been taken out of the bag he kept under his bed. As Joe Stebleski was still hanging around at the time, trying to ingratiate himself with Bob, it was on him that Bob's suspicion first fell.

Despite all that had happened, the scene had not changed.

Bob called in his daughter, Cedella, and questioned her. He felt somehow that Rita may have sent her to bring the bag to her, as only he and Rita knew where it was kept. We were never able to pin it down, however, and so we just let the matter drop.

Bob spent his days planning his future tours, records and concerts, breaking off occasionally to take Chris's boat out as far as he could go, and while his companions fished, he would enjoy his spliff, his meditation and the writing of the outlines of the songs he would use on his *Kaya* album.

Meanwhile I had actually managed Bob for some three years without anything but a gentlemen's agreement. In fact it was not until November 1976 that Bob confirmed my management position by writing a letter which was required in order for David Steinberg and myself to be accepted as Bob's authorized agents. This would become my 'letter of agreement'.

> 19 November 1976
>
> Mr Oscar Cohen
> Associated Booking Corporation
> 445 Park Avenue
> New York, NY 10022
>
> Dear Mr Cohen:
>
> Please be advised that Don Taylor and David J. Steinberg, Esq. still represent me in the capacity of Personal Manager and Attorney respectively.
>
> Therefore, any matters with regard to my interests may be handled by them along the lines of their employ.
>
> Yours very truly
>
> Robert Marley

Following our meetings in Nassau Bob and I agreed that we would leave for London in January 1977. So I put all the arrangements in place for the entire band to head to London. We had just released *Exodus*, which stayed on the British charts for fifty-six weeks, and the resultant success and hype had led Bob to begin the planning of *Kaya* and *Survival*.

The band this time consisted of Alvin 'Seco' Patterson, Carly and Aston 'Family Man' Barrett, and Tyrone 'Organ D' Downie. Donald Kinsey was still scared following the assassination and had decided not to accompany us, so we arrived in London in dire need of a guitarist. This was what led to the hiring of Junior Marvin as a session musician.

Bob had also decided that in the laying down of the tracks, he would fly in the personnel as he needed them, and this is what he did with the I-Threes, and any other personnel we needed.

From the time Bob arrived in London to take up residence at the Oakley Street apartment (he had asked for a place as close as possible to Battersea Park, so that he could indulge his other passion – soccer), he seemed to be in a calm and mellow mood. I myself had taken an apartment at No. 1 Harrington Gardens, as I felt that Bob wanted some privacy. His side of the Oakley Street apartment building had its own exclusive entry, which was separate and apart from that used by the rest of the band. Additionally, he had contracted Lucky Gordon (of Christine Keeler fame) to be his personal cook.

He seemed to settle almost immediately into a satisfying routine. He would be in the studio from the early afternoon, say 3.00 p.m. until the early morning, and play soccer from 10.00 a.m. to about 12.00 p.m. He might also socialize with other musicians on the London scene, such as the Clash, for the era of punk was developing.

It became increasingly clear that he had entered a calmer phase, and he seemed to be in love not just with life, but with all the special women in his life, both from the past and into the present.

On the one hand, there were Cindy, Virginia Burke and her sister Nancy, and entering the scene at the same time was Princess Yashi.

Yashi was an excitingly beautiful young woman of money and class. Her father was the Oil Minister of Libya. She was a tall, slim, striking Arab beauty standing some five feet seven inches in height, with a smooth olive complexion and the gait of a thoroughbred. She walked with assurance and purpose, and her smile lit up every corner of her face, while her dark eyes twinkled with the laughter of a bygone era of conquest, reminiscent of a Delilah looking for her Samson.

She had just started boarding school in London, and was enjoying her freedom, although somewhat restricted by the security permanently assigned to her as the daughter of the Libyan Oil Minister. I remember it was Yashi who made Bob buy the one and only suit that I ever knew him to own. It happened when he decided to take Yashi to Tramps, then the most fashionable nightclub in London. He felt that he was required to wear a suit and tie. When I saw him the following day, he was on an unusual high, having consumed about four bottles of Dom Perignon champagne, two of which were a gift from the club. He recounted all this to me the following morning, while still in the suit. He had actually slept in it all night. I never saw him in a suit again.

Bob went on to become Yashi's constant escort, and together they often made the London scene, and became a hot item.

The last time we met was in Miami when she came to visit Bob and we went to dinner at the Forge on 79th Street, and Yashi, who drank only the best of wines, ordered her favourite, a 1953 Chateau Lafite Rothschild. When the bill came it was for thirty-five thousand dollars. Bob glanced at it and handed it to me and asked me to put it on my American Express card. I looked at the bill and asked Bob, 'Do you know how much this is?' Bob said, 'Nuh, three thousand five hundred dollars.' I said, 'No, Bob, is thirty-five *thousand* dollars.' He said, 'What!' and, not wanting Yashi to see this side of him, he got up and called me and the waiter outside, and said to the waiter, 'Nuh, mistake you mek,' whereupon the waiter said, 'No, Mr Marley, that's the price,' and Bob replied, 'Then 'ow yu know mi could a pay the bill?' The maître d' replied, in the usual pompous kind of voice, 'Mr Marley, we know who you are, and your credit is always good.' It was a good ending to an enjoyable evening.

As was usual with Bob, however, he had to have as many women as he could get, so despite the presence of Yashi he still sent for Cindy to come and visit him in London. He had by now become so absorbed in the London life that he became even more mellow.

To my eyes he seemed to have put the trauma of the shooting incident behind him, and had moved into a whole new arena of creativity.

And so, with his thoughts now turned to love, he was inspired to write such songs as 'Is This Love', and most of the other love songs that were on the *Kaya* album. It was during this period that the memorable way in which Bob always wrote his songs was demonstrated.

It would start with Bob going into the studio and beginning to pick out a rhythm on his guitar. Then Carly and Family Man would come in on the rhythm, and once the rhythm was established Bob would lay down the lyrics, which would all come from his head. Bob never put his lyrics on tape during my time and I have often wondered how he did it. I felt it must have been a result of the bitter lessons he had learnt from the likes of Sims and Nash and Chris Blackwell, who was never able to find out from Bob how his lyrics were created.

So perhaps the fact that he never wrote down his lyrics was an extension of his inherent mistrust of the music scene, or it may have been the result of his uncanny insight. As things turned out, much more would have been exploited after his death had he operated any other way.

As Bob stated on different occasions and repeated in different interviews, 'If Jah hadn't given me a song to sing, I wouldn't have a song to sing. The song comes from Jah, all the time.'

At that stage, Bob was a happy man, he was really into life, and rid of the daily Hope Road pressure. Cindy was in London with him and he was making progress with his work. It was at this time that he offered Blackwell *Babylon by Bus* (which was a live two-album release) as part of our ten-record deal, hoping that because it was a double album which would be counted as a single record Chris would accept it, although as a live album it would not normally have been acceptable. Bob was anxious to be rid of Chris and the Island deal, so we made the offer and it was accepted.

One night while we were out, however, the police stopped us because some of the band members had ganja in the car. Bob claimed ownership as part of his Rasta religious rights and was fined fifty pounds. He felt that he stood a better chance in court than any of his colleagues, and it was a typical gesture for Bob. I can still remember the knowing smile that crept across the judge's face when Bob explained that he used ganja in the practice of his religion. The judge informed him that he would have to suspend his religious practices while in the UK.

It was also during this period that Bob met the Crown Prince of Ethiopia, Asfa Wossen, who approached him for assistance in bringing Haile Selassie's family out of Ethiopia, including Selassie's goddaughter.

Bob reacted without a minute's hesitation, giving him fifty thousand dollars to bring the family out. I realized that this was something he felt so strongly about that he would never refuse a request, no matter how large or small, to assist the Selassie family. There were several calls for such expenditure and Bob was quite sure that to acquiesce was his duty to Rastafarianism and his beliefs; indeed he even felt that perhaps this was his destiny, his reason for being, and he never wavered in his faith and only seemed to grow in his religious beliefs.

As a token of his appreciation, the Prince gave Bob a ring

(the same one Bob was buried with), saying that it had been passed down to him through the family. Needless to say, Bob saw this as a sign and a crowning affirmation of his faith, and from that day on the ring never left his finger. Indeed Bob saw it as a manifestation of his youthful promise, as did those close to him with whom he had a common religious bond and who knew of his dreams and visions. Much has been said about these visions, but very little by Bob. He never spoke much about them to me, but I do know that on his death the ring created a controversy, as many of his family and friends seemed to feel that he should not have been buried with it.

This whole London period had begun to worry his traditional admirers and some of his close advisers, who began to feel that he was losing his edge. The feeling was becoming quite widespread, and many felt that Bob needed to return to Jamaica as soon as possible, so that he could get back the special edge to his music.

By then we were almost finished with the album, so we stayed in England for only another month or so, completing the album and putting in place plans for another European tour, at the end of which, we decided, we would return home immediately.

By the end of this month Bob seemed to be moving back into his revolutionary mode, perhaps because Prime Minister Michael Manley had come to England after having won the 1976 elections which followed the State of Emergency, the shooting and the concert.

A few days before our departure from London I was advised by the Jamaican Embassy that Manley wanted to see us. It was a Saturday in the summer of 1977 when Bob and I met with Michael, who told us that we had to come back to Jamaica. He tried to justify this by saying that it was important for Bob.

He also told us that the shooting had had definite US/CIA connections, and that the CIA had become involved in the shooting because they did not want Michael to retain power. He said that he felt sure that we would want to know who was responsible for the shooting and its true cause.

This was a confirmation of the story going the rounds that Manley and his colleagues saw the shooting as a plot, by the CIA and supporters of the JLP, to kill both Michael and Bob. This was also the line carried by an article in *Penthouse* magazine, which said that the CIA wanted Manley out because of his socialist plans and his affinity with Fidel Castro.

He did not tell us that the shooting had not been solved by the Jamaican police, or by the government of Jamaica, which is still the case today. It was our friends in the ghetto who were able to crack it for us, much later, bringing the culprits to ghetto justice.

In any case, we had the second European tour before us, and I had by now assembled the full tour group in London, ready to start.

This was our follow-up tour, and this time around, we would be touring from July to August, visiting Paris, Stockholm, Belgium, Holland, Munich, Hamburg, Berlin, Copenhagen and Gothenburg, after which we would return to London, where we would break up, to reassemble after a month for the USA leg.

Accompanying us on the road was the group called Steel Pulse. This was their first major tour.

This time around the whole tour had been booked into larger venues, in keeping with the growing demand for Bob and reggae music; in fact when we got to Holland, the demand for tickets was so overwhelming that the show had to be moved to a warehouse in The Hague, about one hour's drive out of Amsterdam. The warehouse was packed with twelve thousand fans, who created the kind of vibe and reception which had to be experienced to be believed.

But it was almost as if the rainclouds were forming from

the moment we arrived in Paris, which was the first stop on the tour.

As was our custom, we had taken the Presidential Suite at the Hilton Hotel, near to the Eiffel Tower, and not far from the park where, just as in London, Bob could play soccer. The three bedrooms in the suite were shared by Bob, myself and the usual political friend that we took on tour, this time a little youth from Trench Town called Lip. Rita as usual was downstairs – two floors down.

Any indications of a return of Bob's revolutionary mode notwithstanding, he was still occasionally manifesting his calm *Kaya* spirit. Whenever Bob and I went to Paris we would meet Mrs Carmen Parris, Jamaica's ambassador to that country, who had become a close friend of Bob's. This time during our visit to her I invited her to the Island party, which was being held that night. When we arrived at the party, Bob and I were welcomed by Chris Blackwell and Bianca Jagger, who had flown in from Brazil. Princess Caroline had also flown in from Monaco. It was a real jet-set party. Shortly after our arrival Mrs Parris arrived with Laurel Williams, a former Miss Jamaica, and a young Jamaican Chinese girl named Sandra Kong, who was a Miss Jamaica Body Beautiful. It was an open secret that Bianca Jagger had come there with her eyes on Bob, as had Princess Caroline, but as it turned out, all Bob was interested in was Sandra Kong. Sandra was also a friend of Cindy's and, needless to say, a relationship ultimately developed between them. But that was Bob. Sandra certainly fitted in with his new mellow and loving mood.

The clouds, however, began to get darker and the hand of Rita Marley again entered the game.

I remember sleeping well into the afternoon the day after the party. Bob had woken up early as usual and gone across the street to get in a game of soccer.

I remember being woken up by a rather hysterical Rita

Marley, who summoned me to the living room where Bob was sitting with his foot up. I watched as Rita went over to Bob, who was lounging in the chair with his feet raised on the arm of the chair, and pointing to his toe, said, 'Look ya Don, look ya, look how Bob toe a rotten off.' I had a look at the toe, which was still sweaty from the soccer game. When I asked Bob what had happened he explained to me that the toe had been in this condition for many, many years, ever since he had kicked it one day in Jamaica while playing soccer. He explained that every now and then it would hurt and open up and then it would heal, and he kept insisting, 'Rita Marley, nothing don't wrong with me toe.'

But Rita insisted that it was more than that and that I should get a doctor.

Considering that we had just spent six months in London, where Bob had played soccer almost every day, I was more inclined to side with Bob, who said, 'Nothing don't wrong with mi toe Rita Marley, everytime I play soccer it sweat.' I guess I should have heeded Bob, but instead, I went to see a doctor. It was about 6.00 p.m. I told the doctor what was wrong, and asked him to come up to the suite and look at Bob's toe. After looking at it he told Bob that he would be back the next day to take care of it. I thought very little more about it and went to sleep to get some rest, and to prepare for the concert which was going to be the following night.

When the doctor came back the next day he injected the toe with something that was supposed to numb the toe, so that he could take the nail out. After injecting the toe, he proceeded to take the nail out, after which he bandaged it.

I will always wonder about these events, as from the day this doctor put his hand on Bob it took exactly thirty days for Bob to be diagnosed with melanoma cancer in the same toe that this doctor had treated.

We went on to finish the tour with Bob's toe in bandages, and from that day, Bob was never completely healthy again.

The long tour was indeed taxing for Bob and when it ended he left for Delaware to stay with his mother, as we had a thirty-day break in between the European segment and the USA leg.

While in Delaware, he again indulged his passion and played soccer, which he had not done for about thirty days, both because he had been waiting for the toe to heal and because we were continuously on the road. After about a week in Delaware, the toe seemed to have healed, but in fact, it was only on the top of the toe that a scab had formed.

Predictably, he hurt the toe again, but this time it became of great concern to him as the pain increased and it now refused to heal. He told me this by telephone at the same time that he informed me that Claudie Massop, who was now out of jail, was supposed to be going to London. He told me that he had decided to meet Claudie and the other guys in London to discuss the possibility of bringing both political factions together and starting a peace process. So I got him his ticket and he went off to London. While he was in London dealing with Claudie Massop he called me again, but this time it was about transferring some money to him in London – a large sum of money.

At first I thought they had held him for ransom, but when I checked it was no such thing. It was the revolutionary spirit at work again. In fact, this was the beginning of the plan to hold a peace concert in Jamaica on his return. Apparently Bob had now decided that in order to defeat Babylon he would have the warring political parties come together directly.

It was then that I asked Chris's assistant Denise Mills to take him to a doctor in London to have both the toe and Bob examined. I was becoming quite concerned about the toe, and the Paris incident with the doctor still worried at the edges of my mind.

Denise took him to the doctor and Bob called me from the doctor's office in a panic, saying that after the doctor had examined his toe, he had taken Denise Mills into another room and told her that it was either the 'toe or the tour', as the X-rays had shown that he had melanoma cancer. Bob also told me that he had heard the doctor say he would have to amputate the toe to stop the cancer from spreading, but if he did, it might not heal in time for the tour. Bob told me he had overheard all of this when he went to listen at the door. He was clearly in a panic and I advised him to return to Miami immediately.

I then contacted Dr Bacon in Miami by telephone. Dr Bacon was the doctor who had operated on me for the gunshot wounds. I told him what had happened and he said that it did not sound right, because black people don't usually get melanoma cancer, which is strictly a white skin disease. (This theory has, however, been recently challenged as some North American and Australian studies have shown that in dark-skinned people the tumour is most frequently seen on the sole of the foot or the nail fold.)

I called Bob back and explained what Dr Bacon had told me. I told him to pack a shoulder bag, leave everything else and come to Miami to see me.

When he arrived I took him to Dr Bacon's office. I had asked Bob to bring back some slides from London, which Dr Bacon proceeded to check. To his surprise, the slides confirmed that it was melanoma cancer.

All this led to a great deal of speculation, with everyone trying to explain how Bob had contracted melanoma cancer and whether he actually had it. The main explanation was that, being 50 per cent white, it was possible that he *could* get it. I, however, have my own suspicions to this day, and cannot simply accept this or any other explanation that I heard.

What all this meant was that we had to cancel the tour while I took Bob to stay at my house and we also had to ensure that the matter was kept out of the press. So we agreed to keep the information a tight secret and limit the number of people who had to know about it.

The following day we went to the hospital, and Bob was admitted, so that Dr Bacon could conduct several medical tests, especially now that he was sure that Bob had cancer.

While all these tests were being carried out, there was continuous excitement. The first manifestation of this came from Gad Man, the leader of the Twelve Tribes of Israel, who on learning of the problem came up to Miami to tell Bob that a Rasta can't have cancer.

During that period, as I was the only person actually living in Miami, I had to handle everything along with my wife Apryl. Because Gad Man said a Rasta couldn't have cancer, he told Bob that the doctor did not know what he was talking about, and that it was nothing but 'buck toe'. He convinced Bob that he should send down to Jamaica for the Rastafarian doctor called Pee Wee, who was a friend of Bob's and also a member of the Twelve Tribes of Israel, before we allowed Dr Bacon to do anything.

Bob spoke to me about this and, based on his feelings and the urgency of the matter, I arranged for a chartered plane to go to Jamaica for Pee Wee. When he arrived I picked him up myself at the airport, got him settled and then took him to see Bob, and to meet with Dr Bacon. Dr Bacon, in agreement with the British diagnosis, also wanted to amputate Bob's toe once he had confirmed that it was melanoma cancer. He had gone even further and said that the possibility existed that he might have to amputate the whole foot, to make sure that the cancer did not spread.

Bob and those close to him made it clear that they did not want the toe to be amputated, much less the entire foot. So Dr Bacon decided, after several conversations, that he would pierce the toe instead and keep cutting until he got clean corners, which he would patch with some skin; in fact he would do a skin graft. He said, however, that if he did not get clean corners he would have no alternative but to cut off the toe. Bob accepted this plan of action.

The following day Pee Wee, whose real name is Dr Carl Fraser, again went to see Dr Bacon, who had arranged to take him to the Jackson Memorial Hospital so that he could see the slides for himself. Having seen the slides, instead of telling Bob straight when Bob asked him, 'What do you see Pee Wee?', he said to Bob, 'Well, boss, if those slides that they show me are yours, then you really have cancer!'

Pee Wee, perhaps because of his own Rastafarian beliefs, apparently had his doubts on the matter and seemed not to want to face the medical truth; and not knowing much about Dr Bacon, he seemed to wonder if Dr Bacon knew what he was doing. A graduate of Howard University, he called up his teacher there, a professor at the Howard medical school. As it turned out, the professor told Pee Wee of his great respect for Dr Bacon, and confirmed what I had told him: that Dr Bacon was in fact one of the top ten orthopaedic surgeons in the world. He had been in the military for some twenty years, during which time he had been the orthopaedic doctor for the US Army. He had then moved down to Miami to set up practice and his record was unimpeachable.

This at least put an end to the immediate arguments, and allowed us to proceed with the operation. As it turned out, the doctor was able to save some of the toe.

After Bob had the operation he stayed in the hospital for about a week, after which I took him to my house to recuperate. The recuperation took about three months. Rita came up to visit occasionally, as did Diane Jobson and the kids.

During those three months Bob spent most of his days in my garage reading his Bible and playing his guitar and many evenings he could be seen pushing a stroller around the neighbourhood in which would be comfortably ensconced my recently-arrived son Christopher. During this time he became very close to my wife Apryl, and due to my own long absence looking after his business, the rumour-mongers got to work, saying Christopher was Bob's child. But Apryl made sure that Bob stuck to his recommended diet of liver, as directed by Dr Bacon. It was also during this time that Bob asked me to find a house for his mother in Miami, so that she could move from Delaware, as the cold there was affecting her arthritis. When I asked him what kind of house he wanted for his mother, he said he wanted one as big as the ones she used to clean for white people.

While he recuperated, Bob continued to work on his albums and to finalize the plans for his return to Jamaica. By now he had completed his plans for the peace concert, which had taken on major proportions, as he moved totally from his mellow mood to his revolutionary role, that of the peacemaker for the oppressed, especially as Massop had fired him up with the ghetto's zeal for peace.

The concert was actually a continuation of the original peace movement, which had been developing spontaneously out of the Kingston ghettoes and which was led by Claudie Massop of the JLP and Bucky Marshall, now a leading don for the PNP. They had apparently heeded Bob's words that the way to defeat Babylon was to avoid 'politricks'.

However, Bob now became the major player in the peace movement, single-handedly backing it, both in capital (the concert would cost some US$50,000) and by his personal involvement, as he became the major link between government, opposition, and the ghetto. In fact the unity he had been hoping for in the fight against Babylon now seemed to be manifesting itself. The ghetto's energies would now be turned on the true enemy.

> 'Well I would not support anyone. I'll support
> myself, a Rasta, you know what I mean? Only
> Rasta, no one else is what the people want.
> Everything's our territory.'

It was clear that Bob wanted a revolution which would stop the exploitation of the oppressed and the neglected from the ghettoes of Kingston and indeed the world; and the gang leaders who hung around Bob represented not only the living product of the ghetto, but also provided the constant link to the resources necessary to fight such a revolution, whether it was a revolution of the mind or, if necessary, a physical confrontation.

Bob had analysed all the stories that followed his assassination attempt, and had begun to realize his power. After all, prime ministers had catered to him and pleaded with him and indeed the whole world was responding to his lyrics and his philosophy. I began to see the same Bob Marley who, all his life, had preached of the evil of politicians, become a better politician than Manley or Seaga, I saw him elated and inflated with power as he virtually became judge, jury and executioner, and I saw him getting close to achieving what he wanted: the reversal and overthrow of Babylon.

I remember Customs Officer Laurie Foster starting to go through Bob's baggage on our return to Jamaica; Bob turned to him and said, 'Bwoy, give me this blood claat,' and picked up his things and walked out of the Customs hall, without anyone saying a word to him or trying to stop him.

The implication of this was underlined the next day when I received a call from the Collector of Customs, who said, 'Don, we know Bob can do anything and nobody will challenge it but ask him not to embarrass my officers that way.'

Obviously Bob's connections with the political hierarchy and his control of the toughest of the tough from both the JLP and the PNP, people like Claudie Massop and Tony Welch, meant that you did not take too many chances with Bob.

Many of these dangerous hangers-on themselves feared Bob, and as that fear grew so did the manipulative nature of

Bob, who found that he could get them to react to all his whims. And it was not clear how they themselves would react to what they considered as disrespect shown to Bob, so most people started handling him with kid gloves.

Besides the ghetto toughs, Bob also had policemen and other loyal fans of his music in his following, and he obviously felt he could overthrow both Jamaican leaders and lead a religious revolution of the Rastafarian faith. And although he would always say, 'I don't want to be nuh leader,' I personally wasn't fooled because he never failed to use his economic power to retain control.

Some people were still reluctant to participate in the concert; one such person was Peter Tosh, who kept saying that he felt very strongly that anyone who took part in the concert would die. How true that statement turned out to be: both Bob and Tosh are now dead, as are Massop and Marshall. Some even say that Mick Jagger came close to death.

At the time Peter had signed with Rolling Stone Records, and was playing host to Mick Jagger in Kingston. Jagger had come to Jamaica to catch up on reggae vibes, and in an interview with the *Jamaica Daily News*, had referred to Bob as his friend. This prompted Bob to call me and berate me for this statement, although I had had nothing to do with it; he demanded that I follow him to the *Daily News* so that he could tell them that Bob and no man who dressed like a bisexual on stage – as he saw Jagger – were friends, and he wanted it made clear that Mick Jagger was Peter Tosh's friend.

Bob and Jagger had met, but they weren't friends. I think Bob felt more empathy with the guitarist Keith Richard than he did with Jagger – Richard had jammed with Bob at a concert. But Jagger always seems to reach out and go along with what was popular at the time, and he was reaching out to Bob. Bob wasn't interested.

At the concert Jagger was running all over the place,

backwards and forwards. And he had no bodyguards with him. Marshall was standing there watching him. Jagger was like money on legs.

'Perhaps we should get him kidnapped and ask for a few million ransom,' said Marshall.

I got word of what he'd said and passed it on to Bob because although they might have said it jokingly we had to take that kind of thing seriously. Especially as the 1976 election cauldron had boiled over but the fire was still not extinguished. Bob immediately sent word to Claudie Massop and Buckie Marshall telling them 'not to make any bloody claat wrong move', and to see to it that Jagger was left alone.

Bob said: 'Hold up, guys. Hey man, don't even think it.' Bob wanted to work in the UK, so he told them to leave Jagger alone. The guys listened to Bob. He was the boss.

For Bob this was further confirmation of the power he seemed to be able to wield with everyone.

The concert itself, held in April 1978, was a musical feast of the best that reggae had to offer, and featured, among others, Dennis Brown, Big Youth, Ras Michael and the Sons of Negus, Leroy Smart and of course, Peter Tosh and Bob Marley himself. Not only was it a homecoming for Bob but the high point was when towards the end of the concert he brought to centre stage both Manley and Seaga, PNP and JLP, and made them shake hands. And finally, at his insistence, he made them raise both their hands in a sign of peace, a most extraordinary and moving moment. Was Babylon ready to co-operate?

Following the concert we put the finishing touches to the *Kaya* album and decided to stay on in Jamaica after it was released. *Kaya*'s release was very much against Chris Blackwell's wishes, as he felt the album was too 'soft', a view which conflicted with Bob's own feelings, that the album would open up new ground for him. And this was, in fact, what happened. We began to get strong feedback from the

aximum dread – Bob in terrifying mood. (© Retna Pictures).

Above: Bob's wife, Rita Marley.
Opposite: Ethnic peoples everywhere hailed Bob as a saviour.

A heartbreaking shot taken of Bob in Paris shortly before his death. (© Rex Features).

:land Records boss, Chris Blackwell. (© Camera Press).

Father and son. Ziggy Marley *(insert)* is carrying on his father's glorious tradition.

Happy days – as we all love to remember him.

Far East, Japan, Australia and New Zealand after its release. 'Maybe if I'd tried to make a heavier tune than *Kaya* they would have tried to assassinate me [again]. I would have come too hard. I have to know how to run my life, because that's what I have and nobody can tell me to put it on the line, you dig? People that aren't involved don't know it, it's my work and I know it outside in. I know when everything is cool, and I know when I trouble, you understand.'

It was around this time, too, that Bob turned back to his African roots, perhaps realizing that since he had achieved some success with the political directorate, he could now return to his Rasta roots. Skill Cole had been in Ethiopia since the Caymanas scam and Bob wanted to see him again, so he broached the idea that he wanted to visit Africa. In any case this was the one continent he had not yet conquered.

In the meantime the ghetto had apparently cracked the mystery of the assassination attempt, and so, one Wednesday afternoon in June 1978, we were called to be witnesses for the prosecution. We were collected by Tek Life, one of Claudie's right-hand men, and taken to a lonely spot near the MacGregor Gully. I should have recalled that Bob, when asked in May 1977, 'Do yu know who shot you?' had replied, 'Yeah, but dat top secret. Really top secret.' So he probably knew or suspected more than I myself knew, for after all he had faced the gunmen. Perhaps he was referring to the secret message sent to him from prison by Claudie.

I did not realize till then that the Jamaican underworld was so organized. For here it was: they had cracked the case which the police claimed they were not able to solve, though to give them the benefit of the doubt the police may very well have been hampered in their investigations by the alleged CIA involvement, and their fear of the US government.

As it was, when we arrived at the gully, they already had three men tied and bound there. One of the young men, whom I knew only as Leggo Beast, told the ghetto court that four of them had been trained as agents by the CIA, who had issued them with guns and unlimited supplies of cocaine to carry out the deed. The accused all tried to plead and explain away their involvement as a situation over which they had no control, while all the time looking at Bob and myself for a sign of help. But ghetto justice was to be carried out.

The court, as constituted, listened to every plea and then passed sentence on the three accused, who confirmed to us that four people were involved in the shooting and that they also knew who the fourth person was.

And so on that Wednesday afternoon between 5.00 and 6.00 p.m., two of the accused were hanged and one shot in the head. I later learnt that the fourth person died of a cocaine overdose. Apparently he was never himself after the shooting and had become quite insane.

I still recall how the ghetto generals offered the gun to Bob before shooting the last victim. They turned to him and said, 'Skip, yuh waan shoot the blood claat here?' I sat and watched as Bob refused, showing no emotion whatsoever, and I realized that he was entering a different phase.

I still vividly recall the rope being placed around the neck of one of the accused, which they used to drag him away out of our eyesight to be hanged. The men were all screaming and begging for clemency. The ghetto court was unmoved. They had wanted Bob to be there to prove that they had had nothing to do with the shooting. I was there not just as an observer – but because I was Bob's right-hand man and had myself been shot.

The men carried on screaming as they were led away. Afterwards we got in the car and drove back to Hope Road. We didn't talk about it; it was never mentioned again. It was as if it had never happened.

The World

12 The First Far East Tour

In 1978 we undertook a somewhat disastrous tour of Trinidad which originated out of an approach made to Bob by Ronnie Burke of Synergy and Reggae Sunsplash fame. Ronnie had come to me to request that Bob perform at that year's Reggae Sunsplash and I had agreed, booking the date for a fee of thirty thousand dollars. Ronnie reluctantly agreed to the fee but, as usual, seemed to find it high. Synergy was always trying to obtain acts at a lower fee by using the argument that we were all brothers together.

In this case, they also went to Cindy and asked her to intervene on their behalf. When Cindy raised this with Bob, he was not happy about the approach and advised her that I was the one dealing with his business, and that was that.

Synergy, having obviously had second thoughts, had a Trinidadian promoter contact me to take over the booking. And the rest was a disaster – lacking both proper promotion and advertisement. We drew about six thousand people, and I had to spend the entire time at the gate ensuring that we were paid. The upshot was that I collected all the cash at the concert, and left the show vowing never to be caught in this way again. This, however, was not the end of it, as when I tried to leave the next day we were taken off the plane because unknowingly we were leaving the country without a tax clearance. We had to remain in the country for some two days until this clearance was obtained.

I vowed never again to be put in this position, nor indeed to allow this to happen to Bob. Until then, I had always been able to avoid, as a matter of principle, this kind of amateur promotion. We returned to Jamaica and almost immediately finalized our plans to leave for Europe and the Far East.

It was in the pre-tour planning for this trip in London that we discovered that Junior Marvin had been convicted for transporting cocaine and had been deported from the USA, which meant we had to go to Washington to get a cultural waiver for him to travel.

The tour to the Far East was, as I had expected, a resounding success. We were doing Auckland in New Zealand, Sydney, Melbourne, Perth, Adelaide, and Brisbane in Australia, and then going on to Honolulu, Osaka and Tokyo, following which we would break before taking on the USA.

All our successes began in New Zealand, where our arrival itself was marked by one of the most unusual welcomes we had ever received. I vividly recall now how overwhelmed we all were when we were met by a large contingent of Maoris at the airport and how they proceeded to crown Bob at a special traditional Maori ceremony outside the hotel, having escorted us there from the airport. In fact they would not allow us to register or enter the hotel until they had carried out this ceremony. It has become one of my most treasured memories, a symbol of how Bob and reggae music impacted on the world.

With respect to the Australian leg of the tour, I will let the following article speak for itself.

The Rastaman in Babylon, Queensland
By Bill Holdsworth of the *Canberra Times*
Bob Marley Concert

What do Bob Marley and the people of Queensland have in common? Simple – opposites attract.

Boring. That's the only way to describe waiting for superstars to arrive. Especially when you are at Brisbane Airport and the bar's just closed. Especially since it's dark and rainy and cold. Every time you look at the screen indicator, the plane has been delayed yet again until it's one and a half hours late.

You stand around trying to glean bits of information from the record company or the tour people. Or you wander over to the other journalists to see what they know. They're holding a contest for the stupidest question to put to our tardy visitor. My contribution is 'Bob Marley, what do you think of Australian beer?' Brisbane is the opener for the first reggae act to visit this country.

Then, just after 11 p.m., well past the stage when you wished you'd stayed home, the plane from Sydney drops through the murky drizzle and off-loads its human cargo. Marley strolls past almost before we realize it. The first reaction is near disappointment. The herbman is small and slight, looking gaunt and exhausted, his great ropes of hair hidden by a dull woollen tam. He has nervous faraway eyes, but where are those religious fires we'd been led to expect?

One reporter has already rushed up to him, grabbed his hand and hustled for an interview. Marley's eyes flick around as if to avoid contact but he says resignedly, 'Yes, on the bus,' then turns, steps into the parking lot and on to the coach. The reporter follows but meets the stiff hand of the tour manager – no interviews. Tagging behind him, we all bunch up around the doorway.

As the rest of the entourage approaches, we end up as some kind of honour guard. The women wear straw coolie hats, the men are in various military styles, faces drawn and tired, framed by hair in all conditions of wildness. They look like an advance group of the Rasta Liberation Army.

Another quiet twenty minutes assures us that

nothing is going to happen tonight so we drift away. My last sight of Marley is of him halfway down the coach, slumped in his seat, silent. I think, ordinary superstars have limousines, but for the Wailers, it's Brisbane by bus.

Next day, the band spends five hours in the Festival Hall rehearsing, indicating some trepidation about this first show. Marley even practises his dancing in front of a full-length mirror. Food is ferried in from a local vegetarian restaurant, Salad Days. They found they had to supply some odd things. The I-Threes, the women who do the backing vocals, refuse to drink tap water; they want spring water.

Showtime is now nine o'clock and there is an SRO crowd of 4,500. Doug Parkinson and his Southern Star Band provided a competent set of sophisticated but accessible jazz-funk but the excitement has been reserved for the Natty One. He arrives to uproar, his Medusa locks resplendently free and flying and a magical night starts appropriately with 'Positive Vibration'. The day's jitters now seem pointless.

Ethiopia is everywhere. That nation's green, gold and red was the background for the BMW tour badges, it was the wool in the headgear worn by the I-Threes, it was the mitten on the bassist Family Man Barrett's right hand. A huge Ethiopian flag hangs at the back surrounded by other drapes – one of Haile Selassie, another saying 'One Love' spanned by the tri-colour as a rainbow and a third showing the black Cross Brigade.

In 'Them Belly Full', Marley exhorts people to 'forget your troubles and dance'. With Tyrone Downie's keyboards adding to the giant rhythm machine of the Barrett brothers, it would have been easy, but for the heavy security. Still, the down-tempo songs are powerfully mesmeric, the rockier ones surge with force.

During 'Heathen', four songs into the set, Marley throws off his guitar, which he was only scratching anyway. Now he's free, and launches into a joyous dance, arms, legs and hair all seeking separate planes. Meanwhile, the second star, Junior Marvin, cranks up his guitar and releases a churning high-note tirade from the edge of the stage. As Marley returns to his mike, Marvin frolics behind him. All this time the pulse beat grows stronger.

Onward and upward, through 'I Shot the Sheriff', 'No Woman No Cry', 'War' and 'Come Lively Up Yourself', the crowd begins to overpower the strong-arm security and everybody gets into gymnastics. When the band departs after 'Jamming', the audience goes bananas.

The encore is even more amazing, hitting a peak on a rabble-rousing 'Get Up Stand Up'. We are doing just that, enthusiastically whooping and singing along, 4,500 people singing about a revolution eons from their lives. All this time, the backdrop of Selassie is spotlighted and the I-Threes point towards it.

The band has gone again and the houselights are up, but the noise barrage indicates that no one is going home. Backstage, they're speechless, ecstatic, slapping each other. The last encore lasts half an hour and they take to the stage for yet another twenty minutes. Island Records rep Phil Cooper says Bob's never done two encores before.

After the concert, hundreds of fans wait at the stage door to cheer. Junior Marvin's showmanship won a lot of attention and he's busy shaking upthrust hands from the bus window. Up front, others are passing around a joint offered up by an appreciative fan and drinking cans of XXXX. ('What do you think of Australian beer?') Later, when two of the band taxi back to the hall, someone else gives them a cigarette and apologizes, 'Sorry, it's only the mild Queensland stuff.'

The morning after, I'm standing in the same airport lounge to see Marley leave. Still tired, by now with flashing eyes, he roams around chatting, laughing, playing with a short ivory-tipped cane. He picks up a paper, reads about the Zimbabwe elections, then crosses to the book stand, where he finds a copy of Lobsang Rampa.

Like all the reporters who have spoken to him, I have trouble with his rastaspeak. He is friendly, sincere and patient but he easily negotiates his way through questions he feels do not require answers.

Your religion is obviously an inseparable part of your music. How do you feel about white audiences here getting off on your music but ignoring the message?

Marley: How do you know they're not getting the message?

Well at the concert last night, I asked several people who Selassie was, and they didn't know.

Marley: Do you know who he is?

Until his death, he was the emperor of Ethiopia.

Marley: To you. It is better that some people do not know who he is than for some to know him in the wrong way. If a guy knows him as he used to be, he will never really know him. He is God Almighty.

Phyllis Diller has just arrived and is climbing into a Rolls-Royce. I'm on my way to the bus stop after

> waving the Wailers goodbye, carrying my very own memento of the Rastaman. It is a fragment of paper on which he's written 'Rastafari is God. Love, Bob Marley.'

But as if the successes of Australia and New Zealand were not enough, we were equally overwhelmed by the Japanese reception where, despite the language barrier, the tour broke all records and left Marley and reggae music as an indelible impression on the Japanese music world – an impression which has continued to grow and which gives credence to Bob's own words, 'Unity is the world's key, and racial harmony. Until the white man stop calling himself white and the black man stop calling himself black, we will not see it. All the people on earth are just one family, and so my music defends righteousness. If you're black and you're wrong, you're wrong; if you're white and you're wrong, you're wrong; if you're Indian and you're wrong, you're wrong. It's universal.'

The final stop before breaking up in Miami was Nassau, Bahamas. I had arranged this as a concert in aid of the children of the Bahamas and in honour of my longtime friends the Knottages; and although the concert was a huge success, as Soldiers Field could hardly hold the crowd, it created a serious political backlash, since in the Bahamas, as in many other Caribbean countries, Rastas were a no-no. So much so that Ruby Knottage became known as the 'Mother of Rasta', which was a label that the opposition party pushed on her in order to gain some political clout with the local population.

One of our longest tours had come to a close, and as was customary we now needed the time to rest and recover; and no one needed it more than Bob, who was looking increasingly tired. Yet in response to the continuous enquiries he would be his usual philosophical self:

'My life here, this flesh; me have to live. Me never say there was no fear of death but mi nuh deal with death. Me have no time to risk this flesh too much 'cause it's this mi have to do it in.'

(November 1979)

13 The Break-up

Shortly after the tour Bob called me in Miami, confirming his intention of visiting Skill Cole in Ethiopia. He wanted to do this immediately after Christmas. I applied to the Ethiopian Embassy for the visas, but after two weeks of waiting was refused. When I told Bob this his reaction was a little surprising. He insisted that he had been told that if we went to Kenya we could apply for the visas from there. Accordingly we set off for Kenya, only to be advised by the Ethiopian Embassy there that they could not grant us the visas.

This did not go down well with Bob, who stormed out of the interview and took off on his own, heading down the main street. It was the first time I had seen him react this way. By the time we caught up with him he was standing in front of an art store talking to a man. As we approached, Bob said to us that this man could get us the visas. My reaction as a worldly businessman and a sceptical street hustler was that this was a scam. I said to myself, 'Whey the man no just beg Bob him two hundred dollars and make us go on.' I felt this would be more convenient than making us walk all the way back to the Embassy just to justify him getting the two hundred dollars. But Bob insisted and would not take no for an answer. It was obvious that he intended to get to Ethiopia one way or the other.

Because of Bob's insistence we reluctantly turned back and walked to the visa office from which we had just come. When we got there, the man Bob had met spoke in Arabic to the same person who had denied us the visas, and the officer, without any further questions, took our passports and stamped the visas.

It turned out that the man who helped us was one of the original Rastamen who had left Jamaica long before Bob was born and that he was married to the Ethiopian Ambassador's sister. He told us that he had come upon Bob as he stood at the art store and, not recognizing the superstar but overhearing him say under his breath, 'Bloodclaat,' he stopped and said, 'You are a Jamaican,' to which Bob replied, 'Yes is mi name Bob Marley.' He then asked Bob what he was doing there, and Bob told him.

It is when I look back now that I realize that Bob did not do one thing; he did everything. He made a statement in one of his songs: 'You ah go tired fe see me face and you can't get me out of the race,' and today I know that no matter what kind of music the world comes up with, Bob's interpretation of reggae will always be remembered while everybody else's may well be forgotten. I always knew that Bob would just get bigger and bigger, but he never seemed to lose his faith in Jah being his provider and guidance.

As he once said, 'I've been here before and will come again, but I'm not going this trip through, for there are two roads. One is life and one is death. And if you live in death then you must be dead. And if you live in life you must live. The way the mouth say, make you live.'

Put together all the extraordinary things that happened to him and you have the combination of shaman and superstar. And in a small way this little incident in Kenya was a classic example of this.

Armed then with our visas for Ethiopia, we set out to visit Skill, who as I mentioned earlier was in that country, having gone there after the Caymanas scam. But we were also in Ethiopia to fulfil Bob's dreams of visiting Sashemene. I had discovered during the build-up to the trip that Bob was secretly planning to build a development at the cost of four million dollars for the Rasta community in Ethiopia.

Again accompanying us from the ghetto was the little

youth named Lip and, as a matter of fact, if anybody can find Lip's girlfriend, she has the only picture of Bob taken in Ethiopia – under an Ethiopian sycamore tree, a photo which Lip took with a little polaroid camera. Lip, incidentally, was later to go the way of so many political adherents of either side. He was shot by ghetto gunmen, after he migrated and was encouraged to return to Jamaica by Stewbert, and ended up in an argument over a gun.

The trip was also memorable for me as we took Malachi from London with us. Malachi was one who never ceased to preach the glory of Ethiopia and who Bob thought would be most suitable to take with us on the trip. We were all surprised when after only two days Malachi started complaining and wanted to go 'home' to England, which prompted Bob to say, 'Then Malachi after me spend all my money bring yu to Africa, yu a talk bout England as home and want to return to London.' I could sense his disgust, as this was an Elder who had preached to him, now referring to England as home.

During the four days we spent in Ethiopia we mainly went about with Bob in Addis Ababa buying art and other cultural mementos. Now that I think about it, Bob's insistence on that trip was undoubtedly due to his need to visit his spiritual homeland and make a pilgrimage in his own way. I think so especially when I remember his description of the Ethiopian experience. 'Boy I really get the recharge from Ethiopia because the song "Zimbabwe" was written in a land called Sashemene. So you can say it is a full recharge, that, and when the song came out it [Independence] just happen. So can you imagine if it was in Ethiopia where you wrote all your songs, then nearly every song you write could happen, then maybe somebody would say "Boy, he is a prophet".'

It was following this trip that our break-up happened. This was why I was not with him on what he later told me was his most satisfying and exciting performance: the Zimbabwe concert.

It is not generally known that my management of Bob was not an exclusive arrangement. I continued to represent a number of other artistes including Jimmy Cliff, whose career and experience with Island Records also reflects Chris Blackwell's way of dealing with artistes.

In 1979, I bought Jimmy Cliff's published work for forty thousand dollars, because no one wanted it. Jimmy was therefore assigned to me and I began to resuscitate his career, which had gone downhill.

Jimmy Cliff, like Bob, had been a part of Island Records, in his case for some fifteen years, and his career now needed rebuilding; we therefore started to work on the album *I am the Living*. I was then seeing Deniece Williams (my wife Apryl and I had been divorced for some time), who helped me with the album production, and I also got Alec Willis, who did work for Earth Wind and Fire, to assist us. This album was instrumental in reviving Jimmy's career; in fact the album went to the top 50 and was Jimmy's first real success since 'The Harder They Come'.

Once again I got into arguments with Chris Blackwell when I discovered he had still not paid Jimmy for his African tour after ten years. Eventually I got him twelve thousand pounds.

The break-up between Bob and me really started on our second tour in LA when I was approached by a guy called Bobette, whom I had not met before, but who in the past had worked for James Brown. This was all I knew then but I later learnt that Bobette was regarded as an informer in the business, having in the past informed on artistes regarding payroll scams. In retrospect I should have been more careful in dealing with him, especially as I had heard rumours of his unreliable behaviour.

This time Bobette was representing a family from Gabon, that of the President, Omar Bongo. I therefore felt he might be genuine.

We had played at UCLA on the previous Saturday to a sellout crowd of fourteen thousand and would be playing that night at the Roxy in a benefit concert for Sugar Ray Robinson. The benefit for Sugar Ray was one hundred dollars per ticket, but you still could not get near the door. It was a resounding success and we were very pleased to hand over the proceeds to Sugar Ray, whom we had all long admired.

That same night Bobette turned up with two girls who said they were the daughters of the President of Gabon. I remember one was called Pascalene. The girls not only wanted to come backstage to meet Bob, they also wanted to invite him to a private dinner. On tour I was always protective of Bob and made every effort to protect his privacy and limit the hangers-on, so I was not too anxious to see him go out with these people. Finally, however, at their insistence, I introduced Bob to Pascalene, which ended up with Pascalene inviting Bob to a dinner at their house in Beverly Hills on Foot Hill Drive.

I accompanied Bob, and because Bob would not eat just anybody's cooking, on the few occasions when we ate out we had to have our host hire a special lady to cook his food. In LA it was a lady called Delrose, who had a restaurant in LA called 'Delrose's Jamaican Restaurant'. She was the only person whose food Bob would eat other than that of his own travelling cooks. So he made it quite clear that he would go to dinner only if Delrose cooked his food.

Pascalene's motives were quite obvious, as she was clearly attracted to Bob; so attracted was she that even after Bob's death she named her first child Nesta. In addition to her obvious interest in Bob, she wanted to hire him to come down to Gabon to play at her birthday party. The bill, she said, would be picked up by her father. Somehow she got both Bob and myself to agree, so we scheduled the visit and the performance, which finally ran into more than US$500,000, because we had to charter all the performance equipment from LA and fly it into Gabon, as there was none in that country.

The person who was arranging all this was Bobette, who by now had revealed himself to be a typical New York hustler.

As it turned out, the money they gave Bobette could do only one show, though Bobette was taking the money from Pascalene and the President of Gabon on the pretext that there would be two shows. After he was told that Bob would not do two shows, Bobette then discussed the alternatives and, knowing that I also managed Jimmy Cliff, he made a deposit with me for Jimmy Cliff to do the other show. Where the second deposit for Jimmy came from I never knew.

I made sure that for this agreement I gave him two separate receipts: one for Jimmy Cliff and one for Bob. Bobette, however, had not told the President of this new arrangement, and continued to give the impression that there would be two Marley concerts, so that when we went down to Gabon, Bob discovered that he was in hot water with the President over the money.

The President summoned Bob and myself to come and explain to him what was happening. I told him that, as the receipts clearly stated, there were to be two shows, one by Bob Marley and one by Jimmy Cliff, and this was my agreement. This was apparently accepted by all, although I could see that Bob was still not happy about it, and seemed to feel that I had siphoned off some of his earnings to Jimmy Cliff. So much so, that on our return flight from Gabon, I sat separately and kept my distance, not even responding when Rita came to tell me that Bob had realized that what he was accusing me of was really not true.

As my personal management agreement with Bob was due for renegotiation anyway, this really came at an opportune time. I needed to consider my own future and I was seriously wondering if it lay with Bob. I had taken him this far, and his grasp of the business and his ability to handle most of his affairs by his own methods suggested that the time was fast approaching when he would become too big for the independents and people like me to manage. I had in fact intimated this to Bob.

On our return from Gabon in early 1979, I went on to Miami; Bob went to Jamaica. Our separation had begun.

My separation from Bob brought the vultures in. But we still kept in touch intermittently by phone and through his mother. The phone calls were strictly on business matters which he still left in my hands.

The 1980 world tour was actually handled by Skill Cole, who had come back from Ethiopia and taken over tour management with Danny Sims. They were the ones who set up the last US and European tours, and the later tours of the Far East and Africa.

I was fully aware of the fact that all this time Bob should have been seeing the doctors for a monthly check-up. Dr Bacon kept calling me to inquire after Bob's progress. I in turn would call Bob's mother to find out if Bob was following Dr Bacon's course of action, including a request that Bob try to eat eight ounces of liver every day.

In fact it was Bob who declared the following in an interview: 'They don't want to run this thing like how I run it. Them want to run me on a star trip. But I realize my structure run down, I must rest, but they are not concerned with my structure. Dem run and plan a North American tour. I watch Muhammad Ali and Allan Cole, and I see how them athletes take care of their structure. But them people who set up the tour do not work. Them just collect the money and when night come yu find them in bed with two girls while you buss yu rass claat a work all the time.'

It appears then – and I learnt this from one of my usual calls – that the doctors' instructions were not being followed and that in fact, on one occasion, they had even taken Bob to a regular British GP, who simply gave him a physical and pronounced him to be in good health.

The matter rested there until Bob came back to Miami for a break after the 1980 UK and European world tour. It was normal to take a break like this before going on to his second scheduled tour of the Far East.

When he got to Miami, Bob asked me to come to his mother's house where he was staying and meet with him and Allan, whom I had not seen since our visit to Ethiopia. When I arrived, Bob took me over by the pool, where we talked briefly, and then he invited me to his room where he handed me a piece of paper and asked me to sign away any verbal or written agreement we had made. Allan had accompanied us to Bob's room, and even while knowing what might come next, I refused.

Things now became physical, and after a lot of screaming and shouting there was a tussle. Although no real blows were exchanged, guns were drawn by both Allan and Bob, and as I have related in the Prelude, Allan actually threatened my life: 'If yuh nuh sign the blood claat paper me ah go shoot yuh.'

During all this, I happened to look at Bob, in whose eyes I could see a whole world of conflicting emotions, and shortly after the tussle he said to Allan, in an almost total about-face, 'Now that we have everything under control I guess Don Taylor can come back to work for us again.' It was almost as if he considered the whole matter a cleansing experience, after which we could now resume a normal relationship.

I could not help but feel that the failure of those around Bob to grasp his needs was having a serious effect on his mental as well as his physical state. Little did we know how the cancer was spreading.

But this whole episode had finally decided my mind. This latest experience, together with all of our past associations including the trauma of my own shooting, made me tell Bob that I could never resume a normal relationship with him.

Allan would never have hurt anyone, let alone me, and I still firmly believe that Bob would not have killed anyone, and was in fact just being Bob Marley, Tuff Gong, at that moment – perhaps he was even trying to impress Skill himself. As a precaution, however, I reported the matter to the Miami Police and, knowing the kind of people who hung around Bob for their living, I went out and bought myself a .45.

I ended up suing Bob for $500,000 under my contract understanding, which we later agreed to settle for a figure which gave me a cash payment. This was not settled between us before Bob's death, though he had told his lawyer in Miami to settle with my lawyer Stephen Fisher. It was Rita who approached me right after Bob's death, saying Bob had intended to settle with me, and we agreed to a figure which for personal reasons I won't disclose in its entirety. It included a cash payment of US$75,000, which I received from Rita Marley.

14 From Separation to Death

After this incident and my decision to pursue my own career, apart from Bob, I began to take a greater interest in Jimmy Cliff, among others; but in a strange way my friendship with Bob remained, and he did not try to end my control of his personal business. We kept in touch by phone and through his mother Cedella.

Following his collapse in Central Park in September 1980 I was told that his family and Dr Pee Wee Fraser had decided to seek the expertise of one Dr Josef Issels. I was never consulted on this, but Bob was flown to the Issels Clinic in the Bavarian Alps by Concorde.

Bob kept me informed by intermittent phone calls and talked of his personal concerns about the treatment and the response of his family and friends to his illness and possible impending death. Bob spoke to me of the great concern he felt about the wills everyone apparently wanted him to sign.

His mood when he called would vary from day to day, as the tumour was increasingly affecting his brain.

I specifically remember one call when he invited me to Germany to visit him on the pretext that he wanted me to arrange a nine-month tour of the world. I found this totally out of character for Bob, who in all the time I had known him had never wished for a tour to be longer than one month.

I almost made the visit, as I came within some fifty miles of the clinic while on tour with Jimmy Cliff.

In a way I am sorry I did not do so, but I was not sure then that I would be able to handle seeing him in such a bad condition. I also felt uneasy about the news he had transmitted to me that those who should have protected him and seen to his welfare were not doing things as he would have liked. My inclination was to distance myself from the entire unpleasant situation.

In fact the whole scene around Bob had not only changed, following my departure, but deteriorated very seriously. There seemed to be a whole new group that had taken over and there were increasing reports of extensive crack and cocaine use by this new set of people. And I can only guess that the controls I had exercised had broken down completely under Skill's and Danny Sims's new management.

For Bob had left me in January in what I considered excellent health, despite the sick toe which he had lived with for some three years, and by following Dr Bacon's advice and prescribed regimen he was expected to improve.

It was obvious that the rigid medical regimen which had been prescribed had not been followed. In fact it was not long after the British family doctor had pronounced him fit and well that he collapsed in Central Park after his Madison Square Gardens Concert, and it was discovered that the cancer had gone to his brain. And to date, no one can explain the reason for his manager taking him to a British family doctor, and why, of all medical personnel, it was a general practitioner when people were aware that he had cancer. I still recall how horrified Dr Bacon was when he found out that Bob had not been following his orders, and how we had to insist that we be sent the medical photographs that were taken after his collapse in Central Park.

By the time they got the photographs to us in Miami and Dr Bacon had looked at them, it was clear that the cancer was growing, and quite alarmingly too.

> 'Hail Rasta! You t'ink anything can rass kill me?
> I understand that writers and people in the press are
> very interested and concerned about my health.
> I want to say thank you for your interest and that

> I'll be back on the road again in 1981 – really performing for the fans we love. Beautiful y'know. It's Bob talkin to ya, have no doubt. See? Good.'
>
> (November 1980)

> 'I have gone inside myself more. I have had time to explore my beliefs and I am the stronger because of it.'
>
> (March 1981)

All of this vividly brings back a disturbing call I received in my LA office. The call was from Bob to inform me that he was leaving the Issels Clinic in Germany and would be coming to Miami, and that when he got to Miami he wanted to see me. I could sense in his voice a certain resignation, but in addition, a hint of the old Bob Marley with a determination that he would work it out, in his own way. And because of this I found the call comforting.

During the conversation, he made sure to tell me that he had not signed the different wills which were brought to him by various people. He told me that he was being pressured on all sides to sign. He told me that Rita had tried to make a will, as had Diane Jobson, and the Twelve Tribes, to name but a few. He said that he had not signed anything, and that all his companies and everything else were still in my hands.

He repeated his old pleas to me, re-emphasizing what he had told me from day one: that all his money belonged to his children, and I should make sure it went to them. He then asked me to meet him at the Cedars of Lebanon Hospital so that he could talk with me about this and other matters. He had, in his own way, a way I had fully come to respect, once again placed the onus on me and the decisions in my hands.

It was this call and its apparent finality which made me fly from Los Angeles to Miami on the night flight, to arrive early the following morning in dire need of a nap before visiting

Bob. At about 11.30 a.m., I got up, dressed and decided to go to my office before going to see Bob.

If I happened to be in one of the cities where I had an office I tried to be in it by 10.00 a.m. so that I could discuss the day's work with my assistant. In this case, it was Peggy Quattro (now editor and owner of *Reggae Report*) with whom I was discussing the day's plans. Peggy had only just joined me and I guess I was familiarizing her with my routine and some of my deals. But somehow my mind just kept drawing blanks, I could not concentrate, and suddenly it was as if a spirit of some sort hit me. I began to feel bad, and I looked at Peggy and jumped up out of my chair saying aloud, 'I am going to find out what has happened to Bob.' The words were barely out of my mouth when the phone rang. It was Rita asking me to pick her up as Bob had deteriorated and we were to go to the hospital immediately.

The phone call reflected the old Rita I knew. She did not seem concerned about Bob, but more inclined to find out what the business needs were. She told me that she was at Bob's mother's house and I should come to pick her up and accompany her to the hospital.

I began to feel that I had let Bob down. Why had I not gone directly to the hospital on my arrival in Miami, instead of going to my office?

The phone call seemed to trigger something and I began to have this continuous feeling of unease, as if something had taken hold of me, and my mind began operating in flashbacks. I could remember, for instance, details of the time we were buying the house for his mother, Mrs Booker, the same house from which Rita had called and towards which I now found myself heading. At the time, in 1978, it had cost some US$193,000. As I've already mentioned, Bob had told me that he wanted a house for his mother that was as large as the ones she used to clean 'for the white people dem', so I had chosen a house in the most exclusive section of Coral Gables:

Country Walk, where every house is built on no less than two acres of land.

I had not, however, followed his instructions and paid cash, as I had found it better for business to keep the sixty-thousand-dollar mortgage which was costing only 5 per cent while cash deposits in Tortola were carrying 18 per cent. But Bob did not care about this; his aim had been to give his mother a house free and clear. So it had become a major argument between us. 'I don't understand oonu blood claat people who work for me, I don't inna this trus' trus' business, anything I buy must be able to pay for cash.' Bob never used credit cards because he saw credit as a means of slavery. He always felt that if he owed nothing he was his own master. Despite this, I had left the mortgage in place as the business side of things was still important to me.

However, to this day I keep feeling I did him an injustice in this case, as I realize how deeply important it was to him for his mother to have her house free and clear. And here I was heading towards the same house with this great premonition.

Thoughts of the strange happenings involving the doctor at the Eiffel Hilton Hotel on the day when he treated Bob's toe also flooded my mind, raising many questions, as they do even now when I ask myself where are the pictures Neville Garrick took on the thirty-day tour of Europe, which have never been published nor seen the light of day. I was filled with regret that I had not visited him in Germany nor responded to all the rumours surrounding his illness or even what he told me himself about the vultures surrounding him, even though I had known it must have been true.

As I drove up to the house, I saw Rita Marley coming outside, looking crazy as if she had lost her mind, so I said, 'Rita what happen, what happen,' and she said, 'We have to go to the hospital right away, 'cause Bob is dying, and he will not tell anyone anything, and he wants to see you so we have to go.'

She jumped into my car, and I drove as fast as I could to the hospital, but as we walked up the stairs of the hospital, Bob was on his last breath and as I looked into the room, I felt it, I knew he had died.

Before we left the hospital, I basically took charge of the situation. I contacted Grange Funeral Parlor in Miami so that the body could be got ready for burial and I had them work with everyone to arrange the services in Miami and Jamaica. Almost immediately, everybody started to argue about who should be put in charge of what, and who should get what, to the extent that I started to feel a bit confused. But I had to see it through as best as I could. I had to do what I could to see that Bob's wishes would be fulfilled.

I knew that the task ahead was not going to be easy as I was beginning to feel the vibes already. And somehow, I felt the hand of Bob was at work. Was he now sitting back and laughing at the antics of all those hangers-on and scroungers?

Bob's death actually had a profound effect on my life, a truth with which I have only recently begun to come to terms. Bob was important to me not only as a business partner, but as a friend. In all our dealings, there was the placing of this enormous trust in me; the only time we had an argument was regarding the Gabon matter, and this was triggered by the devious minds of those who sought to ingratiate themselves with Bob. At the time of his death, we were in court over some royalties due to me, but despite this Bob never removed my control of his estate, or my control of his accounts.

He had even discussed the possibility of my taking over the Island contract and my taking over the publishing rights from Danny Sims.

Without a doubt there was only one insider and that was me. Bob did not make a move that I did not know about. If he slept with a woman he would call me and say, 'Don, boy, I slept with such and such a girl last night.' I had to know his moves at all times because I had to know where to find him and he had to know where to find me. Rita was not involved in Bob's financial and business affairs. She did not even know Bob's account numbers. It did not matter how much we fought; my name was always on his current account because he never took it off. He did not put on Rita's, his mother's, or his children's names; it was my name that was on it.

The impact of all of this was now becoming increasingly clear to me, as I began to deal with the loss of the person I had loved so dearly.

Aftermath

15 Passing On the Estate – Rita and Me

It was not a smooth road after Bob's death, as different forces started to exert their own individual influences and make their individual demands.

I approached Diane Jobson for advice as to what I should do about Bob's estate, and her advice was that the money for Bob's children should be turned over to the Attorney General in Jamaica. This advice, however, was in direct conflict with the argument from Rita Marley that if I resigned and just turned over everything to the Administrator, the children would never get the money because of the government's bureaucracy. I thought about it and knew that I wanted the children to get the money. So I said, 'OK, leave it with me and let me think about all the different factors and persons that would be entitled.' I was, of course, referring to such persons as Rita Marley, Mrs Booker, Diane Jobson and the children.

I had decided that after the funeral services and Bob's burial, I would sit and deal with each person individually after obtaining their points of view.

In the meantime, I continued to set up things for the services. As there was a new government, the JLP – Eddie Seaga having given Michael Manley a resounding beating at the 1980 polls – I spoke with Babsy Grange, who was a Minister of State in the Prime Minister's office, about the government's offer to have a state funeral. The family agreed to this.

Rita then came to me and said she had to have access to some money over that period of time, and as there was approximately four hundred thousand US dollars in the Island

Records account in New York, I released that to her. But on top of that, she asked me to release another one million US dollars to her; I agreed to this, and sent a fax to our lawyer in Tortola, stating that I wanted to transfer this sum to Rita Marley and requesting legal advice as to how to proceed.

Rita, not having any financial experience or any contacts, asked me to help her set up an account, so I flew with her to Nassau where we went to the Bank of Nova Scotia's main branch on Bay Street to meet with a Mr Roy Curry whom I always dealt with (I myself also had an account there). Mr Curry proceeded to make all the necessary arrangements, and the money was transferred to Rita from the Barclays bank in Tortola. So she had her first million dollars of Bob's money.

Rita immediately began flying family and friends from all around the world for the funerals. It was about a week later that we had the first of the funeral services in Miami at Bob's mother's house, and about four or five days after that the official state funeral was held in Jamaica.

Our arrival in Jamaica for the official funeral was fraught with tension and excitement. To begin with, it had been only six months since Jamaica had witnessed the bloodiest election to date, with about eight hundred political killings taking place in the six-month period leading up to it. I guess one could say that the peace concert had not worked.

The usual arguments developed concerning the method of administering the official funeral, which in reality was being officiated over by the very 'Babylon' with which Bob had never been in tune but which now saw fit to award him the Order of Merit, the highest award available.

Hypocrite and parasite
Will come up and take a bite
And if night should turn to day
A lot of people would run away . . .
('Who the Cap Fit')

The ecumenical service saw the participation of church and state and the joint participation of the Twelve Tribes and the Ethiopian Orthodox Church. I guess in a way Bob had indeed brought them together, if only for a day.

Needless to say the whole country turned out to show respect for Bob, lining the roads for a full sixty miles as the procession wound to Nine Miles in St Ann, where Bob was to be buried.

It was the rousing reception that Michael Manley got at the funeral service that created some problems for me with the new government, as some persons in political quarters (perhaps Rita herself, who was becoming very close to Babsy Grange and Eddie Seaga) suggested that I had something to do with it.

Maybe my dislike for some of the JLP politicians was obvious. After the state funeral in Jamaica I went back to Miami to await the return of Rita Marley so that we could discuss the terms of the transfer of Bob's assets to her.

During this period, I continued to have conversations with Mrs Booker, who was concerned about being left out of any decision regarding Bob's assets because she did not trust Rita. I recall her telling me that she needed about three thousand dollars a month to live on, which I got Rita to agree to give her, taking care of this immediate problem. Actually Mrs Booker had hinted that she would have preferred to have Cindy Breakspeare as the head of the estate instead of Rita. Her comments about Rita were always the same: 'So she black, is so her heart black.' She had said this several times on and off, especially when she was upset. However, Cindy was definitely not an option, because my lawyer had advised me that whereas I could put the estate in Rita's name because she was legally Mrs Marley (even though we knew the real nature of the relationship), I could not put it in anyone else's name.

Rita intimated that she did not want to bring the entire

estate into Jamaica, because of the strong currency restrictions at the time. I told her that if she opened accounts in the Bahamas in each of the children's names, appointed their mothers as trustees, and then transferred their fair share into the account, then that would satisfy me. I was still, as always, trying to ensure that the money and the estate would remain with the children. Rita said that was fine with her.

We both then went back to Nassau. This was about two months after Bob's death. I took her to my Bahamian attorney, Mrs Ruby Knottage, whose firm was then known as Knottage and Miller. I went over my proposal to the lawyers and Mrs Knottage helped advise Rita. We then went to the bank and opened accounts in all the children's names. We opened them with about ten thousand dollars per child and Rita was supposed to transfer the rest of the money after I had resigned and nominated her as President. It was also agreed that Rita would take the books to Ruby Knottage, which I believe she did.

I then started a six-month trek of introducing Rita to all the people involved in Bob's affairs, and putting everything into her hands. We made several trips around the world in the process of doing this.

We made one particular trip to Los Angeles because of Bob's publishing contract. The right to administer Bob's publishing companies (separate and apart from his management and recording companies), which were known as Bob Marley Music and Tuff Gong Music, had run out prior to his death, and was never renewed, because of his illness. So I took Rita out to Los Angeles to meet Mr Freed, who was the head of the A&M recording company. I had begun to deal with A&M some eight to ten years before, and had developed a good working relationship with them. David Steinberg accompanied me on that trip, during which I renegotiated the contract, which now provided for Rita to get a one-million-US-dollar advance immediately with the proviso that each time they released a record and the advance was recouped, A&M would re-advance her another hundred thousand to a million dollars, depending on the strength of the sales of the record.

At the time no one could accurately determine Bob's worth, and how fast the money was going to come in, so we had to base our numbers on some estimated data. (In fact, as it turned out, within thirty days of advancing Rita the one million dollars A&M was able to recoup it. This alone reflected the value of Bob Marley and his music, a fact many were now acknowledging.)

David Steinberg was present at all these meetings. In fact, all three of us stayed at the Westwood Marquis Hotel while awaiting the closure of the deal.

It would be wise for me to note that although Bob and I had always used David, he was not very close to Bob in his lifetime, and indeed from my early days of dealing with him he was never really very close to me either; before Bob's death, David was making only about ten thousand dollars a year from our account. That was the most he could make from us, and he had to work all year for it. I therefore found it strange, although I said very little, that all of a sudden, in less than a year, Rita was paying him hundreds of thousands. He seemed to have just come in and taken control of Rita. I had always had this lurking feeling about Rita that she had this mental thing about white people that Bob did not have. I guess that is how they were able to deal with her.

After confirming the agreement, we all went out to dinner that night to Mr Chow's restaurant in Beverly Hills. This was a famous restaurant popular with people in the music industry. It was also owned at the time by the President of A&M, Jerry Moss, with whom we had just completed the deal. The group who attended the dinner included Maynell, an attorney whom I was dating at the time; Brenda Andrews, Vice President of Irvin Almo Music; Rita and David and, of course, myself. It was the kind of night that remains with you always. I think the bill came to about four thousand dollars with all the wine and champagne. After dinner, we all went back to the hotel, and waited for the paperwork to be done and the cheque to be issued. Maynell and myself left the rest of the party at the hotel, and went to a club called On the Rocks, which is on top of the Roxy on Sunset Boulevard and is a very famous club, where all the big names hang out. It was in fact the club that John Belushi was at just before he died. The people who owned On the Rocks were friends of mine, Elmer Valentine and Lou Adler. Lou was the person who developed the career of Carole King. It was an exclusive private club – a key club. You could not buy your way in, you had to be a chosen member and when so chosen, keys were given to you.

That night, for perhaps no other reason than the company I was with, I was encouraged to use cocaine for the first time. It had always been around, but I had always steered clear of it. On this particular night, however, they offered it on a plate, and I took a little. We stayed at the club for about two hours and then left for her apartment in Beverly Hills where we had sex, to me the greatest sex I had ever had; those who have experienced sex after having cocaine for the first time will appreciate what I am talking about. In fact, it really is never the same again, and it is almost as if you spend the rest of the time using it in a vain attempt to recapture the pleasure of that first time.

The following day, Rita, myself and David went back to the company, picked up the million-dollar cheque, and Rita, pleased and smiling, went shopping. A&M paid me thirty-five thousand US dollars for putting that deal together for them. I took no commission from Rita Marley on that particular job, as I was paid directly by A&M.

That night I went out again to a friend's house to get something to eat, and unknown to me a lot of cocaine was sprinkled on the food, which made me really high and paranoid. I went back to the hotel but was in such a state that I had to be taken to a hospital where the doctors, recognizing my problem, gave me some valium and sent me back to the hotel. Those two nights marked my first experience with cocaine, and led to an addiction which would later get out of hand, as I used it fairly heavily for some three years before I realized how damaging it was. I have not been using it for about five years now.

During that period Rita held certain private meetings with David Steinberg that neither of them wanted me in on. With our business concluded, however, David left for Philadelphia and Rita and myself for Miami, from where she proceeded to Jamaica. I joined her later to continue discussions on the estate.

I had by now received the receipt from the bank for having purchased a million-dollar CD in Rita's name. I personally handed this over to Ziggy Marley and a few days later met with Rita to discuss the transfer of the estate to the appropriate persons.

It was about this time that Rita made me listen to what she called the 'deceivers' tape. Apparently while Bob was being treated at the Issels Clinic he had one day left a tape recorder running under his bed. What was captured on the tape alarmed Bob deeply. Comments like 'Why him no hurry up and dead so we can get some of the money' or 'Im deserve it, is fi him fault' were recorded on the tape. What was shocking was that these words came from the mouths of a range of 'insiders' – musicians, cooks, Twelve Tribes family members, people who were supposedly close to Bob. I now fully understood the frantic calls I had received from Bob in Switzerland.

Despite the fact that I had pretty well made up my mind about the matter, Rita was still displaying a great deal of anxiety about whom I would choose to pass the estate on to, and

I have no doubt that she meant the tape to influence my decision.

We needed to decide on a legal firm that would handle the transfer and represent Rita and I suggested that we consult Beryl Murray, a real-estate agent in whom I had great confidence. She had been like a mother to me and the entire Marley family. Any house that was bought for a member of the Marley family was purchased through her, for instance.

So we went to see Beryl Murray, who referred us to a lawyer called George Desnoes; in fact she took us to see him herself. We explained the situation to him and he said he would be honoured to be one of the administrators of the estate. He called in a younger attorney, Raymond Clough, who along with another attorney, a Mr Scholefield, took some notes. Following this meeting I gave them a list of Bob's estate holdings. Desnoes said that we now needed a banker and so we scheduled a meeting for the next day, by which time he promised to find such a banker.

Louis Byles turned out to be the banker that Desnoes found. He was an old and respected employee of Mutual Security Bank, formerly the Royal Bank of Canada. At the meeting the next day at which Desnoes, Byles and I think Clough were present, we went over the notes from the previous day's meeting and I told Byles what I had told the others about where Bob's companies were located, and what monies were held in them.

On hearing all the details and the extent of Bob's holdings, Byles said he would like to be involved, even though it was going to set back his retirement. He particularly wanted to do it, he said, in order to make up to Bob for the bad treatment Bob had received at the hands of his friend, Bob's uncle. I recalled the story of how Bob had visited his uncle, Cecil Marley, a lawyer on Duke Street, to ask him for a loan of three hundred Jamaican pounds to make a record. His uncle had thrown him out and also called the police.

Convinced that Byles was a genuine person, I began to feel

less worried. The following day the bank sent up the estate papers to Rita and Steinberg, who brought them to me. On their advice I called the lawyer in Tortola, and told him to draw up the necessary papers for me to resign and have Rita installed as President and for her signature to be put on to the bank accounts at Barclays in Tortola. Hers was going to be the sole signature on the account.

Maybe I should have had more misgivings about this, especially in the light of Rita's past history, but I was really anxious to be rid of the responsibility for the estate. My own lawyers had warned me that I could get tangled in legal red tape for a long time if I didn't look out. I also felt some sympathy for Rita because of the harsh way Bob had treated her sometimes, and anyway I felt confident that the consortium set up with the bank and the lawyers would ensure Bob's wishes were carried out.

Yet I wasn't really surprised when, after the transfer was complete, Rita, David Steinberg and Marvin Zolt distanced themselves from me. Rita continued to try to involve me in insubstantial matters, but I really didn't care, because I had again been advised by my lawyers to stay far from the estate and in the meantime to make sure that I did everything as carefully as possible.

Slowly but surely I drifted away from that side of the business. Rita tried to hire me for another six months to help with the final clearance of the estate. I told her that there wasn't enough money in the world to pay me but that I would do it for Bob Marley. On the other hand, if she wanted me to work on anything not connected with the estate she would have to pay me my normal commission.

With this understanding she hired me to try and get the Melody Makers a recording contract. I brought them to Los Angeles, where I finally landed a contract for them with EMI USA Records, which gave them an advance of a quarter of a million dollars for their first album.

But the leopard hardly ever changes its spots, and after the recording contract was signed, Steinberg and Rita purposely and successfully undermined me with EMI so as to do me out of the commission that was due on the publishing side. I was also not paid commission on the second Ziggy Marley album for EMI. I found this quite unprofessional, as I had actually got my friend of fifteen years, Thom Bell, to work on the album, which would never have happened without me. Thom had just won a Grammy and was one of the top producers in the US, having produced for people as far back as Little Anthony and the Imperials, the Stylistics, the Delfonics, the Spinners and Dionne Warwick. I had also got Thom to cut some stuff for the I-Threes, which I placed with EMI. And I didn't get paid for that either.

I remember vividly a trip to Nassau with the four of them to make sure the children's accounts were opened. I was struck by the fact that on the trip Steinberg and Zolt were roommates. I found this surprising because about nine years before that, when Steinberg was Thom Bell's lawyer and Zolt was our accountant, they had had a serious disagreement which resulted in Steinberg referring to Zolt as a rogue and expressing a strong dislike for him. When Zolt heard of this and came to me demanding an apology from Steinberg I refused to become involved, but I remember that they couldn't stand each other. Yet here they were, roommates now, after Bob's death.

I also found out that Steinberg had recommended that Rita form a company called Rita Marley Music, which would be located in the Netherland Antilles. It seemed to me that Tortola would have been a more logical choice, but when I expressed this opinion I was told that it was because this was going to be the management company for the Marley estate. So Steinberg and Zolt set up a meeting in New York. Steinberg said that it would cost thirty thousand dollars to form the company. None of the offshore companies I had established for Bob in Tortola had cost more than fourteen hundred dollars to set up. After signing the papers I told Rita that I wanted one of the two of us to go down to Curaçao to check out the lawyers and the people who would be running the company. She agreed, but in the end this was never done.

It was clear at this meeting that Rita Marley Music was being set up in a hurry so that all future payments from Bob's music could be deposited in its accounts. Olner made an arrangement with Citinational Bank in New York for us to make our deposits there, saying that cheques could be cashed there at any time although the money was held offshore in Curaçao. As far as I know this account was handled and maintained by Zolt, who may also have been one of the signatories on the account.

By this time I had physically turned over everything to Rita and the bank and all that was left was the final sanction from the court which would make Rita the legal administrator of the estate. I now realize that this decision from the court which was still pending was what forced them to tolerate me and go through the motions of consulting me. They didn't want me to start objecting to any of their plans. But this was the farthest thing from my mind at the time as I wasn't paying detailed attention to what they were up to.

The only thing I continued to find odd was the apparent closeness between Steinberg, Zolt and Rita. They made frequent trips to Jamaica, Miami and Nassau and were always having closed-door meetings.

The way I had originally set up the contract between Bob and Blackwell ensured that if Bob died the contract would expire, leaving Blackwell with the ten albums that Bob had delivered and nothing more. And within fifteen years of the date upon which the albums had been released they would revert to the estate. By the terms of the Island contract Chris would not own anything Bob had not delivered and had not yet recorded. In fact Bob and I agreed that if Chris ever raised this with him or became difficult Bob could disclaim knowledge of the contract because it was I who had signed it.

I later found out that at one particular meeting in Nassau between the four of them Rita had given Blackwell, Steinberg and Zolt the first album that came out after Bob's death and also the rights to anything that Bob had left unrecorded. She signed a contract to this effect and was paid a measly million dollars, entitling them to rights that I would not have given them, and all of this happened before Rita became the officially appointed executor of the estate.

The person who was privy to all of this was Diane Jobson, but she herself had gone from being one of Rita's most vocal critics to an unquestioning, silent pro-Rita supporter.

I remember an argument between Bob and Rita when he was staying with me in Miami and she came up for a visit.

'Dutty gal why you nuh use yuh name, yuh name is Rita Anderson, mine yu mek people like Don and him wife think you an me is like them.'

He was always reminding her of her subservient status, and I realize now how deeply she must have resented this, perhaps was even waiting for a chance to get revenge herself. I remembered the song Bob wrote about Rita:

Now you get what you want
Do you want more
('Want More')

Yet in all this it seemed to me that wherever he was, Bob was laughing to himself at the greed and the scheming and machinations of those who were once close to him. (Perhaps he was even proving, in his own way, that he was still able to manipulate the scene . . .)

For Bob himself had had no respect for money or wealth. He once told me that he did not sing for money and explained, 'Is true I man no sing for money, but if money come I must get my share, and if I did sing for money I would a stop long time ago, especially from dem early years with Coxsone and the like who use fi give me only five pounds.'

Without Bob around any more I found it hard to deal with the sharks and hangers-on who surrounded him. I was just anxious to wash my hands of the whole business but I could still imagine Bob laughing at the scene and waiting for the right moment to say, 'Don how yu a go decide my business for me.'

16 The Mafia and Me

After all this I basically disconnected myself from the estate and its dealings, but I still found myself involved enough to be the subject of a mob hit.

My final involvement with the estate was to go to MIDEM (the Music Publishers Convention) in an effort to get a deal for Tuff Gong, which I was still representing. Gradually I found myself phased out of even this role until Rita found herself in an argument with King Sporty (co-writer and co-producer of 'Buffalo Soldier') over the masters of that song. She asked for my help and I went to California to see Sporty. I got him to settle with Rita, who paid him US$150,000 against the masters and the publisher's share.

The next thing that happened was that the Danny Sims–Cayman Music affair resurfaced when Sims sued the estate for royalty earnings and Rita asked for my help once again. Once again I got involved, but this time I got a friend, Dick Griffey, owner of Solar Records, and then head of the Black Music Association (who was to become one of Jesse Jackson's personal advisers during his run for the US Presidency), to help me. Over the years Dick had mediated many cases involving problems black musicians ran into in the industry, seeing to it that they would not be financially ravaged by white lawyers. It was in this capacity that I asked for his help and we invited Sims, Rita and her lawyer to a meeting at Solar Records in Hollywood to settle the matter.

We had already informed Rita that the best way to go was to allow Dick and myself to act as mediators. We proposed that all white lawyers be excluded and that the principals involved come to a settlement on their own.

I guess Rita's lawyer, Peter Herbert, was offended by this. Dick and I helped Rita negotiate a deal which would allow Rita to buy back all the Marley songs that Sims owned for nine hundred thousand dollars. This was one hell of a deal, especially when you consider that Blackwell ended up paying Cayman Music five million dollars for it later on. It also would have resolved the long-standing feud over the falsification of these rights.

I was really enthused at getting back those songs for the estate, because it was one of Bob's last requests to me. The meeting, which lasted five or six hours, ended with an agreement to have the papers drawn up the next day, when Rita would have the songs transferred to her after paying the money and signing the papers.

Unfortunately the transfer didn't take place because that night Peter Herbert persuaded Rita that it wasn't in her best interest to purchase the songs. So they broke the deal and didn't turn up to sign the agreement and pay the money the next day.

Now with the conflict unresolved Sims would still have to be reckoned with and I had suddenly become very unpopular with him. I was saddened by this, not only for obvious reasons, but also because I had known Sims since I was a kid in the music business and a lot of what I had learnt came from him.

When the deal fell through Danny decided to report me to some contacts, the Gambino family, allegedly headed at the time by 'Big' Paul Castellano and later taken over by John Gotti. Danny complained to them that I was standing in the way of their earnings and that I had interfered with a lucrative deal, resulting in its falling through. They decided that since I had done this in spite of my acquaintance with them and without any explanation, I deserved to die.

By extraordinary luck I found out that a hit contract had been taken out on me. It so happened that one of the hit men turned out to be a friend of an old friend of mine from my Las Vegas years. The hit man told my friend Cal that he had a contract on me and was just waiting to get certain information. And so it was that I got a call from Cal, who told me what was going down.

I was staying at the Wyndham Hotel in Kingston at the time, and when I confronted an acquaintance I believed to be involved in the affair he admitted to having been questioned by a sharp character. He denied knowing that they wanted to hit me, but I have never believed him.

Realizing how serious all this was, I called up my own Mafia connections, the Gauchi family in Florida. I asked to speak to Bobby, one of the top men in the family and a personal friend, to whom I described the situation.

As fate would have it I ran into Sims the same day at the Pegasus Hotel and went up to him and said, 'What the fuck is going on?' I convinced him to come with me and speak to Bobby on the telephone.

I did this knowing that in the Italian families no one carries more weight than a real Sicilian, which is what Bobby was. As I had anticipated, Bobby informed Danny that he was outweighed and that everything should be put on hold pending a meeting where he would explain the real circumstances surrounding this case. At the meeting he explained to all concerned that I was indeed in the right as Marley was due more money than he had ever been paid and that Sims had never paid him properly or accounted to him. When questioned about this Danny said that the relevant files and documents were no longer available which made it impossible to determine actual figures.

In the end Danny's lawsuit against the estate was held as scheduled in New York and I went to court on behalf of the estate, because as part of the settlement with the Mafia they had agreed that I should honour my commitment to testify, but only on condition that I speak the truth.

On the other hand, because of Rita's attitude Danny was able to get such close friends of Bob's as Allan Cole, Mortimer Planno and Vincent Ford (Tata) to testify on his behalf against the estate.

And although the Mafia were really mad, they kept their part of the bargain even though my telling the truth made them lose the case in the US, which suited my purpose, as it got them off my back. They lost the case on a technicality as the court decided that since Danny had known of the scam for years and had done nothing to stop it he was in fact a collaborator and as such not entitled to compensation as he should have taken action before the contracts had expired.

I had made my peace with the Family and also achieved my goal, which was for Bob to keep his money.

I continued to have problems with Rita although I had patched up my relationship with Danny. She always seemed reluctant to honour her commitments. Based on my agreement with Bob I was entitled to 10 per cent of all future earnings by the estate, up to seven years from the date of the agreement. When I raised this with Rita, however, she said that in the interest of the children she hoped that instead of taking out 10 per cent for me and other sums for Steinberg and Zolt, I should agree to the 10 per cent being paid into a pool from which we could all be paid. I agreed to this, but to this day I have not received any of it and I have not made a fuss about it because I have gotten tired of her obvious insincerity.

In fact I didn't speak to her again on anything close until Blackwell put out the album *Legend*, which had huge sales in the US and Europe and Rita wanted to do a tour of the US. She called and asked for my help and I agreed. The *Legend* tour was a thirty-day affair which she splurged on in the most exorbitant manner. It was the summer of 1983 and we played all across America from New York to the Amphitheater in Universal City in California. Bob would have turned in his grave at the way money was spent on that tour. I was paid US$40,000 for organizing it.

I understood she had to play her game to get back at people, and she was getting back at anybody who had been close to Bob and who she felt had been disrespectful to her. One of the main persons to fit both these categories was Allan Cole, who used to refer to her as 'the gal'.

As the estate grew in value, the whole thing began to take on more sinister and serious overtones and even led to a planned hit on my life by Rita following my exposure of her attempts to defraud the estate of all its cash resources. It began when I got a call from Louis Byles and it really all happened quite by chance.

Byles called me in relation to a personal matter that I was discussing with Camille Henry, to whom he was also close. During this call I asked him about the estate and to my surprise he told me that the estate was broke. I asked him what that meant and he told me that he had only received two million Jamaican dollars from the estate through the Jamaican courts.

I laughed at this at first but then began to question him further. I asked him about the overseas companies, namely, Bob Marley Music and Media Aides Limited, which I knew had had in their account some seventeen million US dollars when I handed it over to Rita.

That's when he informed me that he had a letter dated 1976 which was signed by Bob Marley and notarized by David Steinberg, and that this letter had given all the cash assets to Rita.

I told him that I challenged the authenticity of this letter, even without seeing the documents. I told him that the letter was a phony, as I had handled all of Bob's affairs up to his death, and I would have certainly known of the existence of this letter. I remembered the various occasions when Rita had tampered with Bob's signature over the years. I remembered

Bob's constant refrain that all he had was for his children.

This seemed to support the stories going the rounds that the hard currency, namely, the US dollars from the Marley estate, was being used to do favours for clients of an employee of George Desnoes.

I had, myself, become aware of the illegal sale of US dollars out of the account to various businessmen in Jamaica by an employee of the legal firm of Judah Desnoes Lake Nunes Scholefield, Glen Fettiplace, who was ultimately convicted of this illegality. In fact he once came to me with a cheque for US$50,000 which he was having difficulty encashing in New York. So I told him to come down to Miami, where I took him to Mr Castro at the Bank of Miami and had it cashed.

Knowing of the shortage of US dollars in Jamaica, I had accepted the reason offered, which was that the estate was benefiting from this method of business – the selling of US dollars at a premium – which was used to offset the associated costs of running the estate. But alarm bells were now beginning to go off. It also made clearer to me the need for the Curaçao company.

Byles was beginning to get very upset at what I was saying and I hung up feeling quite concerned and in some way as if I had failed Bob.

I immediately called Rita, who asked me to meet her in Nassau. She had already been alerted by Byles, to whom I had made it clear that I would not keep the matter a secret. In fact, I had followed up the call with letters to the Administrator General, the then Prime Minister, Eddie Seaga – with whom, as I understood it, Rita had developed or was developing a close relationship – and one to Louis Byles and the Mutual Security Bank.

I was livid with anger as I saw all that Bob and I had worked for being lost to the greed of a few.

Bob's words from 1980 kept coming back to me:

> 'They don't want fe trick you, them want fe trick your mind, that's the thing I don't like. Yu have eyes, yu have ears, yu can talk, yu can smell and yet them want fe trick your mind. Is better somebody ask you for something and get it rather than try to trick me fe tek it. I know who God is, now how can yu trick me? I no fool.'

As I thought this over I geared myself for the meeting with Rita which took place two days later in Nassau.

Rita started by asking what she could do for me. I told her it was not really about me but about the children and those whom I knew Bob loved dearly. I mentioned Rohan (one of Marley's sons) as an example who I understood was getting only ninety dollars per month. This did not seem to move Rita, whose main response was to ask if 'is the big pussy girls' I wanted to see get all the money. I tried desperately to explain to her my feeling of commitment to Bob concerning his children and I began to feel angry again at seeing these smart lawyers benefit from Bob's inheritance, so much so that I told her that she was also one of the big pussy women.

I made it clear to Rita that I knew the letter that Byles had was a forgery and that I would not drop the matter. I then proceeded to speak with the rest of the family, and after talking to Mrs Booker, we decided to fly down to Jamaica to see a lawyer. I had decided to ask P.J. Patterson (now Prime Minister) to represent the children. He agreed, but when the matter escalated to include the host of mothers and children and a variety of lawyers, he requested that he withdraw from representing the children and only represent me.

The result of all this was that Rita went to court in Jamaica in 1989 and said that the document she had given Byles was a forgery. The transcripts will show that she was coerced into this. The court then removed her name from the estate.

Not long after this someone decided to take out a contract on my life. As soon as I returned to New York I was warned by Danny Sims that someone had been sent to New York from Jamaica to hit me, and they would be sending someone to my house to protect me. Maybe he did this because he had now become aware that only I would tell the truth about Bob's affairs, specifically the songwriters scam.

He told me that a mutual friend, Kendal Minter, had innocently gone to the airport to pick up a guy, who he thought was a Jamaican ex-Secret Service policeman. He had told him that he had been hired for ten thousand US dollars to take me out. On learning of this, Sims arranged for him to be held until they could resolve the whole matter.

Realizing the seriousness of the case, I reported it to the FBI. In the interim Danny and my own associates, colleagues and friends felt strongly enough about it to assign Bill Underwood to protect me. Bill was later allegedly associated with Nicky Barnes, the black kingpin gangster who at one time had owned the Apollo and with whom I ended up being friends. Today Bill is serving a life sentence in Indiana but we are still friends, and I still visit him occasionally, with every belief in his innocence.

I was somewhat shocked that anyone could go to such extremes. From another point of view, however, nothing that anyone has ever done or said could really shock me. On top of these worries I also had big problems with Rita Marley. Take for instance her statement in the court case in 1989 that she did not trust me: I offer no real comment except to remind the world that if this was the case in 1989, how could she, a few years previously, have signed the following agreement, which I publish in its entirety:

September 26, 1983

NOW AND FUTURE ARTISTS MANAGEMENT CORP.,
c/o Apryl Taylor,
8100 Southwest 81st Drive,
Suite 201, Miami, Florida.

Gentlemen,

Reference is made to the Recording Contract between EMI America Liberty Records and Rita Marley Music for Melody Makers and the Publishing Contract between Almo Music Corp, and Rita Marley Music for Ziggy's. It is agreed that for the services performed by Don Taylor in negotiating and in closing the aforementioned contracts, you will be entitled to a commission of Ten percent (10%) of the net payments made to Rita Marley Music for such contracts. Such commission to be calculated on all forms of payments made to Rita Marley Music including credits issued or any other consideration actually paid to Rita Marley Music. Payment of such commission to be made at such time as Rita Marley Music receives payment and shall be payable for the life of such contract. You agree that for so long as you are entitled to receive commission you will be available to Rita Marley Music for the reasonable periodic requirements of Rita Marley Music in respect of such contracts.

It is further agreed that NOW AND FUTURE is bound to provide the services of Donald Taylor to perform the services here-under in order to maintain this agreement in full force.

It is further agreed that Donald Taylor will on behalf of Rita Marley Music, seek out, place, negotiate and assist in the closing of contracts for talented musical performers, recording artistes, production and publishing companies and further assist in negotiating contracts for the benefit of Rita Marley Music. For each such contract negotiated and completed you shall be paid a commission of Ten percent (10%) payable as aforesaid.

In the event that Rita Marley Music shall require any special or extraordinary services we agree to negotiate in good faith with you in respect of remuneration for such services.

Rita Marley Music agree to reimburse all travel and miscellaneous expenses incurred by Donald Taylor for the benefit of Rita Marley Music provided such expenses have been approved by Rita Marley prior to the same being incurred by Donald Taylor.

It is understood that NOW AND FUTURE shall not make any binding agreement on behalf of R.M.M. without first obtaining the prior written consent of Rita Marley.

If the foregoing correctly reflects the Agreement between you and us, please so indicate by signing below.

Yours sincerely

....

Rita Marley,
RITA MARLEY MUSIC

As I said before, my experience of Rita had led me to expect calls from her only when she wanted something for herself. So I don't know why I was quite surprised, three years later, when she called me in West LA; in fact, I did not recognize her voice at first. When I asked who it was and she replied 'Rita Marley', I asked her how she had got my number. She replied that anytime she needed my number she could get it. She was calling from her apartment in New Jersey.

It was as usual a self-interested call: 'Don, don't testify and bury me, because whatever problems we have we can work it out together.'

She was referring to her pending 1992–93 New York case where Steinberg, Zolt and Rita were facing court proceedings. I responded that if I was asked to testify, I would have to tell the truth. I was never asked, but as it turned out she didn't need my help in any case: the court was satisfied that she was misled. Subsequently in a New York court Steinberg and Zolt were fined one million dollars each for misrepresentation. They are both appealing against the court's findings.

I am sure the world is still looking for a way to understand the maze of Bob's estate and the confusion over who should have gotten what. And it has become even more startling and confusing.

Somewhere around this time there was another court

action, in this case to examine why Blackwell's bid to buy the publishing rights to Marley's songs for twelve million dollars was accepted over MCA's bid of sixteen million dollars.

But Blackwell was smart. He took the line that the sale of Marley's music to MCA would move the ownership out of Jamaica, whereas his purchase of the rights would not only keep them within the country, it would also keep them within the family because by now he had joined his bid with that of Rita and the rest of the family. So by playing up the Jamaican culture and patriotism argument and by using Neville Garrick as a spokesman Blackwell found it easy to win the bid.

Which brings me to Neville Garrick, who continues to portray himself as an insider, although I never regarded him as one. Neville Garrick was not even on the first tour I did with Bob. Garrick begged Bob to be included on the second tour when we were going to play at the NORM convention in the USA. As I mentioned earlier, we promoted the *Rastaman Vibration* album on this tour.

Garrick promptly proceeded to embarrass us by being caught with a powder pan of ganja by the US Customs. He was arrested in Miami and put in jail for four days. We eventually had to get King Sporty and one Captain Curry to bail him out. But because he was an alien, instead of being released after we had put up the bail, he was transferred to immigration and for days we could not find him. The case was tried and he was charged with smuggling ganja into the USA and placed on probation.

Neville Garrick was the only member of the Wailers who ever got arrested. The rest of them had too much respect for Bob ever to smuggle drugs.

Neville Garrick was never on Bob's account and was never involved in any of Bob's business. His job was the album jackets, the backdrops and the lights. Some of Bob's real insiders were people like Family Man and Carly and even they did not know the details of the business. I know some people will say I am wrong in saying Neville Garrick was not an insider, but I know he had no personal relationship with Bob Marley. He was just Bob's key man for art work and stuff like that.

Allan, on the other hand, was an insider. He was Bob's confidant. In fact sometimes I think that Bob really wanted to be the footballer, and Allan the singer. He had the same responsibilities that I had when I took over and more – because he was Bob's intimate friend. I never really had any problems with Allan. He was in charge of a lot of things before I came on to the scene and yet when I appeared he turned it all over to me.

I know I tried to understand Rita Marley after Bob died. I now realize that the only reason she kept me around was because she thought it was necessary. She tried to dismiss everyone else, including the Wailers, and set up her own network, with new people, after suddenly seeing herself in the role of queen. Most people who now worked for her could address her only as Mrs Marley.

Bob's mother Cedella Booker was another character. If I had had any doubts about the stories Bob told me about the relationship between his mother and himself, these were dispelled by my observation of her actions over the estate. I watched her shift support from one person to the next as long as the side she was supporting was working in her own interest.

She started out by being suspicious and non-supportive of Rita and trying to favour Cindy. She kept making out to me that Rita had given her only US$36,000, which was not true, since I found out following the exposure of the fraud that Rita had given her close to one million dollars. Shortly after this she shifted her support to Pascalene Bongo.

As you may recall, Pascalene was the daughter of the President of Gabon who had named one of her children after Bob and was now making a bid to buy the estate, supported by Cedella. Cedella had Pascalene take on the support of her whole family, at one time moving her daughter Pearl to LA to live with Pascalene, who took care of all her expenses. Cedella was urging Pascalene to buy the Marley estate and in fact brought her to Jamaica for that purpose.

When this failed she shifted her support to Chris Blackwell, in return for which he had to agree to pay the outstanding mortgage on her house, which was then some sixty to seventy thousand dollars.

At one stage she aligned herself with Yvette Morris, who had long before established herself as a troublemaker by claiming that one of her children was fathered by Bob. After Bob died she reasserted her claim that the child was his. This suited Mrs Booker, who supported her claim and used it to gain an additional hold on the estate – the child is now on the estate as one of Bob's children.

Indeed Cedella would shift with whatever wind she felt would blow her a benefit, and Bob's words kept ringing in my ears, 'Don Taylor, you don't know my mother.'

I am viewed with hostility by all these competing parties because they cannot buy me. Yet it is only a matter of time before the truth is revealed; and this book will add truth to the body of what has been written about Bob Marley.

17 Reflections

I have never been able fully to explain the implicit trust that Bob placed in me, but I think that much of it lay in our common background, our shaping in the real-life world of Kingston's street university, where the rules of the game are based on trust, where trust and a verbal agreement are as good as a contract drawn up by a lawyer.

This was so much a part of my informal education that when I started managing Bob Marley there was no need for any formal agreement.

Having watched his genius at work, the total informality of his lifestyle and his openness to those with whom he associated, I developed a loyalty and an affinity to his vibes that rose above mere monetary value. He knew I would live by my word and would take only what was mine or what I was entitled to and no more. The endless times he elicited a commitment from me about his children's future impressed upon me the responsibility I had to all his children, and it was a commitment which I accepted and gave unreservedly, until I felt I had discharged my dues as a manager and a friend.

For Bob was one of that rare breed the likes of which we will never see again, and I guess the night of the shooting created an even greater bond between us, for in a sense it was my body which protected him from the bullets meant for him.

The creative and the human moments we shared are beyond any cash value.

I still recall with pride the fact that until my arrival the *Catch a Fire* and *Burnin'* albums were really failures, and it wasn't until I assumed management and responsibility for Bob that they took off. This and more are all milestones in our friendship and association. For in truth and in fact, up until then, the Island contract had done nothing for Bob.

And for me one of the defining moments of our relationship was the day he turned to me and said, 'Don Taylor you know what I like about you is you no lickey lickey.' Meaning that I refused to kiss ass.

I remember my first introduction to Peter Tosh and Bunny Wailer, who were both part of the original Tuff Gong. It was at the first show with Stevie Wonder at the National Arena in Kingston, when both Bunny and Peter came back to the group to do the show; it was immediately clear that their large successful performing egos could not really co-exist on a day-to-day basis. (It was also for this show that I negotiated the largest local contract for Bob: seventy thousand Jamaican dollars. I recall sitting down with Vunnie Isaacs at the stadium while he counted out the raw cash before handing it over to me.)

Peter Tosh always resented Chris Blackwell, whom he referred to as 'Whitewell', and he often said that Whitewell's only intention was to keep them in slavery. Bunny, on the other hand, was more introverted and did not seem to take any specific position or side in the differences between Bob and Peter. His only concern was that he harboured this definite fear of flying in the iron bird, as he called it, a position which occasionally caused some disruption.

Bob set out to learn what you had to teach so that eventually he would be able to meet you on equal terms, armed with the knowledge he had gained from observing your methods. I saw this happen on tours, where he would learn from experience, step by step, covering every facet of the organization, gaining in knowledge and confidence in the music business. He became so adept at using this knowledge to his own benefit that sometimes I wondered if he was now a master politician as well as a giant of a musician.

There was the time for instance after our third tour, when he insisted on flying to Tortola to check on the accounts. This was because I was taking out a mortgage to buy some property we were interested in and Bob objected to my not buying it outright for cash. Bob didn't see the necessity for a mortgage as he felt if you had the cash then you paid cash. So he insisted that we fly to the bank so that he could actually see his money. After we had done this I asked him about it only to be told, 'Yu think me fool to accuse yu early and yu making mi money. But is two tour now, and yu do you thing, yu mek more money. I nuh fool, a mus mek you do yu thing, but we equal now, as yu know me value. So me can check up on yu now. Don Taylor, member say a man can spend him life waiting on a good deal, but anybody wi gi yu a bad deal.'

Bob's reactions to the people around him bordered on the uncanny, and the continuing arguments over his life and the estate bring home to me more and more how perceptive his observations were.

Bob's ability to grasp a situation and explain its ramifications showed an uncanny understanding of the Jamaican mind. There was a time when the group felt that it was necessary to build a fence around the Tuff Gong Studio at 56 Hope Road to control the ever-increasing crowds of uninvited guests and hangers-on who would flood the building at times. Once we were all in Rico's room shooting the breeze at our hotel in Tokyo when Bob left the room. The conversation turned to the fence and everyone expressed his feeling on the matter. I was sitting on the edge of the bed, Tyrone was on the chair by the window and Family Man was next to Carly, who sat intently rolling his joint. We were loudly expressing our views, wondering why the fence was taking so long to go up, when Bob entered, to deafening silence. This was normal because Bob had such a strong presence that quite often no one spoke until he had spoken.

Turning to no one in particular he said, 'What happen, what oonu a talk bout,' and almost in chorus the answer was, 'Nothing,' whereupon Bob retorted, 'Oonu too blood claat lie, oonu a talk bout the fence.

'Oonu want me to lock out people and them kill me for it' (this was after the shooting). 'Mi a go do it piece by piece till dem get the idea, and then nobody will hate me for it by the time it done. Oonu seem not to remember that some of the people we trying to lock out is our bredren who we grow up wid, so we must do it piece by piece.'

I often think about how everything that Bob fought for has been given away by the Ritas and the Neville Garricks of this world. Almost all of what Bob bought from Chris Blackwell has now ended up with Chris once again.

It started with Ian Fleming's house, 'Golden Eye', which Bob had bought for £50,000 through Hugh Hart. Chris's mother, Blanche Blackwell, who was a friend of Ian Fleming's, started to say how much the house meant to her, so she got Diane Jobson to tell Bob that the house had been a bad deal, and that Chris would buy it from Bob for the same money. He now owns it, just as he once again owns 56 Hope Road.

I now realize that although I thought we had outsmarted Blackwell, we really hadn't as he always placed spies on the tours, people like Viv (head manager for Traffic), and David Harper (Robert Palmer's manager), who were placed under cover to report back to Chris.

In much the same way he used Timothy White and Stephen Davis to create an illusion of closeness between himself and Bob. Very little of this was or is true. For anyone who knows intimately the history, culture and politics of Jamaica would recognize as outrageous propaganda much of what is contained in these other writings. But then this is for the reviewers and the critics to decide. What I have given is the real story.

Yet as I sit and deliberate over the time I spent with Marley and attempt to record the truth as I remember it, I realize that to deliberate on the past would be an injustice to all that Bob stood for. For indeed he was a giant in every sense of the word.

My only regrets I have expressed quite openly, and these revolve almost entirely around the ownership of his legacy, and where the ownership is as opposed to where I know Bob Marley would want it to be.

I know for sure it should not be in the hands of Chris Blackwell or the Japanese, or indeed the US or UK or Europe; for although he belonged to the world, he ultimately knew that his home and roots were in Jamaica and with his children.

I recall also how P.J. Patterson told me of one of his reasons why he would represent only my interests and not those of the family.

As he reminded me, I had, following the death of Bob and prior to handing over the estate, arranged for him to come to LA so that I could give him a more in-depth look at the meaning and workings of the music industry and its potential for continuous earning.

As it turned out, he quickly grasped the reality that the present focus of the family (other than Rita), was limited, as they were only looking at the $30 million in the bank, without recognizing the huge potential for the earnings of royalties and other rights income. It also opened his eyes to the different forces that would play a part in the estate.

As he, the now Prime Minister, tells it, on his return after the visit to LA he turned up at his office in Jamaica to find a person who he describes as a seedy-looking individual, waiting in his anteroom. The presence of this person sent up his antennae and he asked the person what the purpose of his visit was. No sooner did the person mention the Marley estate, than Mr Patterson, without replying, asked that he leave his office forthwith; and as he tells it this incident and no other led him to envision the problems down the road and also made him advise me of his withdrawal, except to act on my behalf.

During this time, as was customary, I was offered other artists who people desired to come under my management wing – one such artist was Prince.

I remembered being called by Pepe Willie in Miami, whom I had known as a kid, he being a nephew of Clarence Collins, one of the original Imperials.

He advised me that Prince, in his opinion, would be bigger than Stevie Wonder, and acting on this advice, I acted as Prince's manager for a time, but was myself not fully convinced of his future and was becoming increasingly drawn to the intensity and reality of the demands of Bob's career.

To accommodate it, however, I toyed with the idea of having Prince and Bob do a track together or even do a performance together. I had just finished working with Prince on his first album release, *Soft and Wet*, and he was in LA playing at the Roxy for a promotion I had arranged with Warner, and Bob was also on tour appearing at the Amphitheater in California.

I discussed it briefly with Bob and decided I should have them meet, and so Bob and I took Tyrone along to meet with Prince backstage at the Roxy.

What the result of this might have been, however, I will never know, as when we called on Prince he met us in this skimpy leopard-design G string undergarment, which immediately aroused Bob's Jamaican macho feelings and so our stay was as brief as Prince's G string and Bob's discomfort was shown all over his face.

Of course, immediately on leaving, he turned to me and as only Bob could say it, he said, 'Don Taylor a dem deh man yu want me fe work with? – mi huh in a dem dey batty boy business, mi nuh even wan cum a yuh office an meet dem or even sit inna the same chair as im.'

Perhaps Bob had a point. I myself found Prince weird. He didn't feel emotion. He was a law unto himself – he overspent by $100,000 on his very first album, but it didn't seem to bother him.

I was spending most of my time looking after Bob and his interests, so a young lady who worked for me called Karen Baxter represented me with Prince.

For whatever reason, and this was after some few months, Prince never saw fit to hold an in-depth conversation with Karen and she obviously was finding it frustrating. Suddenly one day, she phoned me quite upset as on this one occasion when he had spoken to her, he advised her that he did not like his sister and he wanted to chop her in five pieces and put her in a plastic bag... My association with Prince ended after that. I never raised the idea of Bob and Prince working together again. I realized that there was much more to Bob's reaction to Prince than a mere macho response, as Bob would indeed leave people to their own devices (as he did with those around Chris Blackwell).

It's amazing the kind of things that would happen around Bob, even before his death; and all revolving around money. I recall the time when it became common knowledge that Bob would have substantial sums of money on his premises or as they would state in local jargon 'A bag ah money up deh', especially after tours and concerts.

It was this same kind of loose talk that, sadly, led to the murder of Peter Tosh on his return to Jamaica, where it was thought that he had returned with lots of cash.

As it turned out in Bob's case, the robbery set up was attempted, but without success, and it led to an exhaustive internal investigation, which Bob requested me to fly down to resolve. My visit and investigation ultimately revealed the involvement of Pearl, who was for a while distanced from the immediate entourage.

Many questions have been asked of me, both before I wrote

this book and while I was writing it. The recurring question is the one that asks why Bob neglected to leave a will. Many people blame him for allowing, as they put it, his Rastafarian beliefs to prevent him from making a will which would have saved the estate and his family the high legal fees and resultant court battles.

In fact, Bob had repeatedly asked Diane Jobson and myself how important it was for him to make a will, and he asked this of Diane even on his deathbed.

As this was Bob's only wish and what he had always expressed to me, it certainly reassured us both.

There is no doubt in my mind that the problems and costs that the estate and the family have had visited upon them were all caused by Rita's dishonesty. She was determined to deprive the rightful owners of their fair and just rights to the money that Bob left and she tried to achieve this by forging Bob's name, thus creating the confusion and problems with the estate.

Yet as Bob himself said, 'The greatest thing them [the Church] can say about death – them say you die – and go to heaven after all this sufferation. To go through all this sufferation for that! It's like after me sick go to the doctor. No, the greatest thing is life' (July 1975). And so I know that no matter what Babylon does, Bob will always live through his music, and in the hearts of those who knew him. And one such person will always be me.

But the last words are best left to Bob himself:

> 'I know I was born with a price on my head, and
> I know that my music will go on forever. Maybe it's
> a fool say that, but when me know facts me can say
> facts. My music will go on forever.'

Appendix: Jamaica – a Historic Capsule

Christopher Columbus is recorded in the annals of history as having 'discovered' Jamaica, which he stumbled across in 1494, when he was lost and floundering in his search for Zipangu in the East. He drifted unceremoniously on to the shores of Seville, in St Ann's Bay, St Ann, not far from Nine Miles where Bob Marley himself was later to be born on February 6, 1945. There, inhabiting the island, he found the peaceful Arawak Indians, who had themselves discovered Xaymaca many centuries before.

It did not take Columbus long to recognize the beauty of the country, when he claimed Jamaica to be the fairest isle his eyes had ever seen. On his second voyage he spent his longest sojourn – one year, before being rescued by Diego De Salcedo on June 28, 1504, one year after he had dragged his water-logged boats on to the Jamaican shores.

As we were told, it was not long after Columbus's arrival and his claiming the island on behalf of Queen Isabella, that the Spaniards saw to the physical decimation of the peaceful Arawaks and ultimately their complete extinction, a truly infamous page in the annals of Jamaica's and the world's history.

The Spaniards left in their wake quaint and recognizably Spanish place names such as Oracabessa, Mount Diablo and Ocho Rios. In the first capital of Jamaica, Spanish Town, there was the impressive Spanish Square which housed the first parliament building in Jamaica and Kings House, the then and future residence of the early governors of Jamaica, from the steps of which the abolition of slavery was announced.

Today those solid brick buildings representing some of the finest examples of Spanish architecture have mostly been destroyed by devastating fires, and remain only as sombre reminders of the Spanish era.

History records that the Arawaks had possibly arrived in Jamaica around 700 A.D. and were, in fact, a peaceful people who cultivated maize and sweet potato as their main staples, and who hunted and fished only to satisfy their needs. They stood in marked contrast to the fierce Caribs of the Eastern Caribbean who would lead warring excursions into the west. The Arawaks would in time become renowned for introducing the Old World to tobacco, a plant which they loved to smoke from their Y-shaped pipes, inhaling with such intensity as to produce intoxication and unconsciousness, after which, at peace with the world, they would laze in their hammocks, a creation they would also pass on to the New and Old Worlds.

> 'Why people drink is they want the feeling I get when I smoke herb. Everybody need to get high, but some people getting high with the wrong things.'
>
> (Bob Marley, January 1976)

The Spanish discovery of Jamaica was a direct result of Europe's insatiable search for gold, which was the real purpose of Columbus's voyages, and to this end the Spaniards continued to have the Arawaks work worthless and unproductive Jamaican mines. Unaccustomed as they were to this hard labour, thousands of Arawaks were worked to death, while thousands more succumbed to new strains of diseases introduced by the interlopers, and many others committed suicide by hanging themselves or drinking poisonous cassava juice.

It was soon realized that there was no gold in Jamaica. So

by 1512 Spanish eyes were turned to Cuba, with many of the Spanish colonists withdrawing to that island only ninety miles away.

In the ensuing years, then, the Spanish did not do much in the colony except introducing banana, plantain, all forms of citrus, and sugar cane to the island.

By 1655, the role of the Spaniards in Jamaica was all but over, and when some thirty-eight ships under Admiral William Penn, sent by Oliver Cromwell to conquer the island of Hispaniola, failed in that mission, they turned to Jamaica as a consolation prize. The by now weak and factionalized Spanish settlers offered little resistance to the British and ultimately fled from Seville in St Ann, a site which was later to be renamed Runaway Bay to commemorate this Spanish flight.

It was, however, the Treaty of Madrid in 1670, some fifteen years after Penn's capture of Jamaica, which formally ceded Jamaica to England.

The British victory over the Spaniards ushered in the notorious era of the buccaneers and would later lead to Jamaica becoming the pirate capital of the world.

The pirates themselves had chosen as their capital the city of Port Royal, strategically situated at the tip of the Palisadoes promontory which juts out of Kingston Harbour. From there they raided and pirated the Spanish and Dutch ships passing through the straits of Panama, violently attacking and plundering their goods and treasures for the British Crown. The most famous of these buccaneers was Sir Henry Morgan. He it was who led the sieges and the pillaging of the Caribbean Spanish Empire, including the burning of the city of Panama in 1671. For this he was made Lieutenant Governor of Jamaica by Charles II, and later bequeathed land on the island, specifically in Clarendon and St Mary, as a reward for his achievements.

The death of Sir Henry Morgan in 1688 helped to hasten

the inevitable passing of this period, as with his influence removed, the strength of the buccaneers was obviously on the wane.

So, when in 1692, four years after his death, half of the city of Port Royal and its eight thousand inhabitants were cataclysmically and unceremoniously buried in the ocean by a violent earthquake, it brought to an end the era of the so-called 'wickedest city in the world', and led to the founding of the city of Kingston, only eight miles away, lying on the sweep of the Liguanea Plain. With the passing of the influence of the buccaneers, the eyes of the merchants and the British realm turned to the unexploited potential of the island for the production of sugar cane.

The growing of sugar cane had in fact originated in the South Pacific and its by-product, sugar, had reached Europe via trade with India. Although the Spanish had introduced the growing of sugar cane on a limited scale to the West Indies, they, in their thirst for gold, had not recognized its true potential.

The British, on the other hand, from as early as 1640 had experienced sugar's phenomenal success on the small island of Barbados. So, Jamaica's comparatively large landmass offered great opportunities for exploitation and economic development of the crop. Being fully aware of the exploding worldwide demand for sugar and the resultant need for increased production, the British were fully prepared to achieve this development by introducing cheap human labour. So it was that this need was filled by the importation of slaves from Africa.

Old pirates, yes they rob I
Sold I to the merchant ships
Minutes after they took I
From the bottomless pit
('Redemption Song')

The resilience and independence of the slaves brought to Jamaica is now historically accepted. In fact, it has been suggested that Jamaica received more rebellious and uncontrollable slaves than any other Caribbean area. This is often attributed to their geographic origin: the majority of the slaves who came to Jamaica were from the Gold Coast and Benin, an area which was home to such strong and resilient tribes as the Coromantees, the Ibos – red and black – and the Mandingos. These were tribes who historically in their own homeland were never prepared to accept enslavement passively. They would thus produce slaves who would continue their fight for freedom throughout the years of slavery in Jamaica, demonstrating a persistence unparalleled in other countries.

Slave driver, the table is turned
Catch a fire . . . you gonna get burned
('Slave Driver')

The final Jamaican slave rebellion was that of Sam Sharpe in 1831, and by its implementation and timing it speeded up the abolition process and led to the 1838 abolition of slavery.

We gonna fight
We'll have to fight
Fight for our rights
('Zimbabwe')

The abolition of slavery, however, left an urgent need for replacement labour, as the freed slaves left the sugar estates to set up their own holdings or, in the case of the skilled, to find work in the towns, a situation which would create its own social problems.

To fill this obvious need for labour and to be able to cultivate some of the now idle lands, the planters and estate owners had to resort to the importation of indentured labourers from China and India, and in later years Germans, who to this day still live in partial isolation in German Town in St Elizabeth.

With the arrival of the indentured slaves came their cultural influences, and some historians have traced the introduction of marijuana, or 'ganja' (which is a Hindu word), to this period of migration.

> 'Maybe you could meditate without herb if you're somewhere that's quiet, but even if you go into the woods there's still the birds. But if you smoke herb the birds might sound sweeter and help you to meditate. The authorities tell you that you mustn't smoke herb because it's bad for you. Yet if they catch you at it they'll carry you off to prison. I think it's better to be smoking herb out here, free, than being in prison.'
>
> (Bob Marley, 1978)

The years which followed the abolition of slavery, up to the mid-nineteenth century, saw deteriorating labour relations; the workers' wages and conditions cried out for attention.

This situation reached its climax in 1865, a year which saw a dearth of good rainfall, almost bordering on a drought. This, when coupled with the impact of the United States Civil War, increased dramatically the cost of food in Jamaica, most of which was being imported. Such conditions, combined with the low wages being paid to the labourers, led to the Morant Bay Rebellion in that year.

This rebellion was led by Paul Bogle and supported by George William Gordon, two of Jamaica's present-day National Heroes; both were executed following the suppression of the revolt.

But the stone that the builder refused
Shall be the head cornerstone
And no matter what game they play
We've got something they
Can never take away

('Ride Natty Ride')

Meanwhile, sugar declined in importance on the world market. As a result of this decline, as well as the continuous social turmoil, the number of estates growing sugar, which had amounted to some five hundred in the mid-nineteenth century, had dwindled to eighty or ninety by 1900.

This void was now to be filled by a new agricultural crop, the banana. The world demand for this product attracted the necessary investments by British and American interests so that by the last decade of the nineteenth century the banana had become the island's most important crop.

So important was the banana as a crop, that Jamaica as a direct result would become the first English-speaking country in the Western hemisphere to build a series of railways. The railway was the safest and easiest way to transport this sensitive fruit from the fields of the estates to the shipping ports of Port Antonio, Oracabessa and Montego Bay.

These developments combined, then, to create the emerging identity of Jamaica's agricultural, political and human landscape. There began an unconscious intertwining of the cultures and beliefs of the British plantocracy and the Irish and Scottish soldiers and farm overseers (acting for the absentee landlords), together with the trading mentality of the Jews and Arabs, the resilience of the Africans and the commitment of the indentured Indians and Chinese.

The modern base was now laid for what would be referred to in later independence years as, 'Out of many, one people'.

Some are leaves, some are branches,
But I and I are the root.

('Roots')

In reality, then, now that the birth of the nation had begun, the voice of the people would have to be heard, and so it was no mere coincidence that at the turn of the twentieth century it was the voice of a short, stout, black Jamaican from St Ann (the same parish in which Bob Marley himself would later be born) that was now becoming known to the Jamaican people. It was the voice of one who would have a deep and lasting impact on Bob's own life.

This was the voice of Marcus Mosiah Garvey, who had bid farewell to his native country in 1916 in order to take on the white world from a base in that increasingly influential country, the United States. Garvey's words in his parting address, 'Look to Africa for the crowning of a black King; he shall be the redeemer,' would become quite prophetic.

Marcus Garvey was born in St Ann's Bay in 1887. When he left Jamaica at the age of twenty-nine he left as a well-read, self-educated man whose strong beliefs were rooted in his slogan, 'Africa for the Africans', which motivated his Back to Africa Movement, launched in New York in 1917, when he founded the Universal Negro Improvement Association (UNIA) in Harlem.

For Garvey and the disenfranchised blacks of the world, the UNIA represented the hopes and aspirations of the awakened Negro.

> 'Our desire is for a place in the world, not to distort the tranquillity of other men, but lay down our burden and rest our weary backs and feet by the banks of the Niger and sing our songs and chant our hymns to the God of Ethiopia.'
>
> (Marcus Garvey)

By the 1920s Garvey's preaching of a black God began to bear fruit and would become more entwined with a rising appreciation for the glory of Ethiopianism. His words took on strength and meaning enough to arouse the spirit of oppressed and disenfranchised blacks, so that Garvey soon became the most powerful leader among the black masses of the USA and, indeed, the world.

> 'The ends you serve that are selfish will take you no farther than yourself, but the ends you serve that are for all in common, will take you into eternity.'
>
> (Marcus Garvey)

It was Garvey's words that developed the black awareness movements in the USA and Jamaica through his newspaper the *Negro World* with its battle cry, 'One God, One Aim, One Destiny'.

Marcus Garvey's worldwide influence grew by leaps and bounds, and although still not fully accepted in his own land, Jamaica, his 'Africa for Africans' cry, and his prophetic words, 'Look to Africa for the crowning of a black King; he shall be the redeemer,' had sown their seeds within the minds of many.

> *A good man is never honoured in his own land*
> *Nothing strange, nothing changed*
>
> ('Survival')

Garvey's preachings and philosophies had by now been borne out by the crowning of Ras Tafari Makonnen on November 2, 1930. By then learned black preachers and historians could prove that Egypt and Ethiopia were, in fact, part of Africa and had only been excised by the Aryan historians determined to divest blacks of their dignity and their history. A fact which Bob never failed to recognize.

Ras Tafari Makonnen was the great grandson of King Saheka Selassie of Shoa, Negus of Ethiopia, who, upon his ascendancy, had taken the name 'Haile Selassie' (power of the trinity), 'King of Kings', 'Lord of Lords' and 'Conquering Lion of the Tribe of Judah'.

Selassie was the 225th in the line of Ethiopian kings, which could be traced all the way back to Menelek, the son of Solomon and Sheba.

Could not one then conclude, as Bob Marley would later do, that the vision Garvey had prophesied had been fulfilled, just as John the Baptist had prophesied the coming of Christ?

Glory to Jah the prophet has come
Give thanks and praises

('Confrontation')

The die, then, was finally cast.

This coincidence of history was, to Garveyites in Jamaica, a prophecy fulfilled, as they pointed to Garvey's teachings which had predicted this crowning almost to the year. Very little outside influence was necessary after this, as the followers of Garvey hungrily clung to all of his teachings, which gave form and shape to the words:

> 'We negroes believe in the God of Ethiopia, the everlasting God, God the Son, God the Holy Ghost, the God of all ages'.

Thus began the Jamaican Rastafarian movement which emerged out of the hills of Pinnacle in St Catherine, led by Leonard Howell, with the master theme being 'Peace and Love'.

The overwhelming influence of these teachings and the historical facts which manifested themselves in these Rastafari preachings, were now carried to the streets of Kingston by such impressive converts as Joseph Hibbert, Archibald Dunkley and Robert Hinds.

Predictably, this rise of black self-recognition and self-esteem was met with great resistance and derision by Jamaican lawmakers and society shapers, who engineered the arrest of Leonard Howell on the trumped-up charge of selling photos of Haile Selassie as passports to Ethiopia.

The reawakening of black consciousness and awareness was taking place against the background of increasing labour unrest in the sugar fields and banana plantations (not unlike that of the Morant Bay Rebellion period), in a new era marked by the rise of a consciously led labour force, which articulated the workers' demand for a place in the sun.

This struggle for self-awareness brought on the labour strikes of 1938 and ushered in the era of trade unions and political parties. It brought to the forefront Alexander Bustamante and the Bustamante Industrial Trade Union (BITU), the People's Political Party (PPP) of Marcus Garvey which faltered and failed and was replaced by the People's National Party (PNP) led by Norman Manley, and its historical opponent the Jamaica Labour Party (JLP).

These social and political developments forcefully emphasized the people's demands for self-recognition and a better way of life.

For the musically and culturally inclined the broadcasting era was beginning to take shape. Radio Jamaica and Rediffusion, an offshoot of ZQI which was an independent amateur station facility owned and run by John Grinan, was subsequently handed over to the government during the war years to advertise the British cause. When peace finally came, however, the British company, Rediffusion Limited, bought out the facilities and in 1950 launched the call sign RJR, utilizing such musical fare as Patti Page, Frank Sinatra, Bing Crosby and the Andrews Sisters.

As Independence loomed, however, it was obvious to all concerned that the rise in nationalism which Independence demanded would not be satisfied by such limited broadcasting facilities, and thus it was that in September 1959 the Jamaica Broadcasting Corporation (JBC) went on the air. The intention was to fill the void that now existed by allowing more originality and creativity to flower, reflecting the diversity and colour of the Jamaican people. This was accompanied by the rising popularity of the American stations beaming out of Miami, such stations as WINZ and WGBS, which boasted an increasingly large listenership. Many musicians would tune in to these stations seeking to catch up on the latest blues and R&B coming out of the USA.

The birth of independent Jamaica on August 6, 1962 was an important ceremonial occasion. The British Union Jack was lowered and the black, green and gold Jamaican flag raised to the resounding refrain of the new National Anthem, 'Eternal Father Bless Our Land', sung lustily by some forty thousand persons. Thousands of young and old and indigent sat with a visiting Princess and a Prince who had come officially to hand back the country to its people, after some three hundred years of British rule. The historic occasion was additionally recognized by the presence of the Vice President of the USA, Lyndon Baines Johnson.

It was the end of the turbulent era of colonialism and Jamaica had begun to govern itself.

The country was being ushered into the global village of the world, with all the trappings of modernity. The development of the suburban areas was now at the blueprint stage – not yet a reality – and the city of Kingston was still confined to an area bounded by the Wareika Hills and Rockfort on the east, and on the west by May Pen Cemetery and the abattoir – the bowels of the city as it became known. To the north and south it was bounded by the Blue Mountain Range of St Andrew and the Caribbean Sea.

Part of this area, St Andrew, later to be called 'uptown', would finally be incorporated into Kingston and St Andrew, forming one city, still referred to as Kingston. Finally it would develop into the present scattered and unplanned city, leaving its downtown area neglected and in need of urgent redevelopment.

But me no have no friend inna high society
Me no have no friend, oh mark my identity
Me no have no friend

('We and Dem')

But already the arrogance and confrontational style of the Jamaican people, of which their Caribbean neighbours would speak, was obvious. Federation had been resoundingly rejected. The rising tide of Independence had come amid a strong economic base of reserves, produced by the exports of sugar, banana and bauxite. The arrogance continued unabated, the reserves of cash were in place. The Jamaican dollar was worth more than the US dollar. The motto seemed almost to be 'Stand back while we take on the world.'

There were some, however, who were reflective and aware that the mere creation of a flag and National Anthem was not enough. Patriotic fervour had to be centred on the island's history and culture and Jamaicans needed, so to speak, to return to base, to identify with and build on their history. Thus they began to dig back into their past, focusing on individuals who had led them to this great moment in their history.

The country now began to learn more of the exploits of Sam Sharpe, Paul Bogle and George William Gordon and the previously untold stories of the revolts against slavery. For it was these who were the martyrs in the cause and in the fight for freedom.

But not surprisingly, it was the charismatic leader Marcus Mosiah Garvey who attracted the most spontaneous and reverent reaction from the populace, for his was the voice that the politicians heard rumbling out of the suffering of the ghettoes, the residence of the oppressed and the poor.

> 'Since the white people have seen their God, through white spectacles, we have only now started out (late though it may be) to see our God, through our own spectacles. The God of Isaac and the God of Jacob, let him exist for the race that believes in this God of Isaac and the God of Jacob. We negroes believe in the God of Ethiopia, the everlasting God – God the Son, God the Holy Ghost, the God of all ages. That is the God in whom we believe, but we shall worship him through the spectacles of Ethiopia.'
>
> ('Philosophy and Opinions of Marcus Garvey')

Bob never failed to articulate these ideas in his life.

> 'I am sure Haile Selassie I is almighty God – with no apologies.'
>
> (Bob Marley, 1976)

The early Nyabinghi Rasta believed that Haile Selassie represented the first coming of the Messiah and that the Babylonian 'Je-sus' was a false god. Out of this belief came the suspicion of governments, and the philosophy to stay away from 'Politricks'.

As their religious beliefs developed and manifested themselves, Rastas adopted the visible characteristic of 'Dreadlocks' – the uncombed and uncut hair which demands much more care and washing than would appear.

> 'All the days of the vow of his separation, there shall be no razor come upon his head: until the days be fulfilled, in the which he separateth himself unto the Lord, he shall be holy, and shall let the locks of the hair of his head grow.'
>
> (Numbers 6:5)

And so this religious vow became the mark of Rastas, who also did not drink alcohol or deal with any form of death, as they went along this ancient and traditional biblical path, comforted only by the smoking of marijuana.

As Bob once said,

> 'When you smoke herb it reveals you to yourself. All the wickedness you do is revealed by the herb – it's your conscience and gives you an honest picture of yourself.'
>
> (September 1980)

Marijuana had been adopted for usage by Rastas as part of their religious worship, a usage which is historically and biblically steeped in the belief that it was given to man by Jah to aid his meditations and open his consciousness to the world. This belief emanates from the fact that it first grew in the grave of King Solomon, hence the name, 'wisdom weed'.

Not all Rastas smoke ganja, but it is commonly used by adherents of the faith. When smoked in a chalice or chillum pipe as a form of worship, it is solemnly passed in strict religious observance from one person to the other as a holy sacrament with each person traditionally giving thanks and praise to Jah. This is referred to as 'licking the chalice' or 'sipping from the cup' and in this respect is comparable to the Christian communion cup.

Accompanying these rituals and beliefs are those concerning food.

> 'Know ye not that ye are the temples of God, and that the spirit of God dwelleth in you! If any man defile the temple of God, him shall God destroy, for the temple of God is holy; which temple ye are.'
>
> (Corinthians 3:16,17)

Thus Rastas disdain pork and shellfish – the meat of so-called scavengers. This is often taken to mean the exclusion of all meat – 'deaders' – though fish is less contemptuously regarded. The total exclusion of salt, which is inorganic, almost completes the diet of eating 'ital'. Ital represents the organically undefiled preparation of food.

The Rasta society that has developed over the last sixty years has given rise to offshoots of Nyabinghi with developed links to the Ethiopian Orthodox Church, which came to Jamaica in 1969. The Ethiopian Orthodox Church is the most ancient and historic of the Christian churches. Its literature includes the *Kebra Nagast*, the book which traces Selassie's lineage to Solomon and Sheba, and records in the Geez language the story of how the Ark of the Covenant was taken from the Jews in Jerusalem and transferred by God to Ethiopia.

In Genesis, Jah created the world through His words. So it was that Rastas would also be required to shape their reality through the use of language and would therefore need to develop Rasta talk, if only to differentiate the godly from the ungodly (especially as Isaiah 11:110–113 confirms that the gathering would begin in the 'Isle of the sun', which as the Rastas saw it could only be Jamaica). And so herb became I-sence – with 'I' taking the dominant role of creating a singular unified identity for Rasta – and Rastas expressed themselves in their I-ssembly (assembly) to sing I-Ses (praises) to I-nation (creation) of Jah.

The phenomenon that was Rasta demanded government attention in the sixties. It was the subject of an official government study by M.G. Smith and Rex Nettleford, especially because it brought with it a strong 'Back to Africa' movement. Another concern was what were considered to be unknown revolutionary intentions as to how to reform the 'shitstem', as Peter Tosh would later refer to it.

And was it not reasonable to conclude, as many of Jah's followers did, that the preservation of the religion which had grown to wide proportions, and which throughout its early life faced, as it still does today, trials and criticisms and which today still draws wrath, especially from the establishment, was proof enough of its genesis and righteousness?

> *It's too late... men have lost their faith...*
> *We no know how me and them a go work this out*
> ('We and Dem')

Meanwhile the changes brought on by Independence being experienced in Jamaica in the sixties were also having repercussions in the Rasta camp, giving rise to new Rasta doctrines being preached in the ghetto. The most influential of these changes was the emerging Twelve Tribes of Israel founded in Trench Town in 1968 by Vernon Carrington, a vendor of juices and herb roots drinks.

He it was who proclaimed that the human race was made up of twelve tribes, each named after one of Jacob's sons. He connected each tribe to a month of the year, marked by a special colour and endowed with a secret blessing, and he related this to the Egyptian calendar beginning in April.

April	–	Reuben	–	Silver
May	–	Simeon	–	Gold
June	–	Levi	–	Purple
July	–	Judah	–	Brown
August	–	Issachar	–	Yellow
September	–	Zebulun	–	Pink

October	–	Dan	–	Blue
November	–	Gad	–	Red
December	–	Asher	–	Grey
January	–	Naphtali	–	Green
February	–	Joseph	–	White
March	–	Benjamin	–	Black

Members of the Twelve Tribes believe that one must assume the name of the biblical tribe which corresponds to the month in which one's birthday falls; and so Carrington, who was born in November, became Prophet Gad, and Bob, who was born in February, became Joseph.

> '... and on either side of the river was the tree of life, bearing twelve kinds of fruits, yielding its fruit every month...'
>
> (Revelations 22:2)

Carrington spread his Twelve Tribes wings widely throughout the uptowners, with many finding appeal in its strong doctrine of anti-Christianity. So much so that the Twelve Tribes became the most highly organized sect in the Jamaican Rasta fold, built on a council of pyramidal structures – which seemed to turn off the traditional Rastas, who felt it moved away from strict Rasta traditions. Mortimer Planno, Bob Marley's spiritual mentor in the early days, was one such person. The movement gained such converts as Dennis Brown, Freddie McGregor, Judy Mowatt, and more importantly to Bob, Allan 'Skill' Cole, who was very influential in having Bob join the Twelve Tribes.

To these Rastafarian believers of the Tribe of Joseph, the second coming had already taken place and thus the 'King' could not die.

The Twelve Tribes stress freedom of lifestyle and appearances and racial tolerance. In their belief what leaves your heart through your lips is more important to the world than what enters it. Being 'born again' they await the time when all tribes will once again be gathered.

> 'For though thy people Israel be as the sand of the sea, yet a remnant of them shall return...'
>
> (Isaiah 10:22)

This sect also takes repatriation to Africa literally, a common trend running through the beliefs of all Rastas.

> *I say fly away home to Zion*
> *Fly away home*
> *One bright morning when my work is over*
> *I will fly away home*
>
> (Traditional Negro spiritual used in 'Rasta Man Chant')

This sect also believes that adherence to the Bible is crucial and that in order to be fully understood the Bible should be read 'a chapter a day' from beginning to end, as the answers to all questions about life can be found within its pages if read that way. Bob never failed to carry out this daily commitment.

In addition to the differing sects of Rasta there was of course the oldest established Christian church, the Ethiopian Orthodox Church, of which Bob also became a member, completing a cycle of membership which would reflect his overriding aim: that of seeking to unite all differing Rastafarian believers under one aim and one destiny, a dream which he sought to fulfil to the end.

MH

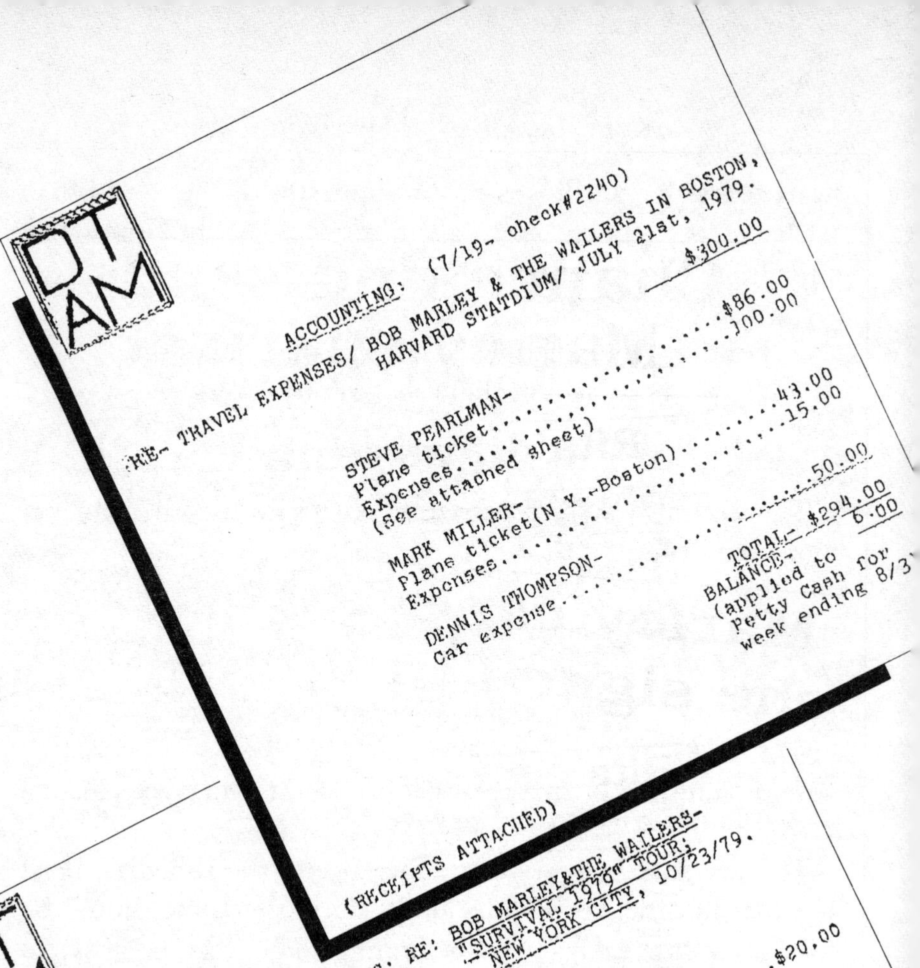

DT AM

ACCOUNTING: (7/19- check#2240)

RE- TRAVEL EXPENSES/ BOB MARLEY & THE WAILERS IN BOSTON, HARVARD STATDIUM/ JULY 21st, 1979.

$300.00

STEVE PEARLMAN-
Plane ticket.......................$86.00
Expenses...........................100.00
(See attached sheet)

MARK MILLER-
Plane ticket(N.Y.-Boston)..........43.00
Expenses...........................15.00

DENNIS THOMPSON-
Car expense........................50.00

TOTAL- $294.00
BALANCE- 6.00
(applied to Petty Cash for week ending 8/3

(RECEIPTS ATTACHED)

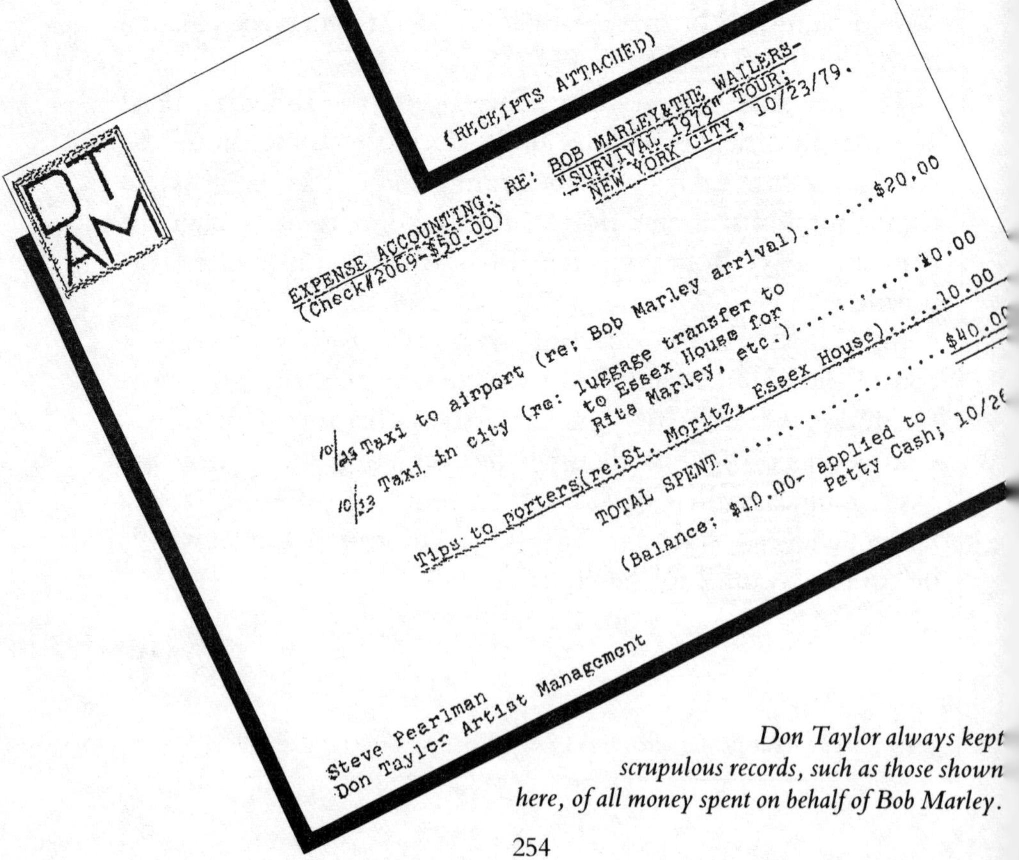

DT AM

EXPENSE ACCOUNTING: RE: BOB MARLEY&THE WAILERS- "SURVIVAL 1979" TOUR; NEW YORK CITY, 10/23/79.
(Check#2069-$50.00)

10/23 Taxi to airport (re: Bob Marley arrival).......$20.00
10/23 Taxi in city (re: luggage transfer to Essex House for Rita Marley, etc.)..........10.00
Tips to porters(re:St. Moritz, Essex House).........10.00
TOTAL SPENT........................$40.00

(Balance: $10.00- applied to Petty Cash; 10/2

Steve Pearlman
Don Taylor Artist Management

Don Taylor always kept scrupulous records, such as those shown here, of all money spent on behalf of Bob Marley.

Chance find sends Marley soaring

The tune was remixed with ...ney Pine playing saxophone ... his first. "Judge Not" (Beverly's) up to his last — a live recording from ... September 23

Rita draws tears

By Virginia Turner & Paul Reid

NEW YORK:— ...

the Marley name. When Rita Marley recounted how in 1976 gunm... attacked the Hop...

Marley case: Rita says she signed in ignorance

— ny in the civil suit brought before ... the Bob Marley Estate ... some

there for the children" and the decision on how much they were to receive was made by Mr. Louis ... of the co-administrators ... and not

"could not be a fact" that the money she had spent had come from Bob's various accounts to which she had signatory power.

Mr. Byles told her to go ahead and settle with the Wailers Band ... had backed Bob

Rita ends tearful testimony

By Paul Reid and Virginia Turner

NEW YORK:

Rita Marley on Thursday ended three weeks of testimony, and cross-examination, on the witness stand, in the Manhattan Federal Court.

"Relief. It was like three weeks of giving my life away," Rita said with a chuckle when asked by the *Gleaner* how she felt. "But, as Bob said, 'not one of my seed shall sit on the sidewalk and beg their bread,'" the Superstar's widow said in a more sombre mood as she expressed the wish that "this thing ends soon."

The trial brought on by the ancillary administrator, J. Reid Bingham, to recover millions of dollars allegedly diverted from the Bob Marley Estate, by his former tax lawyer and accountant continues before Judge Kenneth Conboy.

Mrs. Marley, a third party defendant in this case, told the Court how, despite doubts about the paternity of a child that Yvette Anderson, now Crichton, had after Bob's death, she and her mother-in-law Mrs. Cedella Booker took care of the child and treated it just as they would any of his 10 other children that were born while he was alive.

The family, she said, was not aware of the child, Makeda Jahnesta, until after Bob died and the Estate was compiling the list of beneficiaries. The child, who was born in the United States was brought to Jamaica and Mr. Louis Byles, co-administrator of the Estate suggested that a blood test be done to determine if Bob was the real father and also recommended a doctor who would do the test.

Mrs. Marley said even though she did not see the result of the blood test, support for the child was started and she also signed a letter given to her by Byles saying that she accepted the child as one of Bob's. Makeda Jahnesta was paid all that was owed retroactively from the same time others had started receiving monies, she said.

Falling out

The question of paternity also led to a 'falling out' between Mrs Crichton and Bob's mother Mrs Cedella Booker. They have since reconciled, Mrs Marley said, and at one time both Makeda Jahnesta and Mrs Crichton were living with Mrs Booker in a house owned by Bob in Miami, Florida.

Despite the fact that she never personally sent money to some of the children that Bob had outside the marriage, she saw to it that their needs were taken care of and would include them in things that involved her own children

She said she challenged the amount of money that the Estate had stipulated that each child get as she did not think J$200 per week was enough to sustain a school-age child. To this end, she said, she was always giving the children money, even out of her own pocket, and never thought she had to keep account of that expenditure since they were in effect her children as well, she added.

During cross-examination by her lawyer Kaarie Phillips, of the law firm Graais and Phillips, Mrs Marley explained that she always bought clothes for the children, including Damian, Kymani and Jahnesta, all of whom the plaintiff had suggested did not receive any money since their father died.

Redundant

She also responded to the suggestion that she did not send any cards or presents to them for their birthdays or Christmas by stating that it would have been redundant to send these children cards and presents at Christmas as they were with her and the other children at Christmas. In addition, she said the other administrator saw to it that they always had money.

When it was suggested by the plaintiff, Robert Brundige, that Anita Belnavis and Cindy Breakspeare, the mothers of Kymani and Damian respectively, were 'living near the poverty line,' Mrs Marley said she had no address for Belnavis and so was not able to send any money to her directly but knew she was getting an equal amount as the other children.

Belnavis, who hails from Falmouth, Trelawny, is a former Jamaica table tennis champion, now living in Miami. Mrs Marley said that she did not think Cindy Breakspeare-Tavares-Finson, would have accepted any money for her child from her as, aside from being a very successful businesswoman, she was also married to a successful businessman who was a lawyer, politician and real estate developer.

And, in the case of Bob's mother the US$3,000 per month she received for the upkeep of the house in Miami, that belonged to Bob, and in which she was living was okayed by the administrators.

Mrs Marley added that the children were never envious of their grandmother getting any support or asked that she be cut off or removed from the house.

The legal tussles after Bob's death made headlines around the world.

Select Discography

Albums Produced under Don Taylor's Management

Live!
ILPS 9376 1975
Produced by Steve Smith and Chris Blackwell

This was the album which really launched the song 'No Woman No Cry' as up until then despite being recorded on the previous *Natty Dread* LP it had not created any waves.

This was also the album that caused the first confrontation with Chris, as he had gone ahead and issued the record without our permission and not credited the production to Bob Marley and the Wailers.

Trench Town Rock · Burnin & Lootin · Him Belly Full · Lively Up Yourself · No Woman No Cry · I Shot the Sheriff · Get Up Stand Up

Rastaman Vibration
ILPS 9383 1976

The first album which was credited exclusively as produced by Bob Marley and the Wailers. This change came with the advent of my management. Up until this time Chris Blackwell always placed his name as producer of Bob's records.

This album was a departure from the norm and had Bob reaching for wider audiences and new fields of appreciation.

Positive Vibration · Roots Rock Reggae · Johnny Was · Want More · Who the Cap Fit · War · Cry to Me · Crazy Baldhead · Night Shift · Rat Race

Exodus
ILPS 9498 1977
Produced by Bob Marley and the Wailers

This album, which became Marley's bestseller, was released after the assassination attempt. Side one is a clear response to the event. It was an emotional album for us.

Natural Mystic · Guiltiness · Exodus · Waiting in Vain · Three Little Birds · So Much Things to Say · The Heathen · Jamming · Turn Your Lights Down Low · One Love/People Get Ready

Kaya
ILPS 9519 1978
Produced by Bob Marley and the Wailers

With each album released we sought to show the expansion of Bob's creative horizons; and with *Kaya*, brought out against Chris's wishes, we again broke new ground and opened up a softer side of the market.

Easy Skanking · Satisfy My Soul · Misty Morning · Running Away · Is This Love · She's Gone · Crisis · Time Will Tell

Babylon by Bus
SLD II 1298 1978
Produced by Bob Marley and the Wailers

Positive Vibration · Punky Reggae Party · Exodus · Stir It Up · Rat Race · Concrete Jungle · Lively Up Yourself · War · No More Trouble · Is This Love · Heathen · Jamming · Kinky Reggae · Rebel Music

Survival
ILPS 9542 1979
Produced by Bob Marley and the Wailers and Alex Sadkin

In this album, Bob returned to his revolutionary roots and answered the critics who thought he had gone soft.

Wake Up and Live · One Drop · Ambush in the Night · Zimbabwe · Babylon System · Africa Unite · Ride Natty Ride · So Much Trouble in the World · Top Ranking · Survival

Uprising
ILBS 9596 1980
Produced by Bob Marley and the Wailers

This album is in a real sense the culmination of Bob's musical development, and demonstrates a balance between his serious lyrics and his more adventurous flauntings. This was the last album produced before our break-up.

Coming in from the Cold · Real Situation · Bad Card · Work · Pimpers Paradise · Forever Loving Jah · We and Dem · Zion · Could You be Loved · Redemption Song

After these records, produced and recorded during my time as manager, the albums which followed were *Confrontation*, which is listed as produced by Chris Blackwell and Rita Marley, and *Legend*, which was a mix of previously-released hits avoiding new tracks.

Reference can be made to music catalogues which recall all of Bob's music; the book *Bob Marley: Reggae King of the World* by Malika Whitney and Dermot Hussey can also provide further details, including the pirated records.

The early three albums, namely *Catch a Fire*, *Burnin'* and *Natty Dread*, were all credited to Chris Blackwell as producer.

Index

Entries in *italics* refer to albums and literature.